Gold Man Review

Gold Man Review is published once a year by Gold Man Publishing in Salem, Oregon.

The editors invite submissions of previously unpublished works of fiction, nonfiction, and poetry. Manuscripts can be submitted at www.goldmanpublishing.com by following our submission guidelines.

Copyright 2016/2017 Gold Man Publishing / Gold Man Review LLC.
P.O. Box 21391
Keizer, OR 97307
Printed by Gold Man Publishing
ISBN: 978-0-9969239-0-3

No part of this work may be reproduced or transmitted in any form or by any means, electronical or mechanical, including but not limited to photocopying and recording, or by any other information storage or retrieval system without proper written permission of the publisher. Address all requests to:

Heather Cuthbertson
Editor-in-Chief
Heather.Cuthbertson@GoldManPublishing.com

Contents

Editor's Letter

Does anyone actually read the *Editor's Letter*?

I stress about it every year. Honestly, I never know what to say. I've tried looking at other journals for inspiration and direction and; mostly, the two main choices are either to go an analytical route: diving into a particular aspect of craft or philosophizing on some greater meaning. Or, to talk about what's happening in the political/social environment—all of which leaves me tongue-tied and worried I will offend someone or come off wrong. For this reason, I have historically kept the editor's letter general enough to get by. Maybe it's because, like many people, I fear judgment. So I stay quiet, not saying what I really want to say.

The simplest method would be just to list and explain why these pieces were picked. But, would it be such a bad thing to say some were selected because of a single line that replayed in my mind as I was driving my daughter to dance class? Or a voice I heard long after I finished reading? Or an image that burned into my consciousness? Or the way my heart raced or broke? I know that's not the most mind-shattering thing to say; but, at the end of the day, it was the stories and poems that took hold and kept me there even with my three-year-old daughter blasting *She'll be Coming 'Round the Mountain* in the background.

The truth is, I had a lot more distractions this year, beyond the constant demands from tiny humans. Making a list would be the easiest—the safest. Only lately, life has been anything but easy and I feel if I don't address it, don't at least acknowledge it and try to pretend like it never happened, then I'll be a coward.

This summer, my father passed away. I was there when it happened. I was the one who had to make the call to remove life support, and I will always have to live with that decision—regardless if it was the right thing to do. Losing my father would have been hard enough, except my mother also has terminal cancer and she has spent the last six months bouncing back and forth between home and the hospital. She's in a nursing home now, fighting to live, but knowing it's a losing battle. No one in my family is allowed to talk about the C-word. No pink breast cancer ribbons tagged with her name or Facebook posts asking friends to keep her in their prayers. Photos of her are immediately removed before anyone can see how much weight she has lost. For reasons I don't understand, she wants this struggle to be a secret, which has kept friends and extended family in the dark during a time when I could use their support the most. My mother doesn't read the journal, so this is really the one safe place for me to acknowledge it.

Now that I've admitted what's been happening, I can also admit how hard it has been to keep things going. To act like everything is okay, when everything is falling apart. Despite all this, I made it another year at Gold Man even though I don't know how the issue managed to be completed (mostly) on time. All I know is that it has become special to me. It's become more than just a collection of well-written stories, essays, and poems I liked when I first read them, before things took a turn in my family. I've *identified* with these works. It's become personal. I can relate in a way—loss in its many and varied forms—that I didn't know I would when submissions opened last January. And, isn't that what writing is supposed to do? To connect with others? Make us feel less alone? That someday it will be *okay*?

Okay.

Before I finish the longest (and most private) Editor's Letter I've ever written, I'd like to say thank you to the readers who came on board this year:

Sasha Ives
Chyna Parker
Ashley Rich
Joyce Tomlinson

You four really couldn't have come at a more needed time, and for that, I thank you. I am especially grateful and indebted to Joyce Tomlinson and Ashley Rich who not only read submissions, but also helped edit. You were my literary journal angels.

And thank you to my Issue 6 contributors. You have no idea how much your work has meant to me.

Sincerely,

Heather Cuthbertson
Editor-in-Chief

Gold Man Review Editors

Heather Cuthbertson
Editor-in-Chief

Darren Howard
Managing Editor

Nicklas Roetto
Project Editor

Marilyn Ebbs
Executive Editor

Michelle Modesto
Editor

2016 Gold Man Review Readers

Sasha Ives

Chyna Parker

Ashley Rich

Joyce Tomlinson

The Meaning of Life

Michael Coolen

there is your life as you think you live it
and your life as you actually live it
and the life that friends witnessed and will not tell you
because it would hurt you to hear

and there are those who will tell you
though they don't know the whole story and
would lie about the details
because it would hurt you to hear

Life is ...

רוּחַ
Ruach

Hebrew
"spirit, wind, breath, soul."

"And the Lord God formed a man
from the dust of the ground, and
breathed into his nostrils the breath of life,
and the man became a living soul."

आयुस्
Ayus

Sanskrit
"life, élan, power, health, vigor ... breath"

and among and between all these definitions of life
between the darkness and the light
between life and breath is the true version
the life viewed from ...
where

I don't know where
the *from* is from or the *by* is by
and maybe none of them and maybe all of them together

is life the story about
someone else
in a different time
from a different culture
but really just you

(生き甲斐
Ikigai

Japanese
"a reason for being"
"to get up every morning
and enjoy being alive"

there are those who live to leave a legacy
and those who leave legacies
because of who they were and what they did
and not because of what they needed

and there are those who leave no legacy longer
than the memory of their grandchildren—
which is more than enough for them

بالو
Balu

Mandinka
"life, destiny, what you are meant to do"

there is your life as you try to remember it
and your life as friends think they remember it
and your life others distort simply to hurt you

and there is your life on photos catalogued as
destroy upon my death
that you never intend to look at again but keep
because maybe there's some sort of code or

hidden clue you—and only you and nobody else but you—
will be able to decipher at some point in the future
telling you what your life was/is/could have been/should have been

there is your life as you think you lived it
there is your life as you actually lived it
and among and between all these lives
between the darkness and the light
between life and breath is the truth

When He's in the Room

Alexandra D'Italia

For Andre Dubus' *Fat Girl.*

His name was Andrew. Once when he was sixteen, a girl pulled him under a piano at a party and gave him a blowjob. She was drunk and told him not to tell anyone. Her boyfriend was visiting colleges, but she just loved the look of him.

Andrew's mother had told him to be careful of girls. They always wanted too much. She was overweight and when she looked at him, he could see that she expected him to disappoint her.

It started when he was nine. Girls will want you, just like your father, his mother would say. You have his looks. His father was handsome in an old-fashioned way—like he would look even better with his hair slicked back and dressed in a high-waisted tweed coat. His eyes were intimidating and black. He didn't think he looked like his father at all.

It's not that he thought he looked like his mother. Her features were swollen with the candy bars she kept hidden in her room. Even now, when he was hungry, he'd sneak into her stash in her nightstand or in the shoebox in her closet and eat a Milky Way or a Butter Finger or a Snickers. He had never said anything to his mother about her stashed chocolate. They both had their secrets.

He had his mother's blonde hair, only his curled in ringlets. Like Shirley Temple, his mother said. Like a teen idol, his father said. Everyone, even his teachers, always found a reason to touch it. He had his mother's brown eyes too; they looked like warm cocoa, according to his stepmother. When he looked in the mirror, he liked what he saw. He saw himself as everyone saw him: he was a person to be adored.

He would see his father every other weekend and they would have lunches and days on the lake. His stepmother came, sometimes not. His half-sister came, sometimes not. When he got home, his mother would have baked a cake and they would eat it for dinner in place of meat and vegetables. Wasn't that a treat, she'd say. He'd sit behind her favorite chair in the living room and brush her hair, catching sight of himself in the antique mirror. Then they would switch places and his mother would brush his ringlets until his scalp tingled. In five years, you'll be in high school and you won't want to be with me anymore, she'd say. You'll be into girls. But I love you unconditionally.

Do you know what that means, she asked. Your grandmother only loved me when I was thin. I will always love you; the sun will always shine when you're in the room. He didn't know how to answer her and so like always, he didn't. Girls were already into him.

He got notes in his desk, I love you Andrew. Girls in his class would giggle and try to borrow his sweatshirt. He already got hard when Jessica Pan bent over to hike the ball during gym football games. The hem of the loose dress would flap against her legs as she bent over, "twenty-one, seventeen, hike." Sometimes the wind would blow and he would catch glimpse of her panties underneath.

When his mother fell asleep on the sofa with a crime drama playing in the background—as she often did after her big toe was amputated from diabetes complications—he would go to the attic where she had him store winter clothes in the summer and summer clothes in the winter. She said it was the proper thing to do. Each season, he took one set of his mother's oversized loose dresses and exchanged them for a different set of loose dresses. The attic, besides a storage closet, was a room to call his own. It was where his mother couldn't follow, where she couldn't gaze at him and say, God made you beautiful. Each day after school before homework, before dinner, he'd climb the steep stairs and there in the unfinished eaves, behind the out-of-season dresses, he'd play elaborate war games with his GI Joes. In high school, he'd go there to masturbate. He'd stand behind forgotten boxes of knickknacks, the racks of dresses and jack off to magazines he'd snatch from his father's house. He'd lean into a rack of clothes his mother had never worn in his lifetime: mini-dresses in autumnal colors, velvet dresses that reminded him of Christmas, still others that were cotton and the color of a summer sky. He took to laying in them as he masturbated. He took to removing his clothes and slipping on one of the dresses, a bold plaid that reminded him of a Mondrian painting he had seen on a class trip to a museum; his penis hardened against the satin lining. He'd look at himself in an old mirror, imagine Jessica Pan in a similar dress and think of kissing her.

Like every other girl, Jessica Pan liked him too; at least that's what she said to her friends who in return told him. She was devout and wasn't planning to be interested in boys until college. Andrew didn't need to wait that long. "We could practice kissing," his half-sister had said. She was only one year younger and would sit near him on those weekends he spent with his father. You're always in your head, she said. I can help you, she said.

Andrew let himself be helped right out of his virginity. It wasn't anything he'd been worried about; one way or the other, he knew it would happen and it would happen sooner than most. Yet his half-sister had been determined and after they did it, she cried a little and then wanted to try again. He did but then, when another girl, an older girl, leaned into him and touched his arm, he knew what to do and felt thankful for his half-sister and never fucked her again.

He was popular because girls liked him, and his mother would just shake her head and remind him that girls weren't the answer to everything. She would brush each of his curls and say thank you for letting me do this. I used to love brushing my own hair, but now ... His mother wouldn't finish the sentence, letting Andrew fill in the gap himself. She would avoid looking at herself in the mirror, she would never even catch glimpse in a window; it was as if his mother had lost her reflection. Andrew caught sight of himself all the time, aware, even, when his mother brushed his locks, how his face looked when she did it.

In high school, he and his best friend, Jared, spent weekends riding in a car or going to the movies. Girls were always nearby, ready to smile at him, touch his hand, or depending on the girl, ready to let him touch her. Sometimes, he and Jared just played video games. The female heroes were almost always wearing bikinis and thigh high boots—so beautiful and so lethal. He contemplated how he might look in spandex and boots, but knew Jared wouldn't understand. He knew most people didn't want to wear woman's clothes, and that if they did, they maybe wanted to be with men. That wasn't his thing. Everyone had their own kind of yearning. Jared wanted to be from California even if he didn't really know what that meant. He wore flip-flops in school, even in cold weather. He kept a pair in his locker and said "bra" for "bro" and "dooode" for "dude."

They both were smart and expected to go to good colleges somewhere out of state. Jared became a software engineer and he worked in California making video games. He would eventually marry someone at work and they'd hyphenate their names. When he learned much later of Andrew's penchant for dresses, Jared shrugged and said it wouldn't matter, Andrew would always get laid; women wanted to take care of him.

Andrew and Jared ate lunch together every day, and every day a group of girls would sit nearby and flirt with Andrew. They would ask to touch his curls and ask, what are you thinking? Sometimes, after school, Andrew would meet one of them and make out with her behind the lockers in C wing. I want your hair, she'd say, and Andrew would look at her miniskirt and think of himself wearing it in the attic.

He brought his cross-dressing to college. He took panties of the girl he had escorted to the prom and his favorite of his mother's dresses, the Mondrian plaid, even if he could barely fit into it. He had grown tall like his father. He packed both into a side pocket of his duffel and knew he could explain them away—mementos of sexual exploits. His mother told him she was sad to see him leave because he would find a girl to marry and never come back. God made you to be loved, she said. His father gave him a car like he said he would. His father also gave him a box of condoms and a speech about respectability that Andrew filed away with the dress.

His college was in the Northeast, his father called it fancy, his English teacher called it elite. When he got accepted, his mother cried and said it was from joy. His father was happy to pay. You are going to follow in my footsteps, he said. At college, most kids were from wealthy families. They wore ripped jeans held together by safety pins or ill-fitting pants from thrift stores. Some wore concert tee shirts or tie-dyed tee shirts like it was the sixties. Some had piercings in their face and some had hair dyed the color of Easter eggs. They all wanted to look different and yet they all looked the same. Andrew wore his normal clothes, his jeans and his tee shirts, and the girls seemed to like that. They liked to hang out in his room and watch him not care about their existence.

He thought he might go to law school like his father and his grandfather or maybe he would do something else. He had no doubt he would be successful. College was just a step to the next one. He liked it best when his roommate was out and he could double-lock the door and try on the panties and his mother's dress. The panties never fit. The dress was too tight. Yet he could still feel the satin lining on his skin. He'd masturbate, careful not to mess up the dress, and think of the coeds he would likely get to fuck.

Then he met a girl who was different. She didn't want to take care of him. Her name was Jamie but she went by James and she was too thin and wore thick glasses for fashion reasons. She had to hide her beauty to be taken seriously in a sexist world, she said. She hated that people asked if she were anorexic or why she was in school if she were pretty enough to be a model. She wasn't going to be like her mother who had already had procedures to look like she was still a pageant girl. As if, James said. She liked Andrew because he was as beautiful as she was, perhaps even more so. And he didn't flaunt it; he knew who he was, she said. She never once asked, what are you thinking; she instead told him every one of her thoughts. She told him she lacked an internal editor. He often daydreamed while she talked, and she didn't seem to mind. She planned to be a psychologist or an anthropologist or both if she could do a double major and a double PhD. She told him that she had already researched the graduate schools she'd attend. You can't start planning your life too early, she told him. She had no intention of marrying, so don't get any ideas, she said.

After freshman year, they both moved off campus and did not live together but spent nearly every night in his apartment. It was a tiny studio with mirrored closets to make it seem bigger than it actually was. With James in his apartment so much of the time, he rarely found time to wear the dress, and so he folded it and the panties into his bedside table and touched them each night once she was asleep. Sometimes he'd cut class, risking his grades because wanting to wear the dress was more than he could bear.

They would study and talk into the night. She'd give him a blowjob and he felt like it was rude to ask her to leave. Sometimes he would catch sight of himself in the mirrored closet door as she went down on him. She didn't seem to mind that either. One night, after James had let him try sex from behind, an act that seemed sexist to her, she nuzzled him and asked him what he touched in the drawer after he thought she was asleep, which really, she wasn't. He told her it was a piece of his baby blanket, a token of something his mother had sewn him. It brought him luck; it helped him sleep. She found the story endearing, and he could swear she fucked him harder for it.

They didn't ask much of one another. He liked James even more for not asking about his family. They went to classes, drank too much beer, solved the world's problems, experimented with drugs and talked to their families once a week on Sunday mornings before a diner breakfast. Life unfurled before him as he knew it would. Then one Sunday, James burst into his apartment and told him that her parents were getting a divorce and that it was the end of the world. Her father had been in a relationship with another man for years and her mother had known all along. They had stayed together for her, the sake of the child, she said. Marriage is just another arrangement in life, her mother had told her. James cried so much she shook. Andrew told her what her parents had done was generous and that it wouldn't affect their lives at all.

It changes everything, she said. Andrew held her and wondered if he would get laid that night although he knew that was a bad thing to think. I need your baby blanket, she said. She jumped off the bed and opened the drawer.

Andrew entered a period of his life he would remember always, like someone remembering the year of a debilitating illness. James didn't break up with him, not right away. She said it was weird but really, she had seen weirder. She didn't make him throw away the clothes. She didn't accuse him of being gay, although she asked. She coaxed him to touch the dress and masturbate in front of her, which he found he liked. She asked why he wasn't more open about it on a campus where it was encouraged to be yourself. Did you see the guy who wears a pirate costume to his politics of climate change class? She wanted to know his shame. But he didn't feel shame. It's just something I do that's mine, he said. He wanted to say that most of the people at their college were only pretending to be different than who they were. They wore their ironic tee shirts and protested intolerance, but would they sit down with his mother and let her brush their hair?

James was not a woman to let it go. She said he needed to understand his inclinations. How will you hide this in a night table from your wife, she asked him. It's not a way to live, she said. James devised a checklist of possible reasons and Andrew thought she would be the worst psychologist ever. They fucked while he was wearing the dress and it surprised him that the sex wasn't very good. He didn't want to ruin the dress. She said that clearly it wasn't a sex thing. She checked that off her list.

She had a dress made for him, one that actually fit—a navy blue organza with satin lining. The Internet and I can help you, she said. She gave him silk underwear in his size; she found them in a bargain bin at Macy's. He wore them alone; he modeled them for her. He liked to wear them alone, and she added a note to her list. She showed him how to use concealer to cover his darkening beard if that was what he wanted to do. She did his hair, still longish and curly—like a teen idol his father had always said—in a more feminine way. Andrew didn't like the concealer or the hairstyle and James crossed those off her list. When she would go to class, he would often stay in the apartment and put on his new dress, stare in the mirror and think of James brushing his hair, caressing his face; he'd masturbate to the image in the mirror.

At Halloween, they took the train to New York and he walked down Christopher Street wearing his dress. Did you feel as if you belonged, James asked. No, he told her. He didn't like the crowds. She checked that off the list too. He told her he didn't mind that both men and women looked at him, which didn't make James jealous at all. Maybe you were abused, she said. It's got to be your parents. He told her he hadn't been abused; as a matter of fact, he had been loved unconditionally. His mother was loving and sad in an interminable way he couldn't explain. She eats. She eats candy, alone, in the middle of the night. And she loves me.

Who doesn't, James answered. Then, she asked what his mother wore.

He thought of the dresses for the winter and the dresses from the summer. Loose dresses, I guess, he said.

Muumuus, James asked as if that would mean something.

Eventually, James broke up with him and not because he was a freak, she said, but because she was damaged by her parents' fucked up marriage and their secrecy.

She would always worry that he, Andrew, would be keeping secrets from her. You already did, she said. We're doomed. Andrew watched her pack her drawerful of belongings. Andrew thought of his stepmother who always wore gym clothes and smelled slightly of perfumed body odor and his half-sister whom he had fucked and was now in rehab. He didn't mention those things to James, although he thought it might make her stay, at least for a little while longer. Truth was, he knew his fondness for dresses had little to do with his father's family—they were tangential, like the weekend visits at the lake house.

He filled his grief with college girls who wanted to save him from his sadness. He fucked a girl from every class. Each night he'd put on the dress James had made for him, the panties she had bought him and even the concealer he didn't like so much. He'd look in the mirror and think about James. He thought of calling her and didn't. Eventually, her image would fade and he'd touch himself and feel the silk in his hands and not worry about a mess. He could just buy another dress off the Internet. The magic of those moments in the attic was gone. James's analytical musings had tainted both him and the thrill. He thought of her checklists and for the first time wondered what she must have missed. He didn't know. He tried to remember what he liked about himself: his blonde curls, his brown eyes like cocoa. His eyes were the windows into his soul, women had told him; that's what women loved about him. But when he looked at himself, he no longer reflected the same beauty as before. He saw a man wearing a dress. Now he called his mother more often than Sundays and she would say to him, I miss you Andrew, come home and visit. Let me feed you.

When he went home for Christmas, he brought a new dress he had ordered off the Internet. It was a Mondrian minidress in his size—just like the one he remembered in the attic from all those years ago. On the train, he tried to remain calm. James was going out with someone new, he had seen them together on campus—the guy wasn't nearly as handsome as Andrew had grown to be—and rumor had it he had a gambling addiction. He imagined them fucking and James fixing him with her checklists. He looked out the window and watched the landscape go by in a blur. Unable to fix on the horizon, he became nauseous and it seemed to him that his life was full of nothing.

His father met him at the station and hugged him and brought him to a restaurant with white tablecloths where they split a bottle of wine. You're a college man now, his father said. He asked Andrew about his classes and urged him to go pre-law. He talked of pinots versus cabernets as if Andrew might be tested on them next semester. When Andrew arrived home, his mother hugged him and he noticed she smelled like she always did, of chocolate and shampoo. And, as always, her intense brown eyes bathed him with love. Is it possible you will move back to this town after college, she asked. He shrugged, he didn't know. Do you remember how you loved playing on the front lawn, she asked him, how I'd talk to you about the blue jays and mockingbirds and cardinals I saw on the branches? He didn't remember those things at all. He only remembered the attic and the dresses with near lust. That's where he'd find himself. He'd wait for her to leave him for the couch and her crime dramas. He wanted to return to his world of secret gratification and try to recover the feeling James had stolen from him.

On Christmas morning, he takes care to dress himself. He slips on the silk panties and then the new dress with its white background, grid of black lines, and the three primary colors. He belongs in a museum. He doesn't have shoes, but he likes the look of himself without them. He walks up the narrow stairs to the attic and stands near the rack of old clothes, still unmoved. He looks at himself in the old mirror. He touches himself and feels nothing. He wants to see himself as others see him, as his mother sees him, the sun.

He walks down the stairs. He is hungry now. He wonders if his mother has baked his favorite coffee cake for them to eat by the tree. Of course she has, he answers himself, she loves me unconditionally. In the living room, he gazes at himself in the antique mirror. He is beautiful, he's hard, and he feels James only at the edges of his mind. The dress shimmers in the mirror, the bold lines softening, blurring at the hem. He hears his mother's heavy step on the stairway. And yet he doesn't move. He doesn't want to look away for he is afraid that the nothingness will return. He knows his mother will be shocked but he feels her love so unconditionally that, when she sees him, staring at himself in the mirror, he is surprised to hear her shriek.

Out of Season

Linnea Nelson

you: reticent & undefined
though corners could appear
details of your frame smoky & unuttered
are too early to hold

(i hope you grow all your limbs & come
running unmistaken)

or: a rustling garment not yet
intended for wear
so wait for morning or a solstice
wait for the stain of months on your threads

(then let love wash out of me & irretrievably
hue the landscape of your absolute being)

Living with a Tyrant

Emily Arnick

Cindy's earliest childhood memory at three years old was her father crying because they were leaving. She had never seen him cry before and it scared her. She tried to comfort him and hug his leg as the sun poured in the kitchen window. All his crying didn't keep them there because they left him that day: her mother, her sister Alex, and herself. Her mother's face was cold and unmoving as they drove away.

Cindy looked through her tangle of long, brown hair at Alex, sitting beside her in the back seat, but her sister's face was like their mother's. Instead, Cindy turned to get one last glimpse of her house. Even though the words were never actually spoken, she knew they wouldn't be coming back. When she did, she saw her father chasing after the car, holding her favorite doll.

"Mom, my dolly. I forgot my dolly," Cindy cried.

"We're not going back. Say good-bye to your doll."

After a few hours, they arrived at their aunt's house. While her mother was usually more fun than her father, she wasn't very fun right now. Cindy, Alex, and their four cousins would jump on the trampoline, play hide-and-seek in their huge yard, and climb trees while their mother sat like a stone, staring for hours at a time; Cindy never saw her eat.

Cindy would hear Alex say, "Mom? There's pizza for dinner. Do you want some?"

"No thanks sweetie, I'm not hungry right now."

"Right now" lasted for weeks. After a time, the sight of her mother, who had begun to resemble a skeleton, scared Cindy.

Cindy and Alex eventually went back to live with their father. It wasn't because he missed them. Even at such a young age, Cindy realized they were being used as ploys to hurt their mother, but; ultimately, they moved back because their mother had given them up without even putting up a fight. She had said it was because he wanted go to court, put them on the stand, and force them to tell the judge who they wanted to live with and she didn't want to put them through that. Their mother adhered to that story well into their adulthood, but Cindy knew better.

Living with their father, Cindy met many women. Her favorite was Rose because she would make them breakfast in the morning. Cindy was aware these women were professionals in the biblical sense and doubted that Rose was paid extra to play mommy to the girls in the morning, but she loved it all the same. Alex was not convinced. She refused to give in to Rose's *pancakes-and-sausage* routine and Cindy often felt embarrassed by Alex's rudeness.

Usually, Alex got Cindy ready for school. Even though they were in kindergarten and 3rd grade, they never saw their father in the morning; he would either already be at work or still asleep. Alex would brush Cindy's hair, feed her breakfast, and make sure she brushed her teeth. Cindy could feel Alex's resentment, especially in the mornings. She always said she couldn't find the detangling spray for Cindy's hair and she'd braid her hair far too tight, making her head ache. They were then responsible for walking to school, over a mile away, often in wintry weather. The sister's relationship was forever scarred because Alex had to be Cindy's mother. If Alex was invited to a sleepover, she wouldn't be allowed to go unless Cindy tagged along. Their father said he needed time to *not be a dad* and Alex resented Cindy for ruining her time to *not be a mom*.

Cindy and Alex were responsible for chores and there was no discussion about it. Once, while doing the dishes after dinner, they decided they would talk to their father and ask him if he could take a turn so they didn't have to do dishes every night. His face became the color of a deep red apple and the veins in his neck pulsed like worms under his skin. He never said a word as he reached for a pair of metal scissors on the counter, raised them over his head, and brought them down with enough force that they shattered into a thousand pieces. The girls turned around, finished the dishes, and never spoke of *taking turns* again.

Another morning while they got ready for school, Alex found a rat in the kitchen. Their father retrieved a short 2x4 from the garage and struck the rat until blood splattered the walls, then turned and walked away. Cindy and Alex stood in silence before cleaning the mess he had left them with.

Often, Cindy would have nightmares and try to crawl into bed with her father. Usually he would shoo her away, but sometimes he would let her climb in with him and she'd fall back to sleep immediately; it was the only time she felt truly protected by him. The last time Cindy tried to do this, she crept to his room and saw a woman lying in his bed. She was naked and had long, dark hair and pale, white skin. It wasn't Rose. Her father yelled at Cindy to get out and she did, scrambling into Alex's bed instead. After that, Cindy learned to check the dining room table: If there were empty wine bottles, she couldn't go into her father's room after a nightmare.

Cindy and Alex lived with their father for two years. She missed her mother terribly during that time and felt abandoned by her. She didn't understand her mother was broken, unable to care for herself, let alone fight for her children. When her father had come to her aunt's house and said, "The girls are coming with me" all her mother could muster was "Okay."

In May of the second year living with their father, their mother moved back to the small town where they lived. Cindy was so excited that she brought her to class for show-and-tell. Now that their mother was close, they were able to visit with her every Wednesday after school and all day on Saturday. One Saturday, they went to the beach. Cindy and Alex rolled up their pant legs and played in a stream, trying to catch baby fish to keep as pets. The sun was shining, their mother had made a fire; they roasted hot dogs for lunch and had s'mores for dessert. Their mother watched them for a moment as she sat on a smooth rock before closing her eyes and raising her face to the sun with a beautiful smile spread across her face.

On their drive home that day, their mother convinced them to tell their father they wanted to live with her. When they told him, he'd gotten angry and told Cindy and Alex that he didn't need them; he'd marry again and make a new family. They lived with their mother from that moment forward, visiting their father and his new *families* only occasionally.

After Cindy grew up, she'd look back at her life during that time and honestly couldn't decide which parent would have been worse to live with. While her father was not exactly fit, he kept them housed, clothed and fed; she wasn't convinced her mother was capable of doing the same. Cindy was never angry about how they'd treated her and Alex, at least not until she'd married and had a child of her own. Cindy's love for her daughter was indescribable; she'd throw herself in front of a train for this soft little lump that didn't do *anything*. Why her parents didn't feel the same was a testament to their own selfish tendencies and their complete inability to love and care for anyone, even themselves.

Tribute

Maureen Foley

Ten months exactly after you died, I walk into your empty bedroom. Dark wood floors, no furniture, pale green walls and pink curtains. I open the closet door to grab the suitcase from the bottom and flurries of dust billow up. Late January dawn, thick California fog outside, the neighborhood oddly quiet except an insistent bird. I haven't opened that door for weeks. Christmas looms, two days away. I pull the solitary burgundy faux leather bag out and unzip the main compartment. I stare at all the things you'll never use.

Time to deal. I divide your mostly new clothes and unopened toys into three piles: thrift store, hand-me-downs, and keep. In the thrift store pile, I stack the repeats: an extra copy of *Goodnight Moon* and a board book about a caterpillar, white Gerber onesies, three packs of Dr. Brown's glass baby bottles, an unopened pacifier with the UCLA Bruin on it, two half-used boxes of disposable newborn diapers and a brand new tub of eco-friendly baby wipes. I've already given the home birth kit back to my midwives, opened but unused. The sight of the brown box shipped from the small eco-friendly herbal remedy company in Idaho nauseated me. You were not born at home. You, Jeanette, my love.

The hand-me-downs are easy: a metal xylophone with colorful notes, three knit outfits, seven baby blankets (none handmade), a stuffed animal fox and a plush penguin. A rattle that attaches to a stroller. Teething rings. A scrubby loofah whale for the bath. A small, soft towel with tigers sewn all over it. More toys, more clothes, more objects. Your daddy doesn't know I kept these things this long.

He's asleep in the other room, and it's about five in the morning now. Jeanette, today when I first woke up around three a.m., I registered a pounding head and twisted neck tendons. I slept in a thundercloud last night, awake four times, peed, back to bed to face dreams of snakes tucked into bathroom stalls, losing my train ticket home from Chicago, and being stranded in a darkened parking lot. Now Dad's asleep, and I'm trying to keep quiet. I set down a box of stacking and sorting toys because I can't decide if they should be hand-me-downs or thrift store, and stand up, stretch my arms up to the ceiling and breathe out loudly.

I need a break. I walk out of your bedroom for a moment and creak open the hall closet and reach to the top shelf for the Ziploc baggie with all our prescription meds. I fish out two leftover painkillers from my c-section, reserved for headaches or other nuisances like this one, and down them in one swallow.

The pills go down the wrong way. The leathery aura of the headache combines with the filmy, waxy, dopey feeling of my terrible night's sleep. The meds could just make things worse. My brain was like this when I was newly released from the hospital, unable to remember first names, song titles, anything.

I didn't even pop the heavy shit back then, the narcotics, although I saw the allure. No, I stuck to the Ibuprofen horse pills. In this early morning, I don't want Harold to wake. His Catholic reassurances about Heaven and how you were baptized, blessed, whatever, there is not enough room in my head for all that information this morning.

Back to your bedroom, back to your stuff. I work, quietly focused now, until I whittle it down to the last, hardest pile. What to keep? Finally, I stack only five things. One: a pair of my old booties knit by my long-gone great-grandmother that you wore a few times. Two: a baby quilt my mom sewed the words "Jeanette" into with green and blue and pink and yellow fabric printed with rubber duckies wearing swim caps all over. Third? The Christmas stocking my mom made, too, with leftover fabric from the blanket. Should we hang that up this year? Not sure. Moving on. Fourth: The blue-green rubber pacifier given to you by the nurses in the Neonatal Intensive Care Unit.

And last? The green dress you wore during our family's one and only trip to the beach in Carpinteria, where I grew up. There, done. But not really done, ever.

The dress makes me think of how Harold and I moved back here to raise you beside the sea. The green dress was the one baby thing I'd allowed myself to buy when I was pregnant. I bought it at the fancy baby boutique on State Street, secretly, without telling Harold, with cash from a birthday present from my parents, because I didn't want him to know that I desperately hoped to have a girl and name her Jeanette and teach her to swim and teach her to be brave and tough and sexy, too, because that is what I had always wanted but never said.

Oh, you, the baby, oh you, the baby that died, how you took over. I remember how my water broke a few days after I'd bought the dress. Way too early. Born fifteen weeks before my due date. Suddenly, you, my baby, out in the world but with a ventilator and heart monitor and a collection of tiny syringes. I hold the dress out. The size 0-3 months sundress is cut into a simple A-line shape, without sleeves, and the fabric is light green with white and pink polka dots.

You were six months in the world by the time I wrestled the dress on you. Fall. Wrong colors again for a little spring frock, even for Southern California. A strangely cold day, so the dress's one appearance hidden behind layers of sweater, jacket, leggings and a final hooded sweater zipped by your dad in a final bid to ensure your warmth.

I shake the dress once, and then lay it across the floor. Holding it for the first time since you wore it, I unfold the wrinkled flamingo decoration sewn into the waistline, surrounded by magenta pink ribbon bows. Just beneath the bird, I see a splotch of white caked-on mess. But I can't remember ever seeing it before. Spit-up? You wore so many layers the one day you wore the dress. Bird poop? Dried powder laundry detergent? I hold the dress to my face, searching for a scent, but all I detect is the overpowering artificial hit of the fabric softener Harold insists on using. Then, instead of folding the dress, I balance it on the windowsill. Done.

The baby is dead, but at least her material possessions are sorted. I sigh, too exhausted to feel.

I walk downstairs to the kitchen to find paper grocery bags to contain each pile. I notice the upright vacuum standing erect by the flat screen television. That appliance is my guardian against feeling. I pull out the extension cord and drag it upstairs to the baby's room. The baby's closet needs a good vacuuming. This is all just a simple chore, just a series of jobs that need to be done. Toys sorted, bagged up, I set them by the front door to take out after breakfast. Then, I fold the burgundy suitcase and run the vacuum over the dust bunnies in the corners of the small closet, then the whole bedroom for good measure. Now the room is completely bare, not a trace of my girl left. All done. I clap my hands together three times.

On the third clap, I hit my palms together so hard that my shoulder muscles ache, and the tendons in my wrists jangle like they've been plucked. All is under control. I'm just lonely. Harold won't get it. I want to call my own mother, but it is too early in the morning. I know she's awake, but I'd have to admit something was wrong.

And she'll know just from my voice, remember the date, want to take me out for coffee, fix everything, hug me, tell me, "Oh, Tribute, there's no reason for things like this. It's just the worst thing that can happen to someone."

I want to exit my own body, which feels like molten lead.

"Dear Universe—" I begin, but a strong tingling on the right side of my head stops me. I walk into the middle of the bedroom and turn around, slowly, eyes closed. I open my eyes and turn to look over my shoulder. Someone walks in the room. But when I stare at the doorway, there's no one there. The tingling intensifies. Hot now, shot through with lightning, the right side of my body. I stare, expecting a human, a body. No one appears.

But I hear your voice. Yours, I'm sure of it, even though you never spoke, not old enough.

You say, "Mama, give everything away."

As soon as you speak, the tingling becomes alive all over my body. Then, I see you. But instead of little Jeanette, a healthy baby floats in a body of water, swaddled and tucked into a Moses basket, adrift amid lotus blossoms and lily pads, tall reeds, awake and gurgling, and floating reckless and oblivious. Glowing and golden and gorgeous, a hovering vision just out of reach.

Then, I see myself outside my body looking down as if I've hovered up to the ceiling. Late thirties, brown hair parted on the side and half-covering my face, brown eyes, body a little too thick, short legs and long torso. Wearing jeans, a striped sweater, a slash of red lipstick to fight off winter. Crown of my head flashing magenta strobe lights, and my perfect baby just out of reach. I see it all from above.

"My girl, I love you so much. I miss you, I miss you," I whisper.

The image of you disappears. I gasp, a cry, and I'm back into my body, a heap on the floor, crying, quietly losing my mind. I close my eyes, and the only image is of you sick, dying, premature, a lump in the NICU isolette, a flurry of wires and respirator, tangled, my hands cradling your blue arms and still legs. The nurse making plaster impressions of your cold feet. The memory box. Unhooking all the wires and removing your diaper and taking off the knit cap from your head. Naked, finally, free of all hindrances.

The burning heat in the bedroom rushes through me, singes the hairs on my body. I smell the awful scent of arm hairs curled black. I think of your death: no brain metabolism. No signs of life. Open my eyes again and try to remember where you were before me, soaring, golden, perfect, alive and talking. Too much.

I vanish there with you in that light, that moment. I shriek and wail softly and fall asleep a mess on the floor.

Hours later, not sure exactly when, Harold wakes me up, snoring lightly on the folded suitcase in your room, next to the vacuum, the closet door open, your green dress still carefully balanced on the windowsill. Harsh California midday light floods through your bedroom windows, turning the pale green walls bright through the pink curtains. Just like it was before, still.

"Honey? What's wrong?" he asks.

I hadn't even heard his first-time bathroom door slam, walking down-up the stairs, clomp, clomp, man walk. Or the sound of his overpriced espresso machine whir to life or the shower flood on, the toilet flush, the slap of the mail on my desk, the phone ring, my mother. Breakfast. Breakfast dishes. When did he find me asleep? Why didn't he wake me up? By the light outside, it looks like it's about eleven in the morning.

To tell or not to tell? Not tell. Already, my baby feels so far away again. Dead, I guess that's what they call it.

"Nothing's wrong. What time is it? I just miss our baby," I say.

"Oh," he says. Daddy knows I'm lying. He always does. "It's just about ten. Are you going to farmers?"

"Good old farmers market. Of course. Yeah," I say, trying to right the ship. I stand up, afraid now a little of what I saw. You, alive and hovering. I give the vacuum a little kick, and it topples, face first onto the carpet.

"Hey, can you do me a favor?" he asks. " I want to get Mom one of those cutting boards. Christmas is Monday so this is our last farmers market."

"Got it. From the lemon guy? They're like a million bucks," I say.

"Sixty. Yeah," he says pausing to pick up the dress with the pink flamingo off the windowsill. "I miss her, too, you know."

"I know," I say.

"OK, well I'm going to start cleaning the kitchen and working on that broken screen door hinge. Would it help if I took all the stuff in the bags by the door downstairs to the thrift store? What is it anyway?" he asks, holding up the stocking my mom made, pulled from the keep pile.

"I don't know. Just the baby's things. Kept them for awhile," I say. "Get rid of it, please."

"Got it. I'll take care of it," he says, not needing to know the details of why I'd been buying Christmas presents and saving clothes for a child that no longer lived.

"Wait. Hold on," I say, grabbing back the stocking out of his hand. "I want to hang it up this year."

"So Santa can bring toys to Jeanette?" he asks, looking confused.

"For me. Santa can bring her back to me," I say, my voice cracking as I speak and the inevitable spilling over. Harold stares at me. He feels embarrassed, I can tell. His face turns pale. He coughs.

"It's a piece of shit. A fucking worthless piece of shit, terrible, miserable piece of shit," he says.

"I know," I say.

"I know you know," he says, coughing again. "Farmers."

"Billion-dollar walnut wood artisanal cutting board," I say, slashing the back of my hand across my eyes. I am so done with tears.

"Yep," he says.

"Will you make me pork chops for lunch when I get back?" I ask.

"Yes," he says. "Go."

"Take this, too," I say, handing him the stocking. I can still hear your command faintly: *Give it all away, Mom.*

Before leaving, I fail to change clothes or wash or brush teeth. I fail to see any humor in anything. I fail to tell Harold the truth of your visitation. Instead, I just back the Audi station wagon we bought for your arrival out of the driveway and drive on auto-pilot to downtown Santa Barbara for the weekly farmers market on the corner of Cota and Anacapa Streets and wade through the crush of holiday shoppers for my groceries, a few gifts and last, the royal cutting board.

Fog returned, clogging the sky and making diffuse light bounce off the farmer's blue tent. A chalkboard sign reads: Last Chance Farms. Piles of Eureka lemons cover two burlap tables. Between the yellow hills, two dozen slabs of polished wood boards balance stacked together. From a distance, they just look like regular cutting boards. A smaller chalkboard sign reads: Handmade Walnut Wood Cheese Boards $60.

"Really? Sixty dollars?" I ask a man wearing jeans. Up close, his face looks handmade too. Cobbled. Hammered. Slight redness to his skin, forced cheekbones, shaved head and lots of stubble. Blue t-shirt with the farm's logo of a skull and crossbones, but the beneath the skull are a pitchfork and shovel, instead of two bones.

"Really. They're a nightmare to make," he said. "I spend probably fifty hours on each one."

"What do you mean?" I ask, but a lemon customer thrust two handfuls of Eurekas at him. I wait until he makes change and the lady leaves.

"I mean it's a shit-ton of work. I make them with spare wood from the walnut orchard my father-in-law cut down two years ago. The only power tool I use is a band saw to cut the rounds. Then it's all handwork. Sanding. Oiling the wood. Rubbing it. I make them year-round to get ready for the holidays."

"And in two days, they'll all be gone?" I ask.

"Hopefully. That's the plan. Until next year," he says. Then, to someone standing behind me says, looking at their lemon pile, "Hi. Two-fifty, please."

I pick the boards up to inspect them, turn each over, but eventually I return to the first one I'd found.

"This is it," I say, holding it up. "Can I pay you?"

"Why that one?" asks the farmer.

"The soul feels right," I say, for no reason.

"I know what you mean. Some cultures believe the heart of a tree contains a ghost," he says.

"Really? Which one?" I ask.

"Well, me. I believe that at least," he says.

"Who was in this tree?" I ask, holding it in front of my heart like a plate of armor.

"A baby. Sad, I think. Look, here," he says, pointing to a warp and curve in the tree rings. "Doesn't that look like a rattle?"

I frown and glance to my side. The tingling begins again, deep inside my crown and now the nape of my neck, beginning to burn. For once, I don't feel sad. Just hot. I know this time it's you, my love. You, coming into the physical world and trying to touch me. But I'm not ready for you here, my love, in public. I close my eyes and take a deep breath.

"I lost my ..." I begin "... I lost my baby."

Just like that. Wham. Heat all over. Burning. I don't tell most people about you, Jeanette, just like that. I don't serve them my sinking ship, foist my dense, inelegant heart onto their lives for no reason.

The farmer drops all his lemons and turns to face me.

"Holy shit. I'm so sorry. Recently? Oh, no," he says. He glances behind, looks up to the sky, his hand at the back of his neck. Then he stares directly at me again. "Please just take the board. No charge."

"No, no," I say. But my hands white-knuckle the wooden object, palms hot. "Do I look that bad off?"

"No, it's not that. I make them myself. That's the beauty. I can do this. Shit, I'm such an idiot. About the baby, the rattle. So insensitive," he says.

Are those tears fleeing the far corners of his eyes? Or are they just watering randomly from dust or a caught eyelash?

"Can I give you a hug?" I ask. I'd been on the receiving end of this annoying invitation too many times for the last ten months. It felt good to extend myself out instead. Without a word, he rushes from behind the lemon tables like a man on fire and when he throws his stringy, taut, tree-branch arms around me two things happen.

First, I close my eyes and feel you, my love, my little Jeanette, wash over both of us like energetic lava, doused in a healing rush of sparkling fire-heat.

"You OK?" he asks.

"Sorry," I say.

"No worries."

"What's your name?" I ask just as a mob of Italian tourists stop by, holding up lemons and gesturing and talking.

"Francois," he said. "Francois Chance. As in Last Chance Farm? Let me know if you'd like to get tea sometime at the farm. Or the retreats. Seriously. Look them up. I'm really sorry for your loss. Really."

I take his business card and try, again, to pay for the board but he shoves it toward me, gaping almost, just as the Italians began fumbling with twenty-dollar bills to buy lemons. He walks behind his tables quickly, keeping eye contact.

"I'm Tribute. Bye. Thanks," I say.

Jogging back to my Audi station wagon, my mind churns. Jeanette, let me explain. I am not like those other parents in those dead baby grief self-help groups, not me. No having another baby and moving on for me. Nope. I want to remember my dead daughter more keenly with each passing day. Why can't I just let it go? No. I want to bring her body into clearer focus. I would have tried cryogenics, cloning, anything to bring her back exactly as she was, in the flesh.

All the machinations at planning and independence are feeble attempts to reign in the generalized fear that now wakes me up at night, since having you. Fear underlies every news story about wayward children and flashes in front of me as images of horror spontaneously on the freeway. Right now, it happens again, as a motorcycle speeding surprises me by passing me on the left with its engine all go, and immediately I see myself and a baby destroyed by his wild-spinning wheels. I see these visions of horror everywhere, driving, walking, just standing still. Why, Jeanette?

From nowhere, a voice, "Mama, give it all away."

I think, "I did, sweetheart. Daddy's taking it away. But why do I have to have these bad images?"

This time, nothing.

Driving home, I feel the weight of the day and it sends me straight to the couch. No more outings. I give Harold his board, stash the produce in the fridge, eat some sad soup, fake another migraine, and call quits at five-thirty p.m.

The next day is Christmas Eve and my new global anxiety blossoms, exploding and fermenting into a new blend of panicked second-by-second terror. Instantly awake as soon as my eyes open, I scan the room for danger. All I see is everyday: dark blue quilt made for our wedding by my mom, landscape painting of the Channel Islands, and on our dresser the mini Christmas tree that a coworker gave Harold. A flash in the mirror and you're gone.

Trying to cope, I clamber out of bed and onto the cold, wooden floor, and dig out my favorite sweater, the red-orange one that I wore when I took my pee test that said I was pregnant with you. Long and loopy, the cotton yarn stretches everywhere along the parts of my body that spread out to fit you and never made it back. Black leggings, long gold earrings, the mid-calf sheepskin boots that we wear around here in winter, to pretend it's cold enough for them. Inspired, I even throw on a red and gold bangle bracelet that Harold brought back from one of his public health conferences on whooping cough in Minneapolis.

Harold walks into our room as I'm pointing my hand like a bird beak and trying to shove the wooden ring on my wrist.

"Does this bracelet make my arm look fat?" I ask him.

"What? No. What. Oh, your arm? It's perfect," he says. "Are you trying to pick a fight, Tribute?"

"What do you want for Christmas?" I ask.

"Why are you being so rude today?" he asks.

"Asking you what you want for Christmas is rude? I meant it. Otherwise you're getting a sweater."

"I want a divorce," he says.

"Ha, ha," I say, but he's not laughing. "The gift that keeps on giving?"

"I'm serious," he says.

"Right, you're serious. I get it. You've said this before. It's just your feeling of being trapped. Isn't that what your therapist said?"

"I'm swamped tomorrow," he says. "Tomorrow. Remember? I volunteered to be on call? Well, Phil's sick, and I'm on."

"On Christmas. You're at the hospital tomorrow?" I ask. "Fine, let's get divorced.

I give up."

But we don't really mean it about divorce, Jeanette. We're both just sad and scared right now.

"OK by me," he says. "Let's talk later. Should we do gifts and things tonight? I made us a reservation at the Chinese place. Fake Christmas this year. I haven't done any shopping. I have to do all the nieces and nephews, my dad. You got jam for the neighbors, right? And what do you want?"

"My baby back," I say.

"I know. I heard you yesterday. I can't talk to you. That's not happening," he says, as if I don't know that. "See you back here at five-thirty sharp."

He strides downstairs, slams the door and out he goes into the Christmas shopping frenzy. Alone, again, a swarm of terror.

I know these types of days and they can be calmed by only one thing.

I need to shop for a gun.

I drive the Audi toward the anonymous sporting goods store on Upper State Street. My goal is to buy a gun today, after all.

Thoughts charging, I end up paused at a stoplight behind a red pickup truck with a German shepherd tied to the back. The dog lolls out its tongue in rhythm to its panting. I imagine its teeth tearing a chunk out of a baby's thigh.

Stop thinking.

I turn the knob for the radio and straight-ahead jazz blares alive, Bill Evans, I think.

This is the unlogic of death. Long red light, I watch streams of cars pass, desperate not to envision any more car accidents. I never missed having children when I was in my twenties. Then I decided to become a mother between the red urgency of one period to the next in my thirty-ninth year.

The red light changes to green, and the red pickup ahead of me jerks forward, stalls, and I nearly rear-end the truck in my attempt to jump forward, to move time ahead, to get to the gun store and home before Harold's Toyota Corolla turns into the driveway back from last-minute shopping. I brake and then continue.

Three blocks up, I find a parking spot near the front door. I lock the car quick with the beep-beep of my key fob and dash toward Open Adventures Outdoor Supply. Inside, I veer past giant holiday displays and make a direct turn toward the gun section. As I approach the glass display counter, a man with a shopping cart full of white sneakers in boxes stops me. His nametag reads: Mac.

"We're closed," says Mac.

"What?" I ask.

Mac stares at my breasts and then smiles into my face, "So sorry, ma'am. System is down."

"Oh, OK," I say. System? As in the computers, like the cash registers?

He shrugs and then stares back at the deep v-neck of my sweater. "You're beautiful, gorgeous in fact. One sexy lady. What, like twenty-eight?"

I blush and take a step back. "No. Forty-one. Nice try. Oh, OK. Thanks."

"Will you walk with me to the front? Arm in arm?" he asks. "I'm trying to play my lady. She's in the shoes department."

"No—What? No," I say, suddenly wondering if it's my sweater. Is it too revealing? Is it my boobs? My bra size erupted into a new dimension post-partum and never recovered, and I'd been meaning to toss out a whole load of clothes that would never fit again. The red-orange sweater had been my favorite, and it had special meaning, but it is sort of too tight. I flee the store, noticing only too late that there are no customers inside and there's a handwritten notice on the door: Computers down. Closed for now.

I crawl out of the sweater with my t-shirt pulled up over my head for a second, blinding me. I run back to my car for the second failed attempt at my mission for the day. Time check. Still forty-five minutes before Harold said he'd be home. Enough time to drive home, run to the couch, try to relax and look bored.

Of course, the drive involves traffic. Stuck behind a big rig with a blatantly anti-abortion slogan on the back, I try to check my email on my phone, but I know it's dangerous, so I turn back to the jazz station and tap my fingers in time to Louis Armstrong singing "All That Meat and No Potatoes."

"Is that all about sex?" I ask out loud.

Before the song can finish, I arrive home to an empty driveway and my garden with its hopeful pansies and sad lime tree with three small limes on the tiny tree—three more than last year.

So, no baby, just e-newsletters from baby clothing sales. And a garden with a purple jacaranda tree that blossoms every May, to remember your birth, not your death. I pause in the car to admire the garden through the frame of my windshield. The wrens have left the Tiger's Tail and now a few flit about some camellia blossoms; their weight loosening them until one of the bright pink flowers drifts to the lawn.

Jeanette, your tree is about three feet tall and its roots have grown around and up and through your terrible, terrible ashes buried deep in the ground beneath it. I can't let you go. I watch a swarm of wrens mass inside the camellia bush one last time, but when they hear me slam the Audi's door, they fly off again, en masse.

Inside our two-story white house, I find the respite of TV like an ever-flowing fountain and turn it on. Where has Harold gone now? Empty, white noise, blessed absolution, the careful dissolve of not having to be present or think or plan or decide or disagree. No unemployment. No nothing. Just a reality show about wannabe chefs who are charged with making a dessert using rhubarb.

"Jeanette, I would ace that," I say out loud to the empty house.

Tingle, fizz, a golden orb, and this time I'm not alone. This time, you're with me too.

We Broke Apart

Mercedes Lawry

A ruin of clouds gave us
pause, as if we'd forgotten
about chapters, coyly titled as clues.
Nothing is as abrupt as disappointment.
We observed the fields of switchgrass and chickory,
longing for a further reach, the sky roiling
in blue-black hurt. I gave you
the last chance, with tenderness.
We wore the coming rain as departure
though I still imagined another year
cluttered with sorrow, yet familiar.

Here in the depths of September,
we break apart with no loud crack,
although it seems my bones are separating
as though an alphabet was fractured
into unattached letters, spelling only Babel.

Belonging

Kathleen Glassburn

It was our first time at St. Barnabas Episcopal Church. We huddled in a back pew, my head resting on Mom's arm, Markie fidgeting on her other side.

Reverend Newton stood in front of the altar and announced in a booming voice that made me jerk upright: "The Youth Choir starts today. Besides joy in praising God with song, each member will earn two weeks at Camp Duncan. So, children, see you in the loft." He pointed at three pews to the side.

Gathering her purse and sweater for a quick exit, Mom said, "Do you want to join the choir, Anne?"

I can see myself with pleading, brown eyes, saying, "I really do."

"Your father will have to wait to eat." She cooked delicious Sunday dinners of fried chicken or pot roast. Turning to my little brother, she went on, "If Anne's doing this, you can sing in the choir too."

"I don't want to stay," Markie whined.

"It might be fun."

I grabbed his hand.

We had moved to another Minneapolis apartment, the fifth in my seven years. Dad kept promising that someday we'd have a real house. When he found employment as a bricklayer, he brought in good money. When he didn't have a job, which happened through the winter months, at least there wasn't much rent. He and Mom were caretakers in these many buildings, each a better deal than the last. This Hopper Street apartment, in a gloomy basement, looked out on an alley. The raucous shouts of garbage collectors and the *bang—bang—bang* of barrels being emptied awakened me every Tuesday morning.

It took several minutes for the choir director, Mrs. Ashworth, who had a huge bosom pooching out from a low, round neckline, to organize the twenty or so children gathered. A subdued Markie hovered close to me. The other boys tussled like a pack of friendly mutts. The girls chattered like a farmyard full of hens. One girl, with inky-dark blue eyes and a face blank as an empty page, stood against the wall, watching. She had been in my Sunday School class. Tilting her head toward me, she squinted as if measuring my height.

Eventually, we were arranged in the loft. I was placed in the front pew and Markie at the end of the back pew. He looked ready to bolt. To my right, closest to the altar, sat Emily Price, the watchful girl. She was half a head taller than me.

Mrs. Ashworth took a deep breath, her bosom rising like a bowl of bread dough, and clapped her hands to quiet the ruckus. "I want to teach you one of my favorites—*The Saints of God.*"

This hymn brought pictures to my mind: folks at tea; a shepherdess on the green; a knight killing some fierce, wild beast.

"In a month I want you to sing for the congregation," Mrs. Ashworth said. "Do you think we can make that happen?"

No one responded.

"Remember, participation in choir means two weeks at Camp Duncan."

"Yessss, Mrs. Ashworth," we said in unison.

"*I sing a song of the saints of God/Patient and brave and true ...*"

In half an hour Mrs. Ashworth said, "That's enough for today."

Emily shifted toward me. "You have a really good voice."

"So do you." It seemed polite to say this, even though, while floating off to faraway places with my singing, I hadn't noticed.

"Let's get some cookies."

"Sure, but I have to bring my brother." He was nowhere to be seen.

Upon entering the church hall, I spotted Mom. Markie stood behind her like a shadow. She sipped coffee, listening to a woman who kept waving a hand back and forth as if leading the choir herself. This woman's black hair streaked with gray made her look like someone's grandma.

"That's my mother," Emily said.

Mrs. Price wasn't partnered up with a man. I soon found out that Emily's father, similar to my own, never went to church.

"Can Anne come to play?" she asked.

"Certainly," Mrs. Price said. "How about this afternoon?"

"Do you want to?" Mom leaned close and I caught a whiff of something fresh, like the fragrance of early morning flowers.

"I do." Visiting other people's real houses, with plenty of room for everyone, fascinated me.

I hopped in the backseat of Mrs. Price's blue Oldsmobile next to Emily and gave a cheerful wave to Mom and Markie, standing hand-in-hand on the curb. At the time I failed to see how deserted they must have looked. A pine-smelling cardboard tree hung from the car's rearview mirror. It failed to cover up the odor of cigarettes.

St. Barnabas, with its grand history, stood down the block from our building. The mayor and university president attended. Many of the families lived in mansions on Lake Beckwith Boulevard, a few miles from the Hopper Street neighborhood. In between was Emily's three-story, stucco house on Oldhaven Avenue.

Standing on the sidewalk, I thought, *It's big*. I didn't notice the peeling blue trim.

Inside, Emily pointed to a pink powder room. "Let's wash up." In our apartment there was one all-purpose bathroom with a tub/shower.

On the way to dinner, I peeked at the living room. Hundreds of books filled built-in shelves. We sat at a mahogany table along with Emily's two teenage brothers, Geoffrey and Bradley. I waited for someone to say Grace. Mom, Markie, and I prayed before meals. Instead, Mr. Price said, "Pass your plates" with that same blank face Emily often assumed. He carved the chicken, which looked as dark as a Brazil nut.

Emily and I asked for white meat.

"They want breasts," Geoffrey joked.

Pretending not to hear him, I spread a thick, paper napkin across my lap. Each of the others had silver rings with white, linen napkins rolled inside. Loopy, engraved letters made the rings look like something for royalty. I later realized these were called monograms and that the silver needed polishing.

Once everyone started to eat, I pressed my fork into lumpy mashed potatoes and stirred mushy mixed vegetables. My food tasted as bland as dry toast. Still, I ate everything. A fancy chandelier made up for what the meal lacked. At that time, I didn't see cobwebs winding through the candle-like lights.

Mrs. Price said, "Do you want another serving?"

"Yes, please."

She smiled broadly, showing yellow teeth.

"As much as you eat," Geoffrey leered at me, "You should be bigger than Em."

I scrunched lower in my chair.

Bradley said, "That's rude."

Mrs. Price talked during that first dinner about new altar cloths and people who dedicated floral arrangements and an upcoming wedding of a Lake Beckwith neighborhood couple. According to Emily, she spent all her time doing "guild stuff."

Mr. Price wore a blue sweater draped over his shoulders. He didn't say a word after serving our chicken. By contrast, my talkative father brought up the Democratic Party and upcoming elections and unions while we ate.

I learned that Mr. Price sailed in the summer and skied in the winter and worked in Mrs. Price's father's stock brokerage and seldom read a thing. When we were by ourselves, Emily filled me in on lots of family details.

Near the meal's conclusion, Mrs. Price said, "You didn't clean your plate, Emily. No dessert."

Pushing the last of some peas onto a fork with my pointer, I waited for anything tasty.

Mrs. Price said, "Anne dear, use a bit of dinner roll, not your fingers."

I hid my hands in my lap.

Mrs. Price stepped away and returned with dessert. Bananas and cottage cheese. Not even a cherry. My mother would have put this yucky stuff out as an optional side dish. I took a tiny bite and said, "I'm sorry. I'm full."

Geoffrey said, "It's about time."

"That's enough," Mrs. Price said. "You girls may be excused."

A large room took up almost the whole third floor. Streaky dormer windows faced the street. There were three doors, one to a bathroom. Used towels strewn around made a musty smell like in a swimming pool's changing area. The other closed doors went to Geoffrey's and Bradley's bedrooms. A slouchy, gray sofa sat across from the television. I figured Mr. and Mrs. Price came up here for programs.

My parents snuggled every night on our tan sofa for Milton Berle, *The Honeymooners*, or *I Love Lucy*. In hysterics, Markie and I would roll around on the linoleum when the ditzy lady pulled her antics.

A metal climbing structure, like the jungle gym at the park across two busy streets from our building, filled one corner. A wooden slide, about which Emily said, "Be careful. You might get a sliver," stood beside it. A trapeze was bolted into the high ceiling. "Look what I can do." She hung from her knees. Her dress made a tent around her face, revealing tattered, white underpants. A dollhouse, tucked in a dormer, looked like one of the brick mansions on Lake Beckwith Boulevard. She said, "My grandfather built that for me. It's an exact replica of where Mother grew up."

"Did your father live by her?"

"He came from inner-city Chicago."

I wasn't sure what "inner-city" meant but decided that the Hopper Street neighborhood, with its once-beautiful buildings, might be described this way.

The next Saturday Markie said, "I'll go to Sunday School, but I'm not singing in that dumb choir."

"What about you, Anne?"

"I want to do it. Will I be invited over to Emily's again?"

"I don't know, but you need to reciprocate."

"What's that mean?"

"She should visit here."

"Alright." I looked into Markie's and my bedroom, cluttered with Tinker Toys and Lincoln Logs and trucks, hoping her visit wouldn't happen for a long time.

Mom got a call from Mrs. Price that very day. Afterward I heard her say to Dad, "… awfully bossy …" and "… almost demanded …"

I got to go for a sleepover.

In her second floor room, Emily gestured to a twin bed. "That's yours."

Her carpet, where we sat cross-legged and played Go to the Dump, was dark green and velvety-feeling except on the worn spots. The wallpaper that was coming apart at the seams was covered with lilacs, making it feel as if we were sitting on the ground with high, blooming bushes. Next to the bedroom was her very own bathroom with a claw-footed tub.

Across a hall, wide as the one by my principal's office, was another large room with a single bed.

"That's where Mother sleeps," Emily said.

As I studied the room, she added, "My father sleeps in his den downstairs."

That night, Emily and I ate toasted cheese sandwiches and watched television in the third floor room that we had to ourselves because the boys were out.

I asked. "When will your mom and dad come up here?"

Emily shrugged. "He's always gone on Saturday night—all night."

When we got tired, she led me back down to the second floor. I saw Mrs. Price in her bedroom, sitting on a green brocade-covered chair, listening to what, in the future, I identified as Bach. She never looked up from stitching needlepoint. A crystal tumbler of brown liquid sat on a small table next to her. Beside the tumbler, a matching crystal ashtray held her smoldering cigarette.

"Bradley says Mother's booze helps her sleep," Emily said.

Emily became my weekend best friend—a lucky thing because our family continued to move, causing me to change regular schools and every-other-day best friends almost annually. Music had brought us together, and we continued to sing much of the time. Her favorite pop song was *Blue Suede Shoes*. Emily wiggled her hips and did an imitation of Elvis, dark hair slicked back with her father's Brylcreem. "You can be Pat Boone," she would say. "Your soft hair is the same color as his." My song was *April Love*.

Occasionally, Emily stayed with us. I shoved all Markie's junk in the closet beforehand, and he slept on the sofa.

One Saturday night we piled into Dad's old Ford and went to a drive-in movie. *Raintree County* was playing.

"That was great," Emily said afterward, and I agreed, even though parts had gone over my head.

Before the next day's church service, I heard Mrs. Price telling Mom, "That was not an appropriate film for the girls."

My mother rolled her eyes. Markie and I followed her into a back pew while Mrs. Price and Emily headed for theirs up front.

That summer, we took a bus to Camp Duncan on Woods Lake—a session for girls up to sixth grade. Seven of us, and a teenaged counselor, stayed in each cabin. Emily and I shared a bunkbed with her on top. At campfire singalongs we started out with songs like *John Jacob Jingleheimer Schmidt* rocking our bodies back and forth. Everyone agreed I should do solos. Singing something like *The Saints of God*, I'd tingle from my toes on up to my ponytail. We'd end chanting the "Nunc dimittis" while gazing into glimmering embers, our shoulders touching, and our shirts and shorts and hair picking up the smell of smoke.

"*Lord, now lettest thou thy servant depart in peace ...*"

The last night of camp we had a special program. Each cabin performed a skit and awards were presented. I received Best Singer and Emily received Best Swimmer. A special honor was Best All Around Camper, given to a sixth grader.

The first years of camp were a happy blur. I remember crying each time our session was over, and Emily, close to me on a bus seat, saying, "I wish we could live together forever." But, after our idyllic fourth time, Emily became too busy to talk on the telephone or get together; she and Bradley were crewing on her father's sailboat.

At last autumn arrived. Sixth grade was still elementary school for me, but Emily's sixth grade was the start of junior high. Her brother, Geoffrey, attended the University of Minnesota where he lived in a fraternity house. Bradley didn't go to college or work and still lived at home.

After school started, Emily invited me for a Saturday overnight. She took me to Geoffrey's old room and reached under the mattress and pulled out a worn magazine. "This is *Playboy* ...what do you think?"

A blonde woman spread across the middle pages had a bare bosom, as big as Mrs. Ashworth's, but the rest of her was much smaller. "Didn't she get embarrassed?"

Emily scrutinized me in her blank way before pushing that magazine back under the mattress.

We were in her bathroom, bobby-pinning our hair into elaborate styles that fell out as soon as we moved, when she said, "I'll bet your parents have sex all the time."

I held my comb mid-air. "I don't know."

"They're always hugging."

Mom had told me about sex and said it was special, for when you were married. I thought they'd done it twice because this was the way to get Markie and me.

Emily glanced at me sideways. "Dad does it with Roberta." With my questioning expression, she added, "She's the receptionist at The Club."

"How do you know?"

"Bradley told me she's his mistress."

It was a stifling evening. We sat on Emily's porch swing until the sun went down, singing some of our old favorites, swaying rhythmically: *Mairzy Doats* and *White Coral Bells* and *Frere Jacques.*

Suddenly she dragged her foot, causing the swing to lurch to a stop. "I know what to do with my boyfriend when the time comes ... Bradley showed me." Her shoulders squared for a few seconds before they crumpled. Then she started swinging faster than ever and we quit singing.

After our toasted cheese sandwiches upstairs, we settled into the familiar twin beds in her garden-like room. Once the lights were off, she said, "I have a boyfriend."

"You do?"

"We've kissed lots of times. I let him feel me up."

I bunched the blanket around my ears and pretended to fall asleep.

Emily's new choir friend, Monica, lived in the Lake Beckwith neighborhood, went to St. Barnabas School, and had a boyfriend too. When I heard that Emily and Monica would be bunkmates at camp the following summer, a gripping pain settled in under my tiny developing breasts. *I'm not going.*

Mrs. Ashworth said, "This'll be your last year. They need your lovely voice."

I ignored her.

My mother said, "It would be a chance to practice your singing."

I ended up changing my mind.

The other girls at camp were paired up, except for me and fat, pimply Frances, who lived by Monica. We were assigned to be bunkmates in a cabin several doors away from Emily's. Everywhere I went Frances tagged along, jabbering, "It's so much fun doing things together."

From afar, I watched Emily and Monica, whispering and laughing and giving each other easy pokes. One afternoon they were missing for hours. Counselors flew into a tizzy until the two showed up for dinner, where they behaved as if nothing had happened.

Frances, who knew everything, said, "Their boyfriends hitchhiked out here and met them in the woods."

A day or so later, trying unsuccessfully to lose her, I headed down a deserted path to the boathouse. There huddled Emily and Monica, smoking.

Frances gave me a nudge. "Should we report them?"

"I don't want to be a tattletale."

Toward the end of our two weeks, Emily approached me. "Come to our cabin after lights out."

"Sure," I said, hoping she didn't see me trembling.

"Bring Frances if you can't get rid of her."

In the dark, Frances and I entered Emily's cabin. Scantily dressed girls carried gleaming flashlights and talked in a garbled way and passed a bottle around.

The counselor, Monica's older sister, Sharon, said, "If you two want to belong in our club, you have to take your shirts off. Show us what you got."

Frances fumbled with a button as I backed away. They would howl at the rolls of fat beneath her large breasts. "You don't have to do this," I told her.

"I want to be part of their club."

"I'm leaving," I said. "You can go with me."

She shook her head.

Emily scowled. "You don't belong here anyhow."

I stumbled out the door and back to my cabin. I scrambled up to my bunk. I listened to the other girls' sighs and snores, trying to fall asleep on my wet pillow. When Frances crawled in the bottom bunk, I smelled something sort of sickly sweet like she'd thrown up. I heard muffled sobs.

We had our special program the last night. All I wanted was to go home. Still, I barely could conceal my disappointment when Reverend Newton handed out awards. A fourth grader who lived close to Frances and always went flat got Best Singer. Monica was chosen Friendliest.

Reverend Newton dramatically cleared his throat and boomed, "I'm proud to announce Best All Around Camper for 1959. This year's choice goes to a girl we all love and respect—Emily Price."

In September, Mom answered a telephone call. After a minute, she said, "I'm sorry, Mrs. Ashworth. Anne can't be in Advanced Choir. We've moved too far away. It won't be convenient to attend St. Barnabas any longer."

She hung up and saw me. Her face turned so red that the freckles disappeared. "You shouldn't have heard."

Truth was my parents were restoring an old brick house in the Hopper Street neighborhood with plenty of rooms for all of us.

I said, "Singing in my junior high choir is better."

The next Sunday morning, while Mom stirred waffle batter in our torn-apart kitchen, I overheard her say to Dad, "I'll never have to put up with that woman again."

For a while, I wanted to see Emily.

For a while, I wished she'd call so I could hang up.

For a while, I forgot about her.

In Motion

Martha Clarkson

After sleeping through take-off, The Screamer starts in again, same as he did at the gate. He's three rows up from us and not really a baby at all I suppose—he must be at least one, although I'm not adept at guessing baby ages. Toddlers can get away with anything on planes. It's not like at home, where mothers can say "I'm leaving you here in the frozen peas section if you don't stop crying" and walk around the end of a display of Cheez-Its, just out of view, until they hear the crying stop.

People shift in the narrow seats. Across the aisle, a man stops eating the bowl of strawberry salad he's brought from home. There are three other small children on the plane but their babble is kept to a din of tiny jabber that sounds like marbles clacking together in a bag.

We've been to visit our freshman daughter at college in Arizona. Tucson is nothing like we'd thought it would be. We imagined palm-lined esplanades, grass kept Kelly green with imported water, small-treed hills curving a lush edge around the city. Instead, it is miles of wide highways with unexpected traffic jams; the streets a monotony of small stucco houses with scrub lawns, peeling paint, and shells of cars in the side yards. Every few blocks, there are rundown businesses—drive-in liquor, the Prickly Pear Motel, Oasis Tailors, Hems While You Wait. It is a pancake of a city with a college full of square brick buildings plunked down in the center.

Our daughter takes us to her favorite places—Quik-Mart, where she buys a diet Dr. Pepper every day after math class; The Blue Cottage serving French toast "almost as good as Dad's," the university outlet of Urban Outfitters, which was her favorite store in Seattle. She tours us through her sorority, which she belongs to but doesn't yet live in and has to use the doorbell because she doesn't want to spend $50 on a key deposit. We've given her a semester's worth of freshman money to manage through Christmas and it's been encouraged that she come home with some left over. The out-of-state tuition sucks up her college fund like a turbo Hoover.

Half Italianate and half California McMansion and taking up a quarter block in the middle of Greek Row, her sorority house imposes itself on the street with four massive white columns. My husband is relegated to the ground floor while Jenny and I troll the upper halls looking for an open door so I can sneak a glimpse into a room.

"I'd knock on a door," she says in a low voice, "but they're all drunk from the homecoming parade." It's 4 p.m. For this, we pay an extra three thousand dollars a year.

The Screamer is still at it. In the aisle seat the father reads a paperback. I can see the mother's head bob as she tries different tactics to quiet him. The plane is his chance to get all the attention away from his six-year-old sister, slouched down in the seat, twirling her airplane wings in a probable state of mortification over her brother's decibel levels. The mother picks the baby up so he's above the seat back, facing the people in the row behind. All the heads in the surrounding rows turn to get a look at him, this tiny monster with the power to wake strangers from their altitude dreams. He has a Silly-Putty-like oval head and ear rims that glow red. So liquid are his eyes, it looks like we're seeing him underwater. The chance to see above the seat does nothing for his tantrum.

The mother gets up. The Screamer's at that Long-Body stage where carrying him is like carrying a duffle bag without using the handle. The father steps into the aisle to let her out. He pats The Screamer's head, his own flesh and blood, as they leave. I'm sure he's a fine father but you can tell he's glad to have the child taken somewhere else. He can return to his book or play a game of tic-tac-toe with his daughter.

Jenny and I played tic-tac-toe tournaments of our own from the time she was four. Cribbage belonged to her and her dad and the three of us were gin rummy nuts but tic-tac-toe belonged to us. On napkins in restaurants, on a whiteboard in my office, on the edge of the morning paper over breakfast. In sixth grade, I got her a three-level set and we played in dimension. As she boarded the plane for college last August, I handed her a square package to unwrap in Tucson—a mahogany board with an inlaid maple grid, heavy stainless steel Xs and Os tucked into a secret sliding drawer. Then, it had been a year since we'd played—she'd been blooming in another direction. Xs and Os meant something different.

In the pen of her dorm room, I see the board lodged upright on a bookshelf, partially hidden behind an empty bottle of Corona beer. The plastic wrapper is still on and I know she won't ask me to play.

Her roommate's name is Vine and she goes to Mexico every weekend, across the border to Nogales where the drinking age is null. So far, Jenny has not let herself be talked into this popular excursion, where the bus down cannot always be counted on to be the bus back. Most girls, she tells us, return with an MIP infraction—minor in possession—adding up to two hundred hours of community service all from a chance to eat the worm.

Jenny shows us the two fraternities that have the best parties—sake-slush nights and Commona Wanna luaus. A block away she gives us a cursory run through of the science library—so she can make sure we understand she knows it exists.

Remaining mum about her schoolwork has always been Jenny's way. In seventh grade, she even ventured to tell us the computers had broken at school and her report card would be late. All that just because of a C in math. She's the daughter of a Rhodes Scholar father but we have set no bar for her. She sets it for herself but often finds it sky-high. "It's hard," she admits over tacos, "but I'm doing my best." More than anything, she wants to be a nurse, but things like microbiology and chemistry are getting in her way. She just wants to take care of sick people. The old women she fed and bathed all summer at the nursing home cried when she left for college. If only there weren't the endless lists of muscle names, the study of mitochondria, the memorizations of drugs, like learning a foreign language.

At five years old, she clomped around the house with a toy hypodermic from her doctor kit giving us shots, including the cat. I'd be her patient and pretend to be afraid of shots. "There, there," she'd say, her still-pudgy hand rubbing my arm with a dry cotton ball, "no need to be afraid, it's just a schneedle." And to my arm would go the blunt blue end, like a gun muzzle more than a shot. I'd smile to show it didn't hurt and all was right with the world.

I ran a hand along her spine in what I think of as an affectionate-but-not-cloying gesture. "We know you're trying," I said, but was ashamed of the feeble sound of my reassurances. Over breakfast, at the French toast place, we empathized with the setting of priorities, how much she was dealing with all at once. We understood it more than she can imagine. It was too early to tell her I got a D in biology my first term at college. We expected her to settle and rise, in some fashion, but didn't say it.

The mother takes The Screamer to the back of the airplane. Another group about to be disturbed. Maybe she'll cloister the two of them in the miniature bathroom and let the screams ricochet off the molded plastic walls. Maybe the flight attendant in her tiny stainless steel lair will have a magic remedy. We can only hope. Sympathy, somewhere in the back of my brain, eludes me just now.

Within minutes, the woman and the child return, making a silent processional up the aisle. She taps the father on the shoulder. The child is dead-out, lopped across his mother's shoulder like thunder couldn't wake him. Adult heads around them are lolled back, this way and that, returned to their slumbers of work and money dreams. Our ears plug on the descent. In accidental synchronization, my husband and I yawn to clear them, our daughter six hundred miles behind us.

Thanksgiving 2015

Heidi Seaborn

"Best wishes from our family to yours."
—Hallmark

Brutal: derived from a king slayer, warlord, philanderer,
who turned coat, turned his back, turned on
the trusting hearts hung near his own.
My sister's brute sharpened heart, a weapon to drive
deep between the ribs of the man she once loved.

Not behind closed doors, a quiet killing.
No, a spectacle worthy of the Romans.
As our family gathered to give thanks for another year
of living, of loving, of one another.

Birth gave us front row seats in the Coliseum,
to watch a man bloodied by the ravages
of thirty years of unspoken stories.

I am the Hiritus of this moment, chronicling
what remains as Caesar shops for a new home
and the garden goes untended.

Hybrid Vigor

Leah Freiwald

My parents would tear out their tongues before they'd say a word against my marriage. Snug in their liberalism, they raised me to respect different cultures, ethnicities, lifestyles, orientations, and they insisted that I learn about all religions. World peace will come, they think, only when sects and factions recognize their commonality. For themselves, lifelong atheists, they forswear religious practice.

"All religions have good teachings," Nora says whenever the subject arises.

Ben then winks at me. "If you can ignore the nonsense about this or that supreme deity."

"And the Inquisition and the jihads." Nora abhors cruelty.

"Let's not forget the smiting of the Egyptian babies in the Passover *Haggadah*." Ben always mentions the dead Egyptian babies. Nora always nods. "So sad, so tragic for their parents."

As a mother now myself, I understand my parents' struggle to exemplify their ethos. They do not observe Christmas, Hanukkah, or Kwanzaa. Because my brother and I were both born in December, for a long time Nora claimed the fuss was in our honor. "All that tinsel. And the lights. It's for the two of you, darlings." She tried to convince us I was the Virgin and Jonathan the Prince of Peace everyone was singing about. To a child, that hardly compensated for the fact that Santa never came to our house.

In grade school, Rosh Hashanah stirred up a minor crisis. Ben explained it this way. "Yes, we're Jewish. But we don't belong to a temple, we don't attend services. So it's wrong to skip school." We did, however, live in a suburban Jewish neighborhood outside Chicago. Almost every other kid was out for the High Holidays. The teachers, who looked forward to an extra couple of days off, were not thrilled the Kaplan siblings, along with Stanley Li, whose parents owned the one Chinese restaurant, showed up.

When we moved to San Francisco, the issue resolved itself: there are no Jewish neighborhoods in San Francisco.

You'd think with such well-meaning open-minded parents a child would have nothing to rebel against. Not so. At eighteen my brother, Jonathan, signed up for an outreach program aimed at unaffiliated Jewish youth. The hook—a free trip to Israel.

Ben was suspicious. "They'll brainwash him. He'll come back a religious zealot."

"Don't be silly, dear. It's only a summer." Nora tries to see the best in people, a central tenet of her trust in a perfectible society. "It will be good for him. Expand his horizons. And, anyway, most Israelis are not religious."

It turned out to be worse than Ben imagined. After the tour ended, Jonathan did not come home. He passed an intense language course and, in a show of solidarity with those he now called his "brethren," joined an elite unit of the Israel Defense Force.

Nora was distraught. She wandered about the house, forgot to water the plants, burst into tears, steeled herself against the urge to pray for his safety. "I don't understand. Why can't he tell them he's a pacifist?"

"He's not a pacifist, Mom, you are." I held her hand, fed her aspirins. "You and Dad taught him to think for himself. Guess what? This is what he thinks. Besides, would you rather have him wandering the Judaean hills without a gun?"

Ben was, in his way, distraught as well. "We should never have let him go. It's like he joined a cult."

Ben and Nora flew to Israel. I don't know what arguments they used, but they returned without my brother. Ben refused to talk about it. His hair grayed noticeably. Nora consoled herself by mailing Jon all five volumes of Joseph Campbell on multicultural myths and Gandhi's autobiography.

This was before webcams and Twitter linked far-flung places on the globe. Once a paratrooper, Jonathan rarely wrote; and when he did, he skimped on details. Nora managed to find a bright spot. "At least we know he's exercising." She spent hours in her bedroom looking vacantly out the window, as if waiting for the small child Jonathan once was to come up the drive again, hiking up his jeans, dragging his book bag.

I was preoccupied with my own life, more so once I was miles away at a small college in New England. The first semester I was homesick. Appalled at the naiveté of my fellow freshmen, most of them overprotected overachievers who'd never seen a psychedelic shroom or had a pervert open his raincoat on the bus. Away from parental eyes they reveled through the night. The noise and impositions on my privacy were constant.

At the weekly mixer I cringed when asked to dance and the first question was—"What does your father do?" This concern for status always put me off. Where was the liberal spirit that ought to flourish amid the liberal arts? After a pause I'd say, "Oh, he's a lawyer." My partner would visibly relax. Maybe the black lacquer on my fingernails didn't reflect my politics. "A civil rights attorney." Then, quietly, "My mother's a union organizer." If he pictured five-foot tall Nora leading burly pipe fitters out on strike, I didn't correct him. Head of the teachers' union might pass for respectable.

"You can come home, you know," said Nora whenever I phoned to whine. "There are lots of colleges in California."

"Give it some time," said Ben. "Tough it out."

By the end of the year, I'd adapted. There were benefits: the change of seasons, angels in the snow, fine teachers, a few less preppy friends. An internship at a primary school decided my vocation. The more deprived the kids, the better. "I'm so proud of you," Nora wrote.

Perhaps due to an improved attitude, my social life blossomed. I happily sampled experience, free of faith-based restrictions. Every male who seemed attracted to me was a potential lover. Coffee with a turbaned Sikh? Why not? Lunch with a Saudi playboy? My pleasure.

It was as much a surprise to me as to anyone that I fell in love with Matt. Matthew McDonald, sixth generation Yankee, Scots-Irish with a smidge of Algonquin. He's blonde, blue-eyed, a ringer for a young Brad Pitt, superficially as preppy as they come. He's also kind, generous, strong in his own principles, and, most important, he loves me, too.

Junior year, I brought Matt home for spring break. Ben treated him like a second son. They played chess ruthlessly. Matt indicated he might go to law school. Ben smiled. "How do you like California?" He took Matt down to meet the other partners at his firm.

Nora cornered me. "Tell me, Deb. Is this as serious as it looks? I mean, I know you're always serious, but this?"

"He's the one, Mom. Isn't he gorgeous? And don't fret, he's not as conventional as he looks. He walked a precinct for Al Gore."

"That's a relief."

I sensed she wasn't saying everything she was thinking. "What is it? What's bothering you?"

"Oh, well, I mean—you say he's a lapsed Baptist."

"Right. You know that."

"Well, what if—maybe—don't you worry a little that he might relapse?"

"You're kidding, Mom. Please say you're kidding."

"I'm kidding."

When Jonathan completed two stints of active duty, he entered a yeshiva in New York to become a rabbi. Ben and Nora were stunned. They phoned me at 2 AM my time.

"Where did we fail?" Nora said. "Tell me where."

Ben didn't wait for my opinion. "It's some sort of weird karma. The kid's punishing us. Who knows why?"

"Hush, Ben. Maybe Debra knows. That's why we're calling her. Maybe he's told her why he hates us."

"Don't be melodramatic. He doesn't hate us. He's rejecting us, yes. Rejecting what we stand for. He's acting out some bizarre post-teenage Oedipal impulse."

"Yoo-hoo, you two." I raised my voice. "Listen. It's not about you guys. Honestly. It's about Jonathan. This is what Jonathan wants to do with his life. If you don't want to lose him, alien as it seems to you, you have to respect his choice."

Nora gasped. "Lose Jonathan? What do you mean? He's my child, my first-born."

"I don't know what I mean. All I know is—this is his decision. You'd better get used to it. And he's not a child."

"Of course, you're right." Nora hesitated. "Oh, well. Thank goodness he's back in this country. Only five hours away by plane."

Yet despite the number of flights from New York to San Francisco, it seemed Jon was too busy to come home for a visit. "I have a lot of catching up to do, you know," he stalled.

To me, he said, "How can I tell them I can't eat in their house? Are they suddenly going to keep separate dishes and cutlery? They think the laws of *kashrut* are remnants of barbaric tribal totems."

"Is it possible you're underestimating them? They're basically nice people. Remember? And they love you. You might talk to them about it."

"I can't. Believe me, they can't either. What I'm doing is anathema to them. I know that. You know that. They simply don't approve of me."

"That's pretty funny. They think you don't approve of them."

"Ah. And how about you, Deb? Do you approve? I mean, really. Or do you parrot whatever the parents say?"

That stopped me. Was it possible that I, who'd been taught to respect all religions, who lectured Ben and Norah about the need to respect Jon, that I, Miss True Blue California Lefty, was not respectful of Jonathan's newfound religion? Did I even understand why he embarked on this spiritual journey? Had he found something lacking in our childhood?

"Listen, Deb, this is not a joke. I am not a joke."

In May of that year an elaborately engraved letter arrived. Jon was requesting we attend his Bar Mitzvah. Ben said, "Whoever heard of a twenty-four-year-old Bar Mitzvah Boy?" He pounded on the table. "You'll have to drag me up to that altar," he thundered at Nora, "if you think I'll recite that mumbo jumbo."

Nora said, "We have to be there."

In the end, we all went. Ben performed his part: he read the transliteration of a psalm, his voice a hoarse croak. Nora and I sat in the women's section. My mother gripped my hand fiercely. At a distance, Jon seemed like another person: thinner, a sparse beard, a receding hairline. His speech acknowledged his parents' role during his childhood, but he very much regretted that they failed to make a Jewish home for him. He had, he said, to find that path on his own. From the corner of my eye, I saw Nora blanch.

Afterwards we lined up in the meeting room, Jonathan stiff beside us in his pristine white *talis*. People embraced him, congratulated us. My parents maintained fixed smiles. Strange as the proceedings were for them, how could they hold out against their only son? They acquiesced for the sake of family, even as Jon repudiated their most precious family values.

Once ordained, Jon accepted a post at a *shul* on the east coast. "He has his work now, the work he's trained to do," Nora said. "My son, the rabbi." She sighed. "We must resign ourselves to being on the outside looking in, tiny dots on the periphery of his life. We can't expect him to have time for us."

"I've no idea what to expect from him anymore," Ben growled.

Fearful of a misstep, feeling more and more excluded, they avoided subjects that might widen the gap—the crevasse, Nora said—yawning between them. "I dare not express an opinion about the poor Palestinians or those rightwing evangelicals who pretend to love Israel. Anything I might say would make him angry."

Over the months, I too avoided angering my brother. I didn't tell him Matt and I shared an apartment a few blocks from the parents. He wouldn't be happy for me. For Jon, my happiness was taboo. On occasion he brought it up.

"Are you still seeing the WASP?"

"He's not a WASP. He's Scots-Irish with a—"

"I know. Blond. Blue-eyed. Spare me."

And so I did. Inevitably we spoke less often. I immersed myself in the small, small world that was my class of eight year olds—immigrant Chinese and Russians, Hispanics, Samoans, three Caucasians, various racial mixtures, children with two mothers—assembled in proportion to the city's rich diversity. I loved teaching, loved Matt, loved my life. Still, I missed the older brother I'd always idolized.

Did Jon miss me? The parents? Had he found someone also, or was his an ascetic existence, devoted to good works for his congregation? It seemed, at times, as if our nuclear family had shrunk to just the three of us: Ben, Nora, and me. I did my best to be a good daughter, and I knew my presence was for them a support. But I also knew it was not good enough. The absence of their son was a never-ending ache that only Jonathan could heal. When Ben went into the hospital and came out with half a colon, I asked Nora whether I should tell Jon. "No, no," she said. "We don't want to disturb him." The worst of the pain for me was watching my mother's pain. He hadn't bothered to acknowledge the gift she sent on his birthday.

Tensions flared when Ben took on *pro bono* a suit to remove the words "under God" from the Pledge of Allegiance. For Ben, it was the principle, separation of church and state, so dear to his heart and to his hero, Thomas Jefferson. CNN carried the story, interviewing the man who wouldn't allow his daughter to recite the pledge in her kindergarten class. Jonathan, in one of his rare phone calls, accused Ben of courting publicity. His anger blanketed us all with scorn.

"I'll bet Mom is behind you on this, isn't she? Ready to call out the troops for a godless America. And Deb? Where does she fit in? Is the girl in Deb's school? Don't tell me. You're all a bunch of kneejerk—"

Ben hung up on him.

Before my brother could refuse, I flew east. The taxi dropped me at a cottage on a quiet tree-lined street off a village green. Jon picked up my bag, kissed the *mezuzah* on the doorpost, and ushered me inside. His beard had filled in; he looked tired, gaunt.

"In a few hours the Sabbath will begin," he said. "Here are the rules—no car, no electric lights, no exchange of money. I hope you brought more modest clothing." I tried to pull down my skirt.

That evening and the next day until sunset, Jonathan led services in the synagogue. That he was well regarded, even loved, was evident. He introduced me to the congregants, among them a young woman, Eva, whose gaze tracked Jon alone. Back at the house, I teased him about his admirer.

Jon flushed. "Her father's president of the board. We work together closely."

"How nice. But I was asking about Eva."

"Yes, well, we'll probably be married. I want to start a family. We both do. Family's important to both of us."

"That's wonderful. I'm so pleased. The parents will be delighted when they find out." I reached to touch him.

He smiled shyly. "You really think so?"

"I'm positive. Why wouldn't they be? They've already welcomed Matt."

In an instant the smile vanished. “You mean the WASP? You're going to marry him? And they're pleased about that? Of course. They would be. How stupid of me.”

“I'm sorry, Jon. I've been meaning to tell you.”

“And now you have.” He climbed the stairs to his bedroom and shut the door.

I called out. “It would be so great if you were pleased for me, too.”

The night passed slowly. I couldn't sleep. What had I thought I could accomplish? That I'd find a trace of the brother who encouraged me to try again when I failed the swim test at camp? Who let me stay up to watch Saturday Night Live when he babysat? Maybe I hoped to see a glint of his sense of humor. How foolish of me.

How was I going to tell Ben and Nora? How could Jonathan insist family was so important to him and in the next breath ostracize his family—his parents, me? Was his religion—making a Jewish home, whatever the hell that was—more important than we were to him? Through the night I wept for us, and I wept for him, too.

By the time I pulled myself together in the morning, the smell of coffee gave me an excuse to face Jon in the kitchen. “I'll be off to the airport soon,” I said. “You know, coming here I had a crazy hope you'd officiate at my wedding.”

He didn't respond. The coffee mug commanded his attention.

“Well, OK,” I said. “Be that way.”

The taxi honked. Jonathan shook his head as if to clear his thoughts. “One thing, Deb. You should know that whoever is your husband, your children will be Jewish. According to rabbinic law, the children of a Jewish woman are Jewish.”

“Screw you, Jonathan. You don't even bother to find out what sort of person Matt is and why he's my soul mate. All you see is that he isn't Jewish. I'm afraid you've become an intolerant prick.” I shouldered my bag. “Now you listen to me. My children will be hybrids. You know what a hybrid is? A blending of the best traits from two parents. My children will get the best from Matt and from me.”

Plans for the wedding came together smoothly. Matt hired a DJ, and our friend Christa had herself ordained online. Christa is half-Jewish; it's the other half that named her after Christ. We booked a former disco dancehall; and we wrote our own vows, combining bits of Buddhist, Jewish, Baha'i, and Native American lore. Emma, Matt's widowed mother, held his arm down the aisle. When Christa placed the wineglass on the toe of Matt's shoe, he stared at it for a long minute, then let it roll off and stomped on it.

Jonathan did not attend. He and I have not spoken since my visit. Ben can't bring himself to accept his son's silence. “Jon claims he's a religious Jew, but in the name of religion he shuns his sister. That's simply wrong.” When Jon married Eva, only Nora went.

Without my brother—and his future family—it's as if a major limb of the Kaplan tree has been lopped off. What's left is an unremitting phantom pain. Even so, we find occasions for good feelings. Matt finished law school and joined Ben's firm. We've devised a holiday schedule that is equitable: Thanksgiving with my parents, Christmas with Matt's mother; my birthday with my parents, Matt's with Emma.

Mother's Day is a little tricky.

When Jenny was born, Matt and I, Ben and Nora, Emma, too, were joyful. We all view her as a genius, a princess, the most remarkable child in the world, if not the universe. In December, the Christmas muzak blaring everywhere, I say to Nora, "I won't tell her she's the Virgin, but I will tell her she's the best present I ever had."

"I've been thinking. This year why don't I make a Hanukkah party for her? You know, *latkes* and maybe a *dreidle*."

"I don't know. A *dreidle* is innocuous, I guess. But the warlike Maccabees—how does that sit with your pacifist beliefs?"

"If you don't like the idea—"

"No, I like it. Why shouldn't Jenny be exposed to Hanukkah as well as Christmas at Nana Emma's?"

And so on the first night of Hanukkah, we gather for an ethnic, cultural, seasonal festivity. Nora does not go so far as to set up a *menorah* and pray over the candles. When we're all seated, she brings a platter of golden *latkes* to the table. In high spirits, we lavish sour cream and applesauce on the hot potato pancakes. I blow on a forkful and offer it to Jenny. "Yum," she says.

Ben leans over and in mock-somber tones says, "When you're older, Jenny dear, you'll see Hanukkah for what it is—a historical footnote ballyhooed to let Jews join in the consumerism of the season." Jenny giggles.

Matt finishes his sixth *latke* and refuses another. "What do we do now?"

"I'm not sure," I say. "We're on unfamiliar ground. Did you find a *dreidle*, Mom?"

"Oh. No, but that reminds me. There's a present for someone out on the patio."

"For me?" Jenny jumps up. She grabs my hand and Matt's. "Let's go see."

We stand in the darkness while Ben pulls up a large unwieldy object. Nora switches on the patio lighting. Jenny runs over and begins to rip the wrapping paper from a pink two-wheeler, just the size for a five-year-old's first bicycle. It glitters in the half-light; purple streamers dangle from the handlebars.

"How beautiful," I say. "Isn't it, Jenny?"

Jenny stamps her foot. "Take it away. Take it away right now." She bursts into tears and runs to me, burying her head in my side.

"What's wrong, sweetie?" Ben seems dazed by her reaction.

I hold my daughter tight while she begins to scream. Wordless, shattering screams. What is this? She never throws tantrums. Higher and higher, her voice hurts my ears. This is a full-blown tantrum. After several minutes she calms herself, snuffling against my skirt.

Matt puts his hand on Jenny's hair. "Tell us what's the matter," he says.

"Oh, Daddy." She rushes into his arms. "I asked Santa for a bike. He's going to get me one. It's already on his list."

I stare at my husband. "What's this about?"

"It's OK, Jen," Matt says, rubbing her back. "My fault, folks. When we were at the mall last week, she wanted to sit on Santa's lap. I'm so sorry. I didn't think."

"Well," I say, "we can tell Santa you have a bike."

"No, no, no," Jenny starts to scream again. "It's too late. He's not at the mall anymore. He's back at the North Pole with the elves."

Matt picks her up and carries her into the kitchen. He takes out his cell phone. "Look here, sweet pea. You've seen me check my messages, haven't you?"

Jenny bobs her head.

"That's all I have to do. I'll text Santa. Tell him your grandparents gave you a magnificent bike for Hanukkah. He'll understand."

Jenny looks at Matt. She seems to weigh his words. At last she smiles. "Do it. Do it now, Daddy. Tell Santa."

"First, blow your nose. Then thank Grandma and Grandpa for your Hanukkah present."

I look around for Nora. She's slipped away. I find her in the dining room, gazing at the *latkes*, now cold and hard in a congealed pool of oil.

From Earth

Tara Ballard

You see the stars
only
when dew-drop   comets
                    give themselves

to find rest
above a halo   of trees:
their purple-dark

smudge of leaves
breathing warmth
to a soil-rich bouquet,

and even on nights
like this   one,

the mantis   in prayer

may
pause   to whisper the words

of the prophet
weeping

for this breaking   of heaven
and light.

In the Aftermath of Grief

Briana Loveall

On the day that Christopher Harper-Mercer shot and killed members of his English composition class, I was applying for a job as a writing teacher in a local hospital. While we discussed specific job duties and the emotional detachment that necessitated working with sick children, Umpqua Community College students huddled together, in the aftermath of one man's rage, in grief. Later, I picked up my six-year-old daughter from school and held her too tightly until she complained and squirmed away. She is still young enough to live unaware of the dangers she faces every time she walks through her school door.

Like many Americans, I've seen too many depictions of shootings. I've seen them acted out in movies and YouTube with sad music in the background. I've looked at low quality images taken from a phone, secreted beneath a desk. It is too easy to imagine what happened at Umpqua.

A typical day that starts with roll call, the teachers go over the lesson plans, there are papers to turn in, please gather into small groups now for discussion. Someone walks in late and you don't pay any attention because college students are nothing if not notoriously late. But then the atmosphere changes, things are suddenly charged and there is a sense that something very bad is about to happen. Your classmate, the guy no one really likes, the one you try to avoid after class because he makes you feel weird, is standing in the doorway with a gun. You think this should be a joke. You're waiting for the part where he takes off the mask of fury, acknowledges the poor joke, and then sits in his seat to discuss the critical essay. But he begins yelling and suddenly everyone understands the joke was in believing such a thing as safety existed.

Media following the shooting shows students clinging to each other in grief, shoulders hunched forward as they attempt to bear the weight of death without relief. I watched those clippings on my phone while waiting for my own college classes to start. Later, I would walk to my car with my mace unlocked and clenched in my fist.

I was raised in a world filled with the boogeymen parents warn their children about, the same monsters I teach my daughter about now. I have listened to Amber Alerts, read obituaries of classmates, and watched students on TV huddled together for comfort. I live in a world inundated with events called horrific, unjust, and deplorable, but each day, when I pull through the valet line at my daughter's school and watch as her braid and pink backpack disappear into the mob of other small children, and I wonder if my last words to her, that I will see her after school, are true. This chill of uncertainty settles over me like an impenetrable mist that no amount of logic can eradicate.

I struggle to find comfort here.

The names run together in a stream of nightmarish flashbacks: Columbine, Virginia Tech, Sandy Hook, Umpqua, Oikos, and Red Lake. Knowing even half of these names means I have become accustomed to the possibility that my life, or the lives of those I know, might end within the safety of a school classroom.

The shootings are often used for platforms to launch political agenda. Politicians and angry parents stand in front of cameras and make declarative statements with attempts to sway a nation to change. *This is a gun control issue, this is mental health awareness, this is having parents in the home, this is knowing what your teens are doing with their free time, video games, media, gangs, culture, self-protection, constitutional rights, human rights, inalienable rights, you have the right to remain silent, you have the right to a fair trial, you have the right to a last meal.*

Where is the right for safety?

I have sat in my own Graduate English classes, ones that now include a lock on every door, and struggled to remember exactly when they were installed. I have overheard teachers recount stories of calling security on angry students, and then dismiss the event with a shrug or joke.

The real story is this. A man once walked by my class. He was good looking and tall, hardly someone I expected to walk in and start shooting. He held a paper in his hand and peered into the room. His face was taught and grim and I became distracted by the intensity of his stare. He walked away from the window and I was drawn back towards the lecture. He'd reappeared in the corner of my eye and I felt the familiar fears from a lifetime of horror stories fall over me like a shield.

What would I have done if he'd walked in and started shooting?

I like to pretend that I am just paranoid, one of those helicopter moms who would rather insert their child into a protective bubble than send them into a world that hurts without remorse. Or someone with an overactive imagination that runs unlikely scenarios through my head as a form of entertainment. But when I live in a world where I have to ask myself if the images I've seen, of college students crouched together in front of buildings, will someday be a picture of someone I know, or if the lockdown drills my daughter practices at school will ever be necessary, I don't know that I can blame all of my fear on strict paranoia.

Instead, each shooting seems to reinforce my inability to understand the world. So I watch the news clippings of Umpqua students huddled together, their college sweaters the only thing distinguishing them from any of the other school shootings. I sit in my own college classes and struggle to focus on the discussions when the loud voices of students down the hall startle my heart into overtime, and I watch my daughter's small figure recede into the montage of bright jackets and sneakers, and hope, that I will see her again soon.

Signs of Grace at Hotel San Gil
City center, Sevilla

Jeffrey Alfier

I. Daybreak

On the patio, Balkan students slump
in plastic chairs. Traveling cheap, they reek
of wine, canned meat, pilfered cigarettes —
their clothes a mélange of charity shops.
A young woman with disheveled
hair, thin as rickets, ambles over to them
with her sleep-dumb eyes, her face the warmth
of some beautiful hurt. I envy them,
all their laughter and complacent ecstasy.

II. Nightfall

Rough words from a room down the hall —
a woman scolds a man as if he were a child.
One floor below, quick footsteps thud, like baggage
lobbed into airline cargo decks. The sounds
are balanced by soft talk that leaks over a balcony
across the street. From a low rooftop,
strung laundry takes the sound of fluttering sails.
Streetlights and a soft breeze throw twisted
shapes, like smoke, against my window.

Syntax Error

David Shrauger

Tim had loved the library before the accident, but now it was his prison. It had become a place they put him during recess so that he didn't have to watch the other children playing hopscotch, tetherball, and tag.

Accident. That was what they called it; the word everybody had agreed upon to describe it, as any other word would require more explanation than anyone was comfortable with.

He was propped up in front of the Apple II, the only computer the elementary school owned. It was 1987, but Cedar Creek Elementary was hardly on the cutting edge of technology. Tim looked at the dark green screen of the computer, its cursor flashing at him with mechanical impatience.

"You leave me alone," Tim heard a girl scream from the playground. He turned to the window to see two boys running past as fast as they could. He looked down at the cast that held his leg in one straight line. It itched, so he poked a pencil underneath it in a futile effort to relieve it.

In a little plastic tray next to the computer, there was a stack of black floppy discs. He pulled one out to take a closer look at it.

"Create with Garfield," its label said.

He inserted the floppy into its drive and closed the spring-loaded catch. Looking at the impatiently flashing cursor, he tried to remember the command that would activate the software. He didn't know how to operate the computer, but he had seen it done before. He could have asked the librarian for help, but he didn't want to seem stupid. He'd had enough of that. Tim was ten years old, not a baby anymore.

Play Garfield, he typed.

"Syntax Error" was the computer's response.

Start Garfield.

"Syntax Error."

Run Garfield. Tim struck the keys harder than he had to.

"Syntax Error."

One week ago, Tim had stayed up too late. A girl named Jessica had fallen down a well, and Tim's entire family had been glued to the television set waiting for news of her rescue. It was a school night and Tim had drifted off to sleep on the couch in front of the television. The next day, he fell asleep in class, and the teacher grabbed him by the ear and dragged him to the principal's office. He told Mr. Doubleday what had happened, but the man wasn't moved. Tim would have to come in that weekend for detention.

He had never fallen asleep on the school bus before. It seemed an impossible thing to do, as the bus that took him up Highway 9 five days a week was a raucous and rowdy experience. He had never missed his stop before that day, always hopping out next to the natural gas pipeline that ran near his home. It didn't change the fact that on that day he had slept through his stop … and the next … and the next.

It was the silence that finally woke him. Not one child's voice was to be heard. When Tim snapped awake, he had never felt so alone.

"Last stop," the bus driver shouted. Tim was surprised to find that it wasn't Dixie's voice.

Dixie was a large, soft, impossibly kind woman who had endless patience with the children on her bus, but in her place was a hard, blocky man who couldn't have been more rugged if he was carved out of wood.

The brakes hissed and the door snapped open, but when Tim looked around, there was nothing but trees. He made his way toward the front, rubbing the sleep out of his eyes as he walked.

"Please, sir," Tim said when he reached the driver's seat, "I missed my stop. Could you please take me home?"

"I'm sorry, buddy," the driver said. "I'm not headed back that way. I'm headed to the bus depot and the district doesn't let me drive students in my car. Maybe your parents can come and pick you up. Go on, get out now."

The bus driver's tone seemed impatient and he scared Tim a little, so he did what he was told. He stepped off and the doors snapped shut behind him.

As the bus took off, he realized that he had left his backpack. He waved and shouted for the driver to stop, but it was too late. He hadn't even slowed down.

The road he had been left on wasn't paved and there were no power lines on either side of it. Tufts of grass grew in a little stripe down the center where wheels never touched and the trees that bracketed it seemed a thousand feet tall. There was nothing to do but begin walking back, so Tim started backtracking the direction the bus had taken—his grass-stained Chuck Taylors kicking up dust and dirt.

Tim didn't see any sign of a house or a paved road. He listened, but he didn't hear any traffic. He hoped to hear the telltale sound of the log trucks that constantly roared down Highway 9, but there was nothing but the sound of birds in the trees.

It was getting darker, but he couldn't tell if it was from the sun going down or because the trees blocked out the sky. His heart sped up and then all but stopped when he heard the first coyote howl.

"Syntax Error" remained on the screen.

He knew he had made a mistake, but he didn't know what it was. The device was asking him to do something simple, but he didn't know what.

Looking down at his cast, he saw the words his classmates had written on it his first day back. It was covered with well-wishes and get-well-soons. Some of the scribbles were rubbing off.

"Syntax Error."

The cursor on the screen continued to flash with the same mechanical beat like an impatient teacher tapping their foot, waiting for an answer that was too slow to come.

He felt one of his attacks coming on. Attacks. That was what the school counselor called the fits of blind terror that had come and gone since the "accident" out in the woods. His chest began to tighten and he swallowed uncontrollably. Tears pooled in his eyes, and he squeezed them shut in an effort to keep them from rolling down his cheeks.

Hey there, buddy. You need a little help?

"Syntax Error" was all the screen offered.

Just as dusk was beginning to cover the woodlands of the upper Skagit River, Tim found a clear-cut. The smell of cedar had filled Tim's nostrils and he followed his nose until he found it just as the sun was going down. It had seemed much darker in the tall trees that towered over the dirt road, but when he saw the rosy glow just over the unfamiliar hill, he took a moment to appreciate the beauty of what he was seeing. For that moment, things didn't seem so scary.

The forest was decimated. From his vantage point it looked as if a great beast had taken a bite out of the entire landscape. A muddy creek ran down through the center, with a kind of improvised wooden bridge placed across it. The loggers who cut the trees needed to get them to the mill and, for that, they needed a road. Tim knew that if he could find it, he could find his way home.

Tim traversed the clear-cut by jumping from one enormous stump to the next. The abandoned detritus of the loggers fluttered all around him as the wind blew: empty potato-chip bags, soda cans, clusters of chewing tobacco containers and cigarette packs. He kicked over cans that he found sitting on the stumps, spilling foul brown liquid. It was the closest he had come to having fun all day, and certainly since he had been kicked off the bus.

He knew that his mom would be home by now. She always got home from her job before it got dark. She had to be worried, but she would probably beat him with the belt when he showed up. In his imagination, he chopped down trees and lashed them together into a raft that he could use to light out for the territories. There were not any territories to be had; however, and he was not Huck Finn. He had no choice but to go home.

On the other side, he found a road. It wasn't Highway 9. But it was gravel instead of packed dirt. It had uphill and downhill routes; he chose to go downhill. While he walked, he first realized how thirsty he was, and cold, and hungry. He heard the coyote howl again, and another answer. Darkness had crept up on him until it finally fell on the gravel road. The howling got louder and closer.

Tim had never seen a coyote, but he was as familiar with their song as he was with the mournful wail of the train that rattled past his home at night. They both had a way of keeping him awake. He had found bloody evidence of their activities when he played with his friends in the woods. He needed to get home, or someplace safe, before he ended up on the receiving end of the teeth that turned those forest creatures into red scraps.

The gravel road wound down an endless hill. The trees got smaller, thinner, and he could see the moon through their branches. It was just a sliver of itself, but it was better than no light at all. He could see his breath as he exhaled and he wrapped himself a little tighter in his coat. He thought that he heard the sound of a car, but when he stopped to listen more closely, he heard nothing.

It was an hour later when he found a paved road, honest-to-God asphalt. The sign said "S&S Grade Rd."

"Syntax Error," the dark screen told him in its green letters.

Tim wiped away his tears. He had forgotten what he wanted to do with the computer. He was typing whatever came into his mind.

Help me.

"Syntax Error."

Save me.

"Syntax Error."

Why?

"Syntax Error."

Don't be a stupid little boy. Don't you know what happens to stupid little boys?

"Syntax Error."

The headlights surprised him, coming around a sharp blind turn of S&S Grade Road. A foot to the left and the vehicle would have smashed Tim against the railing that protected motorists from a precipitous drop.

The van screeched to a stop, fishtailing a little before going into reverse and pulling back toward where Tim was huddling against the guardrail. Tim waved; relieved to have finally found someone in the empty wilderness. The van pulled parallel to him and the window rolled down. The man he saw was nobody he knew.

"Hey there, buddy. You need a little help?" the man asked with a yellow smile.

"I'm lost," Tim said. It was the first time he had said that out loud, and the first time he had admitted that to himself.

"Well, get on in. I'll get you home."

Something made Tim hesitate. A tiny flicker of intuition or a small, still voice. Something told him not to get into the van.

"My mom told me not to ride with strangers. Could you just tell me which way to go to get to George Road on Highway 9?"

"Don't be a dummy. That has to be thirty miles away."

"I'll be okay," Tim said, although he wasn't sure that was the truth.

The man seemed to change at once. His yellow smile disappeared. He pulled the emergency brake and opened the door to step out. He was huge, bigger than Tim's gym teacher.

"Don't be stupid," he said. "Get in the van."

Tim tried to step back a little, but the man grabbed a big handful of his coat in a huge, hairy fist.

"Please," Tim said.

"Don't be a stupid little boy. Don't you know what happens to stupid little boys?"

"Please …"

"You and I are just gonna take a little ride and … Holy shit!"

The man was startled. Tim couldn't see what he was looking at over his shoulder, but he took the opportunity to get away, pulling himself out of his coat and tripping over the rail. He didn't even have a moment to regret the decision before he found himself rolling down a hill covered in blackberry bushes. He felt himself being torn apart by rocks and thorns alike, then was airborne for a brief moment before landing on his side. His leg was bent the wrong way. When the pain of it hit his brain, he screamed like he had never screamed before.

"You stupid little fucker! Are you still alive down there?"

Tim cried and whimpered. He couldn't move his leg at all. He could hear movement and breaking brush on the hill above him. The man was coming, cursing and swearing at every thorn and blackberry bush on the way down.

He knew that he couldn't run away, but he could crawl. He rolled over onto his stomach and crawled, amazed at the pain, but feeling it awakened something in him. A hard, fast surge of will to survive. There was a culvert running underneath the road, a little trickle of water. If he couldn't run, he could hide.

The culvert was just big enough for a boy, but much too small for a man to squeeze into. He crawled into its darkness, looking ahead to the dim light at the other end. He couldn't see behind him, but he kept crawling. He didn't want the man to reach in and pull him out. He didn't know what would happen if he did, but he didn't want to find out.

"I see you in there, you little bastard." The man's voice reverberated through the culvert as he shined a flashlight into the pipe.

Tim rolled onto his back and lifted his head, putting his chin to his chest. He could only see the man's legs.

"What is wrong with you? If you don't get out of this pipe … fuck! I'm gonna cut your little pecker off for this! You hear me, you little shithead?"

The man continued to curse, but he couldn't get far enough into the culvert to reach Tim. He tried for what seemed like a very long time, cursing and saying even more horrible things. Tim just lay there, feeling the trickle of water down his back. Tim lay in the slime and in the darkness, listening to the reverberating voice of the man with the yellow smile.

Then the man screamed.

Tim looked up and saw the flashlight fall to the ground. There was a sound of running through the bushes, then a rustling noise, then something else he couldn't identify. Something he had never heard before, even in his nightmares.

It was quiet for a time, and then there was a shuffling noise near the opening of the culvert. The flashlight illuminated the face of the coyote, allowing Tim to see the blood on its muzzle. The animal sniffed around the culvert a little more, lapped a little at the trickle of water, and then turned to leave. As he listened to it pad away into the darkness, Tim laughed a strange laugh despite the tears that flowed freely down his cheeks.

In the library. In the culvert. In the school. In the wilderness. In the day. In the night. Awake. Asleep. Lost. Found. Mother. Stranger. Headlights. Road. Pain. Stupid.

Coyote, he typed.

"Syntax Error."

The Boy Graces

Cameron Quan Louie

swapping dramas &
sipping Listerine
on the late bus,
remind each other
what girls like. For two
years, says one boy, slipping
both vowels out of
years, I made it
with a splendid
delivery girl – she
was devoted to
High Life in bottles,
organic tobacco –
for two whole years,
we slept together
without

touching, though
so close, I could glut
my mirth on her sleep,
the compact turning
of her thoughts there
suspended like
a drop of nectar
over my face.
Another boy blinks & eats
the night with his eyes,
the late bus still
gracing the road,
& he & the glad
faced songsters hug
in plastic seats, choir
the tired riders
with sour breath

so brimming and sere
that it could be
love – I'm really so
comfortable here, says
a lady in the back.

All three boys smile
in her direction
so that years go by,
a long appoggiatura,
friends and expensive
sheets worn out.
Look at her, says one,
cheerfully pointing
with his long tongue,
it's cute when they twitch,
is she dreaming,
do you think, of
running, eyes drawn,
through prostrate leaves,
away from home &
its two lit streets?

4.23pm, Wednesday, 21 November, 2014

Sean Hennessey

"Hands are unbearably beautiful.
They hold on to things. They let things go."
—Mary Ruefle, "The Cart"

Timeofdeath:4.23pm Wednesday21November2014intheyearofourmadness

The room is quiet. The window is ajar and the curtains are thrown wide, the blinds are down but they are turned out to allow in the sun. Its reddened light is hard as daggers and chops the still shadows, forcing them back. They cannot engulf us, me, yet, though they soon will. I am here, her body is here, she is not. The room is cold. My breath is a fog. She fails to draw anything in: she emits no air, offers no transience of condensed moisture.

She has given up the practice.

I seal her eyes with my thumb and ring finger. A gentle closing, done with a downward swipe, and the most intimate of our connections is permanently severed. It is a relief, in a way, as their blankness was too much. If the eyes are the windows to the soul, what can they show you when the electrical spark that separates us from meat is gone?

They just stare up into emptiness, refusing to lock hold with your own, their gaze slipping away despite their lack of motion. The room appears clearer now. The shadows in the lower corners dissolve from a stolid black to a more forgiving reddish-blueish, livid, bruising gray.

Her lids rest softly over her eyes. There's no tension there, no strain to keep the timbres of her irises hidden in pretense. No shuffling underneath, no rustling like the sheets above an uneasy sleeper. Her long lashes reflect the light, blue-black with a shimmer of silver where the glint is strongest. Although her lips fade from red to purple to a puckered blue and her cheeks turn ashy, her lashes are full, making them seem ready to open.

3.45pmMonday3May2004ActivatedDimentia

I am alone, but in a minute she will come. We haven't met but it happens soon. Any second now. Not that I'm counting. I'm sitting outside a café in Minneapolis, face-in a book: a poet worshiping an impressionist. It is the first truly magnificent day of spring and the light is warm on my torso, which is wrapped tight in denim and cotton. It's too much for the sunlight but in the shade, well, one never knows. I'm nursing my second cigarette of the afternoon; I'm cutting down from the daily four of the last few weeks to three for the next couple. After that, it will be one, and then, hopefully, none. I'm trying not to think that far in advance. I smoke the last quarter inch of the cigarette with deliberation, hoping to sate at least the mental need for a while, then stub it out before the filter can begin to burn. I return to trying to figure out why I highlighted a specific description in the book. There's no note next to it and the ten years since my studies ceased have erased its significance. I'm considering this when she walks up to my table, her coffee tossing steam into the air. She startles me. I hadn't noticed her coming.

Excuse me, she asks, can I have a cigarette?

I have to pull back from the nineteenth century. I reach in my jeans for my pack and a lighter then hand them to her.

Take what you need, I say, still at a distance.

Oh, thank you, she says back. She sits at the table across from me. I'm not sure if I welcome her there or not. I know that I'm not fully here. She barely seems to be. Between the sunlight and me, she is mostly outline. Dark hair, pulled back into a ponytail that's bound at the base of her neck, a long fringe that caresses her forehead. She's dressed simply. Cotton, mostly, and jeans as ratty as mine, a sweatshirt that reads Property of the Twins with the black X of a permanent marker half-erasing the "erty." In the shade of her face, her eyes are further hidden by large, deep black.

I don't usually smoke, she says, I never really do, but it's been such a shitty day.

I wish I could say the same, I say.

You wish your day has been shitty, too?

No, I smile. I wish that I needed a reason to smoke.

I reach for the pack she has left on the table, standing on end. Is it a miniature wall between us? A pocket monolith? A perverse obelisk to the moment? I take out a cigarette and consider throwing it into the air but without the Tchaikovsky it seems a pointless gesture. So I light it. No one should have to smoke alone, especially if it has been a shitty day.

So, what's so wrong with your day? I ask.

What? Oh.

She drops her hands to her knees, then continues:

I probably lost my job. I sort of ran out in the middle of a meeting and I didn't go back … I have clients, and. I don't know. People have different levels of tolerance, and. I don't know. I think I'm just done, know what I mean?

No. Honestly, no.

No … of course not, she says into her chest, laughing. How could you? You don't know me.

She takes a breath.

Thank you for the cigarette, she says, somewhat more gathered together. I nod and smile. She grins and walks away.

Departures make people clearer. Possession is a gift of the retrospect. As she walks out of my life, she moves into my head, giving me reign to contemplate what had been her reality even as that image fades. For a moment, I consider the possibility of connection: I worry about her job, and then wish her well before dismissing the whole incident and stepping back, through my book, to that gallery in Paris.

4.24pm Wednesday21November2014inAbsentiaDigressive

I want to weigh her. I want to see if there was any heft to her soul or if, as I expect, even a life as beautiful as hers has no weight; life moves with so little momentum that it hits the wall of death and stops. We're all electricity, chemistry, and math, and once the plug is pulled, all that is left is what is distributed into the hearts of those surrounding us, a transient immortality in synapse and brain matter until the switch is turned off on those as well. Then we are truly gone.

I want to weigh her but I can't touch …

—yet—

I'm scared.

And I don't want to remember.

And I want to go home—wherever the hell that is now. And I have to pull away.

She wasn't afraid but she wasn't brave either. She was tired. She had become pain. And now, she isn't even lying serene or resting in pieces. She is just here. She is empty, hollow, reduced, material. Disposable in the way organic matter always seems when it has begun to embrace entropy with clear intent, though there is not yet a substantial change to her features. Her cheeks collapsed during the first round of chemo and never recovered, not even after a hint of ruddiness had returned to them between sessions. They are now shallow and sallow. Their pinpricked blush is fading. She was thin, even before the disease, and it made her unable to digest anything but herself and now there's almost nothing left. She has been pale since the direct sunlight began to hurt, eventually even lamplight did as well. This is the first time the sun has had the gift of falling on her for over a month. She grew weaker faster than we'd hoped; but, in the end, she made it to her day, her chosen time, her hour of departure. Her hair, straight and even from the long, slow brushing she had asked me to give it before she departed, is the only part of her with animation as the breeze plays with it in a way that would drive her crazy if she could feel it. She has given up that control, as well.

It was her hair that stayed with me the longest when we first met. Its luster stayed even longer, enough so that it was the first thing I'd noticed when we met again, nearly a year later, in the same place, the same spot. The *my* seat that became *ours*. It was what we spoke about as I slowly brushed her hair back from her face, a ritual we started as soon as this home became her prison, this room her cell, and, eventually, this bed where she spent the majority of her time. She said she felt lovely and loved when I did it and I was energized by the connection, the continuum of our time together.

The angle of light sliding through the slat in the blind has shifted as the sun treks further west. This time of day, the light starts to bleed a little, and it paints her white visage almost livid, now that it's falling directly on to her. It offers the only warmth in her face. It creates shadows that fall into the gentle creases around her eyes and mouth, marks that there had only been hints of two years ago that now seem carved into the soft marbling of her skin. The fringe of her bangs is animated by the breeze from the window, but she is frozen and the day is almost gone.

11.10amTuesday25June2013AgonizedDiaspora

One month after she has deemed herself terminal, we are in Boston. We are trying to live a lifetime before she becomes too weak to live a day, an hour, before she begins counting the seconds of alertness, made concrete with pain, then sleeping in a narcotic haze. Most of her hair is gone. Her head is wrapped in a muted orange scarf. We're standing before a Gauguin: *D'ou Venons Nous / Que Sommes Nous / Où Allons Nous—Where Do We Come From? What Are We? Where Are We Going?* With her head wrapped as it is, her summer dress hanging loosely on her thin frame, the light sweater thrown across her shoulders, and the alien paleness of her skin, she looks almost as exotic as the women in the piece before us; each of them depicted semi-nude but without sexualization, representing different stages of life, embodying the title.

It is her favorite piece and she has only ever experienced reproductions. Her face is again red but there are no glasses to conceal the impact of the painting in her eyes. She weeps. Gauguin intended the picture to be read linearly, like literature, but from right to left, destabilizing the process for me the way the introduction of a partner obsessed with visual representation undermined my fixation with the codes printed in a book, the way she blew up my black and white world with explosions of color. My way of seeing art came through description, through interpretation. I saw through the frozen, dancing lines on the pages of the books assigned to me. She came from the other direction, unhampered by the weight of literary language, and we learned to compliment each other. She became a lens. I never experienced color before I met her: my understanding was entirely ekphrastic. I'd never even known the spring.

Set against a background of a variety of blue textures, the simplified forms and exaggerated skin tones of the painting's denizens shine like beacons. The central figure reaches for an apple—immediately next to her is a child eating one as well—yet they are never forced away from their paradise. They live in this mute and immobile tale, where time's arrow is superimposition and not movement, and I find myself wishing I could freeze our time as well, and never leave this spot. Be a part of all of our time together at once.

It is here that she makes her request, without turning from the piece before us, starting slowly.

I'm almost ready, she says.

She speaks so softly, the words waft past my ear and I have to search for meaning beyond the kiss of air in the shape of "almost." She repeats it. I swallow.

When it is time, she continues, I want you to do it.

Why?

I need you to give me this last gift.

Why?

Because I know I have the strength to make the decision but I don't think I have it to complete the act.

Why?

Because I need it to be you.

Okay, I answer—it was the first thing I've said outside my head. I will. She takes

my hand. She is warm.
But, she says, let's live for a little while more, okay?

Okay.

4.25pmWednesday23November2014AmortizedDislocations

We came to this house six months ago, knowing it would be where she went to die, because it was all we could afford so late in the process. We came west two years ago, because we knew she could choose when to do it here, because we needed to establish residency to make that choice, because the climate would be somewhat kinder, and because our adventures became too much for her to maintain. We painted her room orange and hung a print of the Gauguin piece behind her bed.

In the remaining light of the day, the Gauguin fades, its blues trend toward black, the details of its figures' bodies grow indistinct, but the tones of their skin are still alive in much of the same way the reddening of the fading sun paints her skin livid, giving the lie of rest to her inertia. Is that why we close the eyes of the dead—so we're spared the emptiness that has replaced our gateway into the heart of our loved ones? Without their ocular expressiveness their passing is all too real but, with it cut off, we can bolster the lie that death is another state of life?

I finally touch her. The tips of my fingers graze the tips of her lashes and feel their pathetic resistance. She fails to wake. The heaviness inside of me pulls me into the seat next to her bed. I hold her hand with both of mine. She is cold.

I rise, pull up her blanket, and tuck it around her shoulders and arms. Then I close the window.

3pmWednesday21November2014AnesthetizedDimensions

The room is bright. She is in her bed, propped up because her neck refuses to hold the weight of her head. It isn't broken but it is finished and now shuns work. My heart is unsteady; she claims hers is not. She tells me it is intact but tired. It is ready for rest.

The room is bright because the house faces west, the window is open, and the blinds are raised. We had moved her bed away from the direct light but she wants to see the day, some, and feel the air. She can roll her head and study the Gauguin print that is usually behind her. She smiles at its colors, how its shades steal luminance from the sun's rays and impress upon them their own signature. Her eyes reflect the warm glow of that light as their movements slowly echo the path of its rays. It makes the room feel warmer. She follows the patterns of the motes in the air with as much interest as she gives the painting. If you count the light as an extension of the art, then Gauguin's flat perspective gains the third dimension it lacked. The motes become the detritus of its futurity. It takes on the width of time.

I'm here, I tell her, it's nice to see you enjoying the painting. You're giving it life. I'm hardly here, she says quietly, and you are indistinct.

Her smile flashes wider and then fades.

I think I'm stoned, she continues. All I can see is the color. I ask: How do you feel? She answers: Hollow.

She has had to define her life as being filled with pain so even being empty is a relief. There's a quiet knock at the door, which then opens despite my offering no reply. Her doctor creeps in around the door. By Oregon law, he can't administer the fatal dose. That is my task, anyway. By request.
How is she, he asks?
I can hear. I think I'm stoned, she replies, slow.
She's okay, I answer. I put my hand on hers. I don't think she's in much pain now.
No, she adds, just floating away. He nods.

4.26pm Wednesday21November2014AngledDistortions

I think it's odd that the few times in life we can be exactly certain of, the ones that we document as precisely as possibly, are the only two events that are guaranteed us. The document, the certificate of her birth that sits in a folder in the desk in the room beyond hers, the one I've been sleeping in, tells me that she came into this world at 4.25pm, December 21st, 1973. She chose to leave it on this date to complete the seasonal cycle but to not be greedy and leave some change. She chose it because autumns always seem to last longer than the other seasons. She chose it because she thought she would still be more with us by that point than not. The pain moved fast, but she was right.

The fact that we perceive time as linear is a curse. It is a fallacy that we use to tell the stories of our lives and grant them momentum—always knowing that we can close our eyes and go back for more details but forgetting that back there, also, we can find the people that we've lost. If only we could find it in ourselves to turn that arrow into a loop, we might never lose them at all.

But time, as we experience it, will not allow that. At 3.30, the doctor left.

At a quarter to four, I helped her out of the bed, out of her nightgown, and into a simple shift and her jeans. Awkwardly, and with more of her weight on me than on her own legs, we walked into the back yard. *I can barely see it but, oh, the light,* she said.

At 4pm, she was back in her room, in her bed. I brought her a basin and helped her clean her face and hands.

At 4.10, I brushed her thin, dark hair, making sure that the fringe just tickled the front of her eyebrows. I held up a mirror for her to see herself, the last time. *I'm beautiful*, she said. *Yes, you are*, I replied.

At 4.23pm, Wednesday, 21 November 2015, I injected my wife with the overdose that killed her. We had overestimated the time it would take to prepare, and for the drugs to do their job, and so lost the last two minutes we had left.

Dusk's Song

Nancy A. Shobe

I deplore chain emails—those banal requests followed by idle threats.

Yet, this email seemed different. It was uplifting, nonthreatening, from a close friend. "I am part of a collective, constructive, and hopefully uplifting exchange … Please send an encouraging quote or verse to the person whose name is in the position below …"

As a collector of quotes, this email was easy to fulfill. So, instead of trashing it, I forwarded Amelia Earhart's quote about courage to the name on the top of the list.

Soon, inspirational quotes were flooding my inbox, including one from a previously unknown-to-me woman residing in Utah. She shared:

> *Once upon a time, when women were birds, there was the simple understanding that to sing at dawn and to sing at dusk was to heal the world through joy. The birds still remember what we have forgotten, that the world is meant to be celebrated.*
>
> —Terry Tempest Williams from *When Women Were Birds*

Perfect timing.

Days prior I had asked for guidance from my now-deceased mom about a tempestuous love affair. Our breakups were many; our highs and lows trying. I loved him; we had much in common, but the dissonance between us made me question our match.

"If there is someone who is better suited for me, please send me a red bird, Mom," I prayed.

I thought I was being clever and a bit funny when I asked for a red bird. I haven't seen a red bird *ever* in my twenty-four years of living in southern California. I knew my mom would laugh at my joke.

I also knew that with no red bird coming into my life, I didn't need to make any changes. I could stay the course—settle in with what was good enough. Change didn't come easily to me. Mom always knew that.

Several days after my prayer, I was standing in a field with my partner, a girlfriend, and her mother when a red-breasted robin flew onto the branch of an oak tree.

"Look," I said as I pointed to it. "Isn't that a red-breasted robin?" My girlfriend and her mom nodded. I watched in awe. Red robins are very uncommon in southern California. In fact, neither my girlfriend, a hobby ornithologist, nor I had ever seen one.

I watched the bird as it nodded its head and then leapt off the branch to another. Was the red robin the red bird for which I had asked?

No. It wasn't a full red bird. It was probably just a visit from my mom. After all, the robin was a symbol of my mom's death.

On an early January day in Michigan nearly two years earlier, Mom commented on how odd it was that two robins were alighting on the rails of her back deck. “I’ve never seen robins while it’s snowing,” she said. “I’ve been watching them all morning; their antics make me laugh.”

During the next two weeks, whenever I called, Mom marveled at how the birds showed up each day. She told me that they spread their wings, preened and chirped and tiptoed about on the crest of the new-fallen snow.

Mom made her bird reports until she became ill with the “flu” and was transported by ambulance to the hospital for surgery. Post surgery, she was admitted directly into hospice with a diagnosis of stage IV cancer.

Mom’s hospice bed overlooked a wall of windows, outside of which stood a maple tree, barren yet clinging to the remnants of snow. When I arrived for the first time in hospice, Mom was upright in bed, chin resting on her fingers, quiet, looking through the window, watching the snow melt into droplets and slide from the branches onto the barren ground.

“Isn’t that beautiful?” she remarked. “Remember to notice the small things in life, Nancy,” said Mom. “They matter.”

Mom’s death was time with wings. The six weeks of Mom’s hospice stay could have been one day or one year. Even a calendar in her room was conspicuously missing.

On April 14, the final evening before her death, a very rare snowstorm fell under an even rarer blood moon eclipse.

As I paced through the dimly lit hallways of hospice, taking a break from kneeling bedside, I stopped to press my forehead against the cool condensation on the wall of glass that surrounded the hospice’s inner courtyard.

I peered through the window. Outside, snow fell like angel tears, filling the outstretched, cupped hands of the stone saint and dappling his eyes with kisses. Eclipse-light streaked across the snow like a chiaroscuro path upon which my hope and faith no longer walked.

I sobbed until my knees buckled and I fell to the floor. The wet prints of my hands slid down the glass after me. I was losing my champion, my advocate, the person with whom I spoke daily. The one with whom I discussed the trials and tribulations of life. What would I do without my mother’s love?

The next morning at early dawn, a few hours before Mom passed, a robin alighted on the outdoor windowsill and pecked its beak against the glass. I heard the tap-tap-tap and turned around from my mother to see it. Through blurred vision, wet with tears, I saw my mom’s robin had returned, this time alone, to take her home.

So, was this red-breasted robin in the tree a sign for me to conclude the relationship I was in?

I didn’t have faith it was the sign for which I had asked. A sign is never a sign until it is believed.

Days later, I awoke in my partner’s house, walked into his kitchen, and saw him watching two birds on a rail outside of his kitchen window. “Aren’t those two birds marvelous?” he asked. “I’ve been watching them since I woke up this morning.”

I looked at my boyfriend and thought how handsome he looked in the morning sun. How the light danced upon his sculpted cheeks and made the merriment even brighter in his dark eyes. Why hadn't love made our relationship easy?

"Look," he said as he pointed to one outside the window. "There's even a red one."

Red Bird Sign #2. Would I listen?

Even though I intuitively knew I should end it because I could no longer stand the discord, I realized I had more faith in hanging on than I did in the signs.

That night, I went for a post-holiday dinner at a restaurant with my granddaughter and good friend. My good friend had purchased a marker set and drawing paper for my granddaughter, who was eagerly drawing out the pens and getting ready for an artistic session.

Without being prompted, she asked, "Noni, will you draw me a red bird?"

My girlfriend looked at me and raised her eyebrows.

Sign #3. How could I not listen?

In a final attempt to refuse the sign, I reviewed my journal. Had I asked that the red bird be a sign to move on or to stay? Like a scientist checking her lab report, I wanted to be sure. I leafed through the journal and realized I was right. I had asked for the red bird if there was someone better suited for me.

What was this fear that I felt inside rising? I had long had an intuitive feeling about the demise of this relationship and now had the signs. But I was questioning everything.

Why didn't I have the courage? Was it a fear of making a mistake, of one day regretting my decision? Was it that I was afraid to go it alone and start all over again? Where had my courage gone?

Just a few days earlier, a red bird flew right past me and landed on a telephone pole. It would have landed on me if I had been a tree. This time I had faith in what I knew, and a tsunami grew inside of me. My mom was speaking to me and it was time to listen. It was time to muster up courage to take the leap.

As I wrestled with the cacophony of noises in my head and the fear that rose in my heart, I turned to the poem that resides in my wallet, the one that I sent in an email to the first person on the list. Amelia knew what it took:

Courage is the price that Life exacts for granting peace,
The soul that knows it not, knows no release, From little things;
Knows not the livid loneliness or fear, Nor mountain heights
where bitter joy can hear, The sound of wings.

—Amelia Earhart

Water-Glass Jar

Lana Bella

When she left,
it was said she had
the fungal blood
of a thousand men
weeping through
her fingertips.
Most days she
was inflamed to
the sky's touch,
waiting for
the bony horizon
to skipper her
towards the rapine
of someone else's
water-glass jar.
But to be not at all
nearest to forward,
she peeled those
cloven fingers
from the gaps of
her thighs,
skinned the hot-
plate of pulses
before the sun's
alkali flow arrived
only to snatch up
her low oxygen diets.
And as if the tender
spores of her were
forgone in profile,
she rose, palms
reached out to
the rivets bytes of
the dulcet shoal,
eyes locked
with the exquisite
corpses of the water.

Circular Logic

Simone Martel

Marquita enjoyed chatting to pass time on the job. Her bus circled through Oakland every hour, picking up school kids, office workers, grannies, and good-for-nothings. Now that old Harvey was aboard, she twisted around in her seat so she could talk to him.

"You know that scrawny white lady with the walker who rides this route every Friday afternoon, the one I thought had polio or MS? She sat behind me today, like you are now—where people sit when they want to talk. Turns out, there's nothing wrong with her she hasn't done to herself."

"You gossip too much, Marquita, but go on and tell me. What'd the woman do to herself?"

Marquita's bottom shifted on the driver's seat as she turned the bus's big wheel. "Wrecked herself weightlifting. She used to teach PE, but now she's out of work. She's had hip replacements, shoulders, knees … See why I don't exercise?"

"You're getting fat, though."

Old Harvey tottered off the bus before Marquita had a chance to tell him about the burly man who'd carried the woman—a bony bundle in an orange tracksuit—out of the apartment building.

"That big man I saw you with your husband?" Marquita had asked.

"Boyfriend. Jake." The woman breathed quick, shallow breaths. She could've been anywhere from thirty to sixty, with a tanned, lined face and short hay-colored hair.

"You should apply for assisted living. Get you a ground floor place. You don't belong—up on what floor?"

"Fourth."

"With no elevator. That's a crime."

"I'm gonna get better once the antibiotics kick in." The woman knocked a knobby fist against her thigh. "Got an infection after my last hip surgery. Doctors are trying to get me into a wheelchair, but I'm not getting stuck in one of those."

"You ain't stuck. You can ride the bus. I take people in wheelchairs all the time." Marquita smiled at the woman, who scowled back.

"They'll never get me in a wheelchair."

She got off at the red brick church on the corner. At the senior center three blocks on, old Harvey climbed aboard. Marquita waited for him to settle himself on the seat behind her before she began: "You know that scrawny white woman with the walker who rides this route every Friday afternoon …"

Miranda leaned on her walker as the bus door wheezed shut behind her. That fat bus driver should get out of her seat once in a while, or else lay off the junk food. Now that Miranda could barely walk, let alone work out, she just didn't eat. Starving her body gave her some power over it still. Though she couldn't escape the wrecked shell, she could fight to keep it lean and mean. She had to stay tough in order to avoid a trap even worse than her bag-of-bones body—the hideous, terrifying wheelchair.

"Coming through." Miranda plowed forward on her walker through the gaggle of tatted and pierced men and women till she reached the brick church's basement door.

"Open up," she hollered. "I gotta sit down."

The doors swung open for her; the other addicts funneled in after. Inside, Miranda arranged her stick legs on a cold metal folding chair. The pretty cokehead seated across the circle smiled, eager to talk, to *share*, though she and Miranda had nothing in common except addiction. Miranda raised her eyes above the girl's blond head to the calligraphy banners taped to the painted brick wall.

"One Day at a Time."

"Keep Coming Back"

"It Begins With You."

A flabby male face leaned into her field of vision.

"Heh, heh, how ya doin'?"

Miranda sighed. "What."

His story was he was broke. And he wanted to sell her Vicodin. At a Narcotics Anonymous meeting. Oh, the irony.

Crappy, she was about to say. I'm doin' crappy. With Vicodin, though, she could cut back on the methadone her doctor had her on to ween her off pain meds. A little Vicodin was healthier than tons of methadone. With the pills, she could take charge of her own health, remain upright and mobile, independent and strong.

"How much?"

Jake's huge arms, biceps like grapefruit, stretched out to the steering wheel. He looked down at Miranda in the passenger's seat beside him.

"You eat today? No? You want me to go in with you and tell the doctor you got an eating disorder, too?"

"Wish I could quit food cold turkey, like I quit booze, but I got to *manage* it, like I manage pain pills."

"You gotta eat to stay healthy."

"Yeah, you gotta exercise to stay healthy, too. How can I get healthy if the doctors won't let me work out?"

"You can't touch the weights anymore, Miranda. No weight-bearing exercise. Maybe I'll take you to the pool tomorrow, if you're good. We'll go to the Y."

Office buildings, trucks and buses slid forward, shifted back. She leaned her head against the cool glass, looking up at the sky. "Beautiful sunny day. You going to the hills this afternoon?"

Sure he was, after her appointment, after he carried her back upstairs and deposited her in front of the TV, he was going to bike the fire trails above Oakland. They used to ride together, the sun burning down on their heads. Now he went alone, and she never left the city.

"Biking is a non-weight-bearing exercise …" She looked sideways at Jake.

"Sure, and you'll get back on a bike soon."

"I miss the hills, the sky. The pool at the Y is in the basement."

At the hospital, the young doctor sat down to tell her the bad news: the infection was eating into her thighbone. He gave her a year before she lost it. They both looked down at her twiggy legs, mentally removing one.

"Can't ride a bike with one leg."

"You can live a full, rewarding life."

"Can't bike the fire trails."

That thought looped around and around in her head, all the way home. Back in her dark apartment, after Jake left, Miranda decided: one more ride.

On a bike, legs pumping, back hunched, she'd fly with a dry whooshing sound over the soft, sandy fire trail. Under the huge sky, she'd chose her own path, winding through golden, grassy valleys, smelling the dust, feeling the breeze on her forehead. She'd dip down into cool dim hollows under scrub oaks, then surge out into the light, powered by her own body, a superwoman.

Miranda's eyes dilated like she was already high. Cupping the pills in her shaking hand, she swallowed all the Vicodin. She'd need every last one to numb her up so she could do this thing, achieve this independence. Miranda pulled on her shorts, her pink and black top. She gathered gloves, helmet and water bottle. She deserved this ride. They were going to take her leg soon enough. All she had was now. Wasn't that all anyone had? Couldn't you die any time, say, hit by a bus? She still had today, though. The doctors couldn't steal that from her.

That night, on a gurney in the emergency room, Miranda wept with pain. A curtain separated her from a muttering old lady on a different gurney. Out in the main room, a kid moaned and doctors moved about while Miranda lay waiting for attention with Jake standing by.

If the rattler, sunning itself in the middle of the fire trail hadn't surprised her, if she hadn't swerved, tipped, fallen onto the rutted ground, landing on her bad leg, even then the ride would have taken a toll on her body, only with all the Vicodin buzzing inside her she wouldn't have noticed until after the damage was done.

"Was it worth it?" Jake sneered, disgusted with her.

"I had a good two hours."

"You stubborn woman, you stupid, stubborn woman."

Two hours, over now. Forever. The ride, Miranda's now, was in the past. Only pain remained. And the precious pills were gone.

"I shoulda saved the pills." She looked up at Jake from the gurney. "That was the plan. I was gonna dole them out to myself, ween myself off of the methadone. With the pills, I was gonna take charge of my own health. Forget the doctors. I was gonna get healthy on my own."

"You got yourself crippled." Jake's bulging arms folded across his tight shirt. His face blotted out the hospital light burning behind. "You had a year, Miranda, and you blew it."

The ex-junkies at the NA meeting shook their heads when Miranda showed up in a wheelchair, confessing to a relapse.

"You listened to your inner-addict."

"Used an addict's circular logic."

"Fuck off." She closed her eyes, focusing on the pain.

"What do I do now?" she asked, in the dark. "I've always been an athlete. It's my profession and my identity. If I'm not an athlete, who am I?"

"You still got your mind."

"Yeah." It was a twisted thing, though, that had rushed her into a wheelchair like that had been the plan all along.

Miranda backed her wheelchair into the bus shelter and watched the street through the rain-streaked, graffiti-marked plastic wall, waiting for the bus, the driver's round face above the wheel. She waited to go around Oakland, O-town, to her meeting, to sit in a circle, with other addicts. A few miles away, dusty fire trails accepted the season's first rain. Rabbits hid in tangled blackberry vines, hawks perched on sheltered branches. Maybe a tough, seasoned athlete or two ran or biked the trails in the downpour, choosing to take the high road up to the rocky peak to witness the rain coming in over the gray waters of the San Francisco bay.

The bus's headlights hit Miranda's eyes and she wheeled out of the shelter. Watching the wheels on the bus go round and round, the babyish song repeated itself in her head, her brain woozy with the pain meds that never stopped the ache.

Marquita waited for old Harvey to fold his umbrella and settle into the seat behind her.

"First rain always makes the roads slick. Hey, that handicapped woman, you know, the scrawny one, showed up in a wheelchair today. Going into assisted living like I told her to. I was glad to hear that, glad she's being sensible at last. I'll be seeing a lot more of her, too, 'cause she's starting a daily rehab program."

After dropping old Harvey at the senior housing complex, Marquita finished her route, gassed up, and then started the loop all over again.

A Shell

Melinda Giordano

Shaped like clenched knuckles
Shrimp-pink and ivory
Pale like whalebone
Tightly bound as a corset
The ringlet of bone twisted and curled
Resting in a cusp of foam
After its travails through currents and grottoes
And the empire of crustaceans
The staircase of its core
Curls like an inner ear
Attuned to the sounds of a salty home
The symmetry of tides
And the puppeteer moon
That twitched the waves
And the indecipherable tides

Lucian and Leigh

Daniel Corfield

I have been standing under this skylight for over three hours, naked. He tells me I have two more hours to go. And that is just for today, the first day. When I look down at him standing there with his palette knife I can't help but feel as if he's more like a surgeon with scalpel in hand, ready to peel me apart, exposing what's underneath.

He works with a good deal of tension, as if each stroke is wrenched from beneath his skin. Having called him my friend these past several months, it amuses me to see him in this light. Of course, I know his work. Indeed there is a bold, gritty intensity in each of his paintings, that, when compared to the man—his soft-spoken tone, his effeminate manner—seems a bit out of a character. But I suppose that's what a great artist can do: become what he is not.

It is what I do, anyway. Or rather, what I attempt to do. Every performance. When I put on the costume and mask, step out in high heels and a dress, I am the first to tell you it's not the real me. But at the same time, it is authentic; I'm creating a form, an image, an idea that is outside of my usual self but somewhere deep within. What would make it truly great would be if the viewer could feel what I feel when doing so. If they were to look and then sense the transformation my soul has undergone in order to prance before them like that, only then I will have succeeded.

I think he chose me because I'm a performance artist. He too realizes that art is not about showing the world who you are but involves creating an entirely new Self out of the part that's been hidden since the day you were born. Listen to me, going on and on like some pretentious authority when the truth is that for many people I am a clown. Not your typical clown, but a clown nonetheless. I suspect to many folks I am pure entertainment, in a Disney-Adorno type way. Art is the furthest thing from their mind, seeing me parade about on a stage providing a chuckle, rather than say, a coherent thought.

So what is it about Lucian that compels him to paint me? That night I met him at the Michael Clark dance performance he scanned my entire body with eyes so wide I figured he wanted to fuck me. What can I say? It was the New Romanticism, the London scene at the time.

But then my good friend Rachel, who knows everybody, told me he's only into women. Okay, then why me? Just me. Not the me in laurel green face or ten-inch stilettos or pink baby outfit with bib, not even the me in the Nazi lesbian costume I wore for that show at SMAct.

"Just me?"

"Naked," she said.

Half-jokingly, I told her that to stand for him like that would be my most challenging piece as of yet.

"Oh, and he will need you for several weeks."

Of course I felt honored. He's only the world's most respected painter of nudes. But six years went by without another peep.

Then one night, he showed up at a gig we were doing at the London Freedom Café. These were the days of my band, Minty, my brief career as a punk vocalist. We had a two-week show lined up, but after three nights the Westminster City Council closed us down. To this day, I don't know what drew this austere quiet man of high culture and fine breeding to the likes of someone like us. Was it the on stage piss chugging contest, the simulated birth complete with authentic placenta, or perhaps the words to our best known song, "Useless Man?"

He was leaning against the bar after the show in his signature ascot, which he wore loosely draped over a cashmere sweater along with kaki slacks and tan loafers. An extremely attractive older man who still had enough hair to be fully manicured. His eyes, narrowly set, were the very definition of piercing. Approaching him still in full costume, I asked what he was drinking before noticing the glass of Chardonnay in front of him.

"I'm fine, thank you."

"Did you enjoy the show?"

He smiled an ambiguous smile for which I could only determine meant he was happy to have endured. To go much beyond that would have been a generous self-assessment. There was a bit of a sparkle in the old fellow's eyes, but what intrigued him most was anybody's guess.

With little else in the way of chitchat he got straight to the point. "I'd like to paint you."

"So I've been told."

He paused, watching for my response, his eyes as wide as can be. It felt as if he was already composing inside that head of his.

"Are you interested?"

Although the show had ended, the club was still very loud, the party long from over. Since I'd known his reputation for work, I figured he'd desire to be up early and painting or doing whatever he needed to do to get things started. He didn't seem capable of shouting over all of the hoopla, which of course was my usual way of conversing, what with the amount of time I spend in clubs. At the top of my voice, I told him that I had my band to consider, knowing, of course, the time commitment he would require.

He nodded as if he understood my biggest concern. "I will pay you quite well."

"Then we have a deal."

I may have been the most famous performance artist/fashion designer/punk singer in London at the time, but I was entirely broke.

The longer I do this, stand here naked, the more uncomfortable I become. I'm not talking about how my eyelids droop, how muscles begin to ache, how minutes drag on into hours, hours on into days. Obviously, posing is excruciating. But this is to be expected, the rigors of nude modeling. What I'm referring to is the way I can't seem to feel safe, emotionally speaking, as if at any moment a flick of his wrist is going to scrape a nerve beneath my skin that will send me reeling towards some psychic wound I've kept buried for years. It's the way he wields those palette knifes.

He'll start a good ten yards away, dipping and swirling, looking like some sort of mad-scientist, before stepping ever so close and diving in.

"Are you going to cut me with that thing?" I jokingly asked him yesterday.

He merely smiled and stared, then took a couple steps back, applying the knife to the canvass. "Please hold still."

With my legs crossed at my shins, my chin down, I stand on top of a draped wooden crate, my baldhead burning beneath an open skylight. I feel like Goliath to Michelangelo's David. Seeing myself looking down on my large frame—I know how imposing I am—I'm reminded of that day I was in Florence, having made the turn to look down the long hall of the Accademia di Belle when, suddenly, I saw him: the perfect man, standing there with his slingshot resting on his shoulder.

I am the antithesis of David, hence, Goliath. Is that why Lucian wanted me? Some sort of postmodern Nuevo-classicism? A gay man no less? A man so bold and outrageous in life and yet here I stand, in utter fear that there is something this scrawny soft spoken painter will see inside of me, and, once revealed, well, then I, Leigh Bowery, will be the one who is slain.

I suppose still-life modeling is somewhat akin to Buddhist meditation. A friend of mine once told me the story of how, in his effort to achieve enlightenment, he sequestered himself inside a Zen monastery for ten days straight. Hour after hour, day after day, he'd sit quietly, for it was against the rules to talk and move about. Apparently, the first five days were the most excruciatingly, mind-fucking, painful days he'd ever experienced. His head would not shut up. He wanted to leave. It took every ounce of strength to keep his butt glued to the floor. At night, while lying awake in his cot, he grew extremely depressed, figuring he didn't have what it took to find oneness.

Then, somewhere about halfway through day five, while sitting before the Buddha, legs crossed, eyes closed, his mind just broke. "I could actually hear it snap," he told me. From that moment on he was happy, entirely at peace. He didn't ever want to leave the temple. It was as if his psyche had done a 180.

I think this happened to me early this morning, for now time passes quickly. If it were not for this one sore spot, the fear of exposure, I can honestly say I am enjoying this project. To be gazed at for hours, after all, is what I've worked for my entire life. I just never imagined how it would feel when it is one set of eyes instead of a thousand.

Lucian tells the most interesting stories when wielding his knife. He comes alive in every way. Seeing as standing absolutely still is my most important task, I am not free to respond. Therefore I listen carefully. Having stood now for seven days in a row, six days, four hours and thirteen minutes, I think I have discovered the secret of Lucian's genius. It's his stories of Francis Bacon and the rest of the gang. Their gambling debts and run-ins with the mob. His, Lucian's, growing up as grandson to the most influential man of the twentieth century. These generous stories have a way of breaking down pretense. They are the last things you'd expect from a man you think you know simply from his work. Of course, there's the champagne he plies me with the moment I arrive, the roasted quail simmering on the stove to be eaten during breaks. It's an entirely fulfilling experience, posing for him, one where, again, with that soft-spoken tone of his, he's constantly encouraging me to be my "natural self."

What is so special about a nude by Lucian Freud? What separates his above the rest? I could go on and on with what the critics say. But you don't need to be an expert to see how his work is far superior. It is something ineffable, but it is there, staring back at you. Something alive. Something real. Something natural.

What is my nature?

I can't help but keep coming back to this. I have this secret inside that is unknown to me but as clear as can be to him. In a roundabout way, I've tried to ask him what it is he sees. "Why do you want to paint me Lucian?"

"Because it's my nature to paint."

I want to push him, for clearly he is avoiding taking this further. Perhaps it's the same thing that keeps a novelist from talking about his book before it's done. And yet, I truly suspect, unlike many novelists, Lucian knows what's at the end, seeing something I don't.

"Are you afraid you might spook me?"

"Shhh. You must stop moving." He smiles his tender smile and then slices his knife across the canvass.

It's an intimate thing to stand naked in front of someone six hours a day, day after day. After all, he is looking at me constantly. How could we not bond? Of course, with intimacy come new boundaries, less formidable ones, I should say. We can joke much more easily now.

"Are you sure you don't want to fuck me? I must say, if there ever was ever a look of gay you certainly fit the bill."

"I don't want to fuck you."

"Then why?"

"That body of yours. It's like a beautiful monster."

He knows I've been told this a thousand times. Hell, that very phrase has been headlined on more than one occasion. Beautiful Monster Steals Show at London Nightclub.

My own art is meant to shock. Where others strive for beauty, I shoot for embarrassment. My parents, god-bless them, have seen this side of me since I was four. They've told me, on more than one occasion, how when all other good Catholic tikes were kneeling and praying in Sunday school, I was flipping up skirts and running amok. To be the center of attention has always been my deepest concern. What better way to do so than to walk into a room so outrageously dressed, so flamboyantly charged that all faces turn red in an instant while, at the same time, the slightest attempt to overt one's eyes merely concedes to the force of my presence? I love the power to be gleaned from telling the world that I don't give a fuck. It's what most people want, but so few actually do, that is, take up the attitude of I don't give a fuck. After all, it is hard to tell oneself over and over again, "I don't care, I don't care, I don't care." And then to show it as well.

I remember the night I was asked to appear on The Joan Rivers Show, how I stepped through the curtains in my sequined mask and yellow tights and immediately tripped and fell flat on my face. How devastating this would have been had I not already expected an audience to be thinking the very moment they laid eyes on me, what the fuck is that thing?

Confusion, embarrassment, shock. Yes, that is what you get when Leigh Bowery enters a room. Of course, I am speaking of the artist Leigh Bowery, the performer, who, as I've already hinted, is not the same as the private Leigh Bowery. Even in those Sunday school days, it was a public persona. The Leigh Bower at home has always been entirely different. After all, my parents have also told me what a wonderfully pleasant little boy I had been.

Yesterday, the tenth day in a row, was an extremely difficult day. I coughed. I kept coughing, thus moving, thus making the entire day of work impossible for Lucian. I am deeply concerned about this cough. I think it is here. Do I tell him?

"Are you feeling any better this morning?"

I assured him I got a good nights sleep and there was no need for concern.

"Listen, we can postpone this. In fact, if you are going to be coughing all day perhaps it's best that we do."

Postponing anything in my life is not an option. The very opposite is true. I must try to do as much as I can before it's too late.

Looking back, I can recall the very first question that popped into my mind when Rachel told me Lucian Freud wanted to paint me. What if he discovers I'm HIV positive? But then, having heard no more of this project, having gone the next six years without a shred of illness, I suppose it became one more thing I just didn't give a fuck about.

But now the constant coughing. I fear it is no longer simply the virus. Will he still want my body when it becomes a shell of what he's accustomed too seeing, the body that has put me on the map of so many artistic genres?

How about when I am as thin as Freddy? Or Adam? Or Trent? Or the dozens of other friends I've lost to this hideous illness. Standing here, I wonder what shade of purple he will use to create the lesions that are bound to form upon my skin. Yes, I should probably tell him.

When I look at the canvass I assume we are barely half way through. What will my body look like two weeks from now? I have seen how rapidly this disease tears apart a human being. It's ironic, I suppose, here I've been, this entire time, worrying about Lucian discovering something I've been hiding from myself, when there is this very real, immediate secret I've been keeping from him.

"Please eat something," he said. We had just taken a break and were sitting down at the small, wrought iron table on his back patio enjoying the fresh air. The sunlight bursting forth and the rich green leaves on the surrounding trees allowed me to breath. Today he served duck rather than quail, but by now my stomach was in full force rebellion. If I were to eat something it wouldn't stay down. Rarely did I even feel hungry anymore.

"How do you like the picture so far?" I asked

"All I can tell you is that I'm entirely absorbed."

I looked off into the trees and watched the leaves flicker, the sunlight sparkling, giving a warm afterglow. "Do you know I am dying?"

Lucian took a sip of tea and looked me in the eyes.

"Yes."

"Who told you?"

"Leigh, everyone knows. It's as much a part of your performance as the high heels and dresses, the Leigh that goes out there on stage every night with an intention to shock."

"Doesn't it concern you?"

"Time is all. Just time. I should have followed up with you years ago."

"So why me, Lucian? What was it you saw? I know I'm the beautiful monster, on stage anyway, but what is it about this body of mine, naked, here, standing tall on this platform you have me perched upon that is so god damn intriguing."

"I'm sorry; I don't mean to upset you."

"I'm not upset Lucian. I'd just like to know. What is it?"

Lucian leaned forward, his eyes bulging wide. Then he said, "I see a man who has never been comfortable with his own body."

Now indeed I was angry for he'd touched a nerve. "You're right Lucian, but how about we stop with the psychoanalysis."

"I'd be happy to." He took another sip of tea, leaned back in his chair, and looked off into his yard.

"Rachel told you I was HIV?"

"Yes, but there were rumors as well. The crowd you run with, people talk I'm afraid."

We sat in silence.

"Perhaps we should get back to work."

I can talk more freely now. I've been posing everyday for three weeks without a single day off. The image of Leigh Bowery has by now impressed itself upon his retinas. It must be frozen like a photograph. Lucian has taken what he's wanted but still I stand here, and will stand here until he's done.

My symptoms worsen rapidly. I've lost an ungodly amount of weight, my entire body aches, swollen lymph glands, sores under my armpits, inside my groin. At night I sweat rivers and shit waterfalls. When I wake up and look into the mirror the person looking back has a skin color that is of no human race that I've ever seen.

Yet Lucian holds to the image of what he saw that first day I walked into the studio. It is as if those palette knives of his are; well, like I said, surgeon scalpels, only now instead of slicing me apart they are keeping me alive. Considering how fast this illness can take a person—believe me, I've seen it, a month or two and they are gone—I am still holding on. I am still performing.

"How much longer?" I ask him constantly.

He simply takes that knife, dips and swirls, presses against the canvas, sliding smoothly, like stitching wounds, and pieces my flesh together.

This morning I told myself that I would ask him one final time why he wanted to paint me and whatever he said I would have to take definitively. It goes without saying that I had yet to be satisfied with what he's told me so far. Maybe I am making much too much of this, that I want some sort of profundity that simply isn't there. But no, this is an artist whose works hang in the world's greatest museums. He doesn't pick his subjects whimsically. I am not his lover, his muse, his child, his best friend, or his worst enemy for that matter. And yet something struck him and told him yes, I will take a month, maybe two months out of life, working seven days a week, six hours a day, whatever it takes to capture this man's image in oils.

Before I asked, I recalled what he said about being at war with my body. He had been right, after all. Standing under this skylight, rotting from inside out due to the worst illness known to man, I slipped back into a childhood memory.

He must have seen a change in my look, perhaps a slight tilt of my head, or a distant gaze that wasn't there before, for he stopped what he was doing and dropped his palette by his side. "What is it?"

I turned my head and spoke. "As a kid I used to look at myself in mirrors for hours on end. I'd start with my eyes, staring as deep as I could, then roam down my torso, my hips, on into my crotch and my thighs. I'd turn this way and that; check out my butt, my hamstrings, my triceps and neck. All the way to the top of my head, again and again. I'd stand there for hours, feeling the day slip away, feeling trapped, somehow. Finally, I'd return to my eyes, looking, looking, looking. Leaning deeply into the mirror, I'd think perhaps I'd see something that was truly me. But then it would flicker away."

Lucian stood there, listening.

"For years I wasted the most gorgeous days looking for something in mirrors that I could never find. I've been doing it ever since, only now, the hours I spend staring into mirrors I see someone looking back. It is the creation, that beautiful, ambiguous monster, and he is looking into Leigh Bowery's eyes, the one and only Leigh Bowery."

"This is what I am trying to paint," said Lucian.

"What?"

"The mystery. This moment you just described. I want the viewer of my painting to see a naked man before him and see whatever it was you were looking at, or, rather, looking for in those mirrors when you were growing up. I want that moment to be seen in each and every stroke."

"Why?"

"Because this is a moment many of us have. It isn't just you, you know."

"But what is that moment? I've always wanted to know."

"It's the mystery of the Self. It's the looking inward and wondering, who is really in there? I think many people, not all, but many do this, some their entire life."

"You think I am someone who does this?"

"You tell me?" he said. Then he stepped back and turned once more to his canvass. This time he had a brush in hand. Like a magic wand, he waved it across the painting.

For the second time since I'd come to his studio to pose, I felt a release of tension that made me think of a Zen monastery. Only this time it wasn't my brain that snapped and fell into a calm peace, it was my body. Standing there, upon the table, my skin rested comfortably and my breath flowed easily. For a moment I simply stood in silence. Then something stirred in me and I had the urge to tell him how I wanted to be buried back home in the lot with my parents when I died.

Lucian nodded. "Okay, but first, there is more work to do."

When I returned to my pose, I didn't feel afraid, confused, or anxious. Nothing was different. I was still naked, still standing in the same relation to Lucian with his brushes and knives. And yet my entire body seemed to have fallen into place, both inside and outside, as if, for the first time in my life my soul and body had become one.

"Very good," said Lucian. "You look natural."

At that moment I realized I could stand like this forever.

On the day of the exhibition, he came to visit me. Lucian and Rachel are the only two people in the world that know I am here. I always knew it would happen fast, but never this fast.

He leaned over and showed me an article in the paper about the opening and how all the buzz was centered on Freud's incredibly enigmatic nudes.

"They would love to see you, Leigh." As soon as he said this I think he realized how awful it sounded. His face turned red and he immediately offered if he could get me something.

I pictured what I would have worn, if, by some miracle I could have pulled myself up and out of this lousy hospital bed and made it to the gallery. "It would be one of my more conservative outfits ha, ha, ha."

"Tell me."

As it was, I could barley lift my head up off the pillow, but he was patient, the words coming slowly. "I see something glamorous, but also horrifyingly twisted, something in contrast to the authentic Leigh that you discovered, something, well, alienating. Perhaps a merging of the clown and monster. Sequins and feathers and makeup. A shrunken human skull strapped to the top of my head. A giant safety pin pierced from one side of my mouth to the other. Yellow tights beneath a red dress. Oh, and lots and lots of polka dots, as always. I'm not quite sure of the fabric, but the design is there, inside my head. Pure artifice, Lucian. Pure artifice. I see myself standing next to your painting, welcoming folks, telling them that this is who I am too, as they sip their wine and eat hors d' oeuvres. Of course they will never be able to decide which me they prefer."

Lucian stood there, his hands upon the cold railing, a look of terrible sadness upon his face. "What would you like me to tell them Leigh?"

Typical Lucian—he had taken practically all my strength, but still he wanted more. I had to think about it for a moment. I didn't want anybody to know the truth. Leigh Bowery was supposed to live forever. "Tell them I am in Papa New Guinea," I said and then closed my eyes.

Now, the Narrowing Time

Sarah Isto

Those to whom I was given have gone silent.
Those whom I chose are winnowed by frailty
and by their own great silences.

My solace wilderness is now unattainable,
the shale too steep, the willows and alders
too stiff to brush aside.

My body surprised by slowness,
my mind by confusion,
my memory by its patchy tenacity.

What did you expect, the faces ask,
life full force straight to nothing—
suddenly the bear's red maw gaping,
or the fatal rage of three-day fever,
or the small plane gone silent, then falling?

Yes, always.

Unprepared for drift,
unmoored from the deeply loved and
the deeply unloved who knew me best,
I am unready to be steered by
a crew of brisk strangers.

My once-intimate hills
retreat in purple distance.

Here in my faltering body,
in my nearly empty room,
little remains that is not tattered

except for an unreasonable fierceness
that will not release my heart.

Hi, Lady

Tracy Snyder

When my son was in grade school, he spoke the vocabulary of cartoons. If something untoward happened, he would reply "Doh!" as if he were Homer Simpson, or interject a nonsense line from Spongebob Squarepants.

One of Drew's favorite lines came from the Warner Brothers cartoon. A minor character in this cartoon was a little girl. She routinely approached strangers with the phrase, "Hi, Lady. I love you. Goodbye." This became Drew's favorite way to address me.

One summer afternoon, the door banged open to admit a dripping little boy. He trotted to the kitchen, grabbed a cookie and scurried to make his getaway. I headed him off at the pass and pointed accusingly at the drops of water on the wood floor.

"Hi, Lady. I love you. Goodbye," he said with a charming grin and wink of his big, blue eyes. Out the door he danced, scot-free.

Disarmed with a single shot.

In middle school, it became embarrassing for a young man to admit he loved his mother, so Drew shortened the phrase.

"Hi, Lady," he would say and then stop. I love you was no longer spoken, but we both knew it was there.

During this time, Drew's immune system went haywire and attacked his own pancreas, destroying his ability to manufacture insulin. At the age of twelve, he became a Type I Diabetic, dependent on daily injections for the rest of his life.

Shortly before we were discharged from the children's hospital, the doctor called me into his office. In an effort to impress the importance of helping Drew manage his illness, the doctor listed, in excruciating detail, all the ways my son could die. I was shaking as I walked back to his room. When I entered, Drew rolled over and looked at me. He was as white as the sheet that covered him, dark shadows smudging his eyes.

"Hi, Lady," he said with a weak attempt at a smile.

I love you; I rehearsed the line in my head. *Please don't say goodbye.*

Years passed since Drew was diagnosed with Type I Diabetes. His blond hair had darkened, his voice deepened and he had grown to a height where he looked down at me. He administered the daily shots of insulin to himself without comment. It was amazing what became routine.

As I walked up to the house last week, I had to smile. The booming staccato of an electric bass guitar could be heard from the street. The sound came up through my feet as well as through the air. I was sure the neighbors were pleased.

I opened the front door to see my son, fingers flying over the strings of his dark gray guitar. Headphones snug against his ears, keeping the metal music he accompanied to himself.

Drew saw me as I entered. He stopped playing and pushed his headphones askew, leaving one ear free. "Hi, Lady," he said with a sweet smile. "Need help with the groceries?"

In a few months, Drew will graduate from high school. Soon after that my youngest, my baby, the one who has needed so much care, will prepare to leave home. When that day comes, I have a good idea what it will be like.

We will stand next to his guitar-laden car. He will flash a grin, give me a hug and whisper, "Hi, Lady. I love you. Goodbye."

1930

Ha Kiet Chau

Last night, I departed Earth and fell into a deep
slumber. Spiraling into the unknown, images
and numbers flashed like camera lights:
cocoa skin, emerald eyes, orchid petals,
and 24 street signs.
Here I was, traveling like a nomad, in and out
of two worlds, teetering on the cusp
of reality and fantasy. In an alternate dimension,
gravity pulled me backwards to 1930.
Life, once a shade of gray, now unfolded
like a Technicolor film.
The streets of Shanghai were humid and smoky,
lined with bakery shops, opium dens,
dance halls, and secret brothels.
Whiffs of herbal incense and sesame buns
hanged in the breeze. Percussion beats
pounded from an opera house.
Beep-beeping up and down the roads,
foreign cars and wooden rickshaws hurried past
strangers with exotic angular features
and brown cocoa skin—women in silk cheongsams,
men in pinstripe suits, *have we met before?*
On 24 Changzhi Road, at a street-side vendor,
I spun three-sixty, bumping into a boy
with eyes that glinted emerald—
a rich hue of jade and sea.
He placed a lavender orchid in my hair,
traced 缘 分 on my palm, and murmured, *zaijian.*
Lifetimes must've passed like rivers between us.
When he fled down a back alley, petals wilted,
and I knew in dreams, nothing good lasted.
As temperature rose and the streets grew hot,
I hopped on a trolleybus—gravity pulling me
out of the city. That morning, after a deep

slumber, I returned to Earth.
Gazing out the window, face to face with reality,
another gray, overcast day—no hummingbirds
singing, no song to ease my morning blues.
Eyes closed, I could feel the faces, colors,
and liveliness of 1930 fading like a memory.
Oh, to be lost in dream state again.

Letter to Jaegermeister

Cecile Barlier

I have you in my head, Mr. Jaegermeister. I cannot help it. Any time I've had to myself in my room upstairs in the attic, I thought of how happy or how angry you were. God bless the work that kept me away from the attic. You see, most of the day I spent planning and cooking your meals, and I needed the good night's sleep. I'm a good sleeper and even you won't change that.

In your house, floors and walls are way too thin, and Mrs. Jaegermeister was always loud. The woman reminded me of the cow, Blümchen, at the farm where I was raised in Tyrol. Her milk was sour even if she ate the same green grass as the others and slept on the same fresh straw. Cows don't act up: Her milk was sour and that's that. You see? A woman no good, like the Blümchen—with vinegar instead of milk. The only good she ever did was to hire me as head cook in your house. God bless her for that.

Bitter, bitter, bitter. Nothing good enough for the woman: not me or my dishes, not you, not her pockets full of gold. Agitated, she was. She'd talk and talk, and screamed when she was done with the talking. You could handle the talk real good, but screaming got on your nerves. And your nerves are fragile like a bull's; I know what I'm talking about. Like they say, yours is blue blood, Mr. Jaegermeister—handle with care, like blood sausage, so it won't burst. With all the screaming, you spent more time outside the house, and so I had to fix it.

It was her money you wanted, 'cause you like it, just like me. I never wasted a schilling in my life. I don't need much, and it's all in my cassette. Good notes won't lie, just like cows; a schilling is a schilling, and that's that. Her schillings were good, but she wasn't, and I know how to read the signs.

Childless like the Blümchen, her belly too tight to bear and too ugly for you to do her. You see, I'm no idiot. I know you like fresh meat in your plate and other places too. You liked Annemarie, the pastry cook. Fourteen and what it takes, where it should be. I made sure she'd be around for you to see. I know you better than you think.

All the others, the ones for service in your house, they looked at me funny. I'm used to it; only cows never looked at me funny.

Do you remember the day you wanted to find out what was for dinner and asked me to your office? You said you'd been to Tyrol and started talking like us out there. That was before. But now, Mr. Jaegermeister, what now?

Like the Blümchen, I made sure Mrs. Jaegermeister was gone with no noise while you were away on your trip. They couldn't blame you for it 'cause you were gone. I thought you'd like the silence in your house.

You want to know how I did it? Even if you don't, I'll tell you anyway, 'cause you should know those things. You see, people like you leave it to people like me to execute all things in your life, and that's what we do. I know what hard work takes, and this took preparation. I had done the Blümchen, but somehow cows and women are different. You don't prepare an apple strudel like you do a Germknödel, and that's that; but how would you know?

Doing Blümchen was mostly physical, and I didn't mind the noise; the stable was far from the farm, and I had the privacy. Mrs. Jaegermeister had to be done silently, since there is no such thing as privacy in your house. Like I said, walls and floors are way too thin and the woman was always loud.

Me, I don't talk a lot, so I have all the time to listen. I knew the schedule of all the people. Most of them jabbered a lot. It's human nature, like they say. You see, I was born and raised with cows, and cows don't gossip—God bless them for that.

So Hans, your carriage driver, is a typical Viennese, and like all Viennese, he's good for nothing. Hans would spend most of his day sleeping in the kitchen by the oven, and even holding the reins tired him. He could only handle one thing at a time, and sometimes he would need to get back to it twice before it was done. One of these days, Hans will fall asleep on the carriage with you in it and then what? But first things first.

When Hans wasn't sleeping by the oven, he liked to sit his sagging behind on the kitchen bench and drink Schnapps and chatter with whoever was willing to listen. You see, no one listened to Hans anymore 'cause he didn't have the most interesting conversations or the most intelligible, especially with the Schnapps. Well, me, I never stopped listening to Hans; I was in the kitchen anyhow, and I might learn a thing or two on your whereabouts. Hans told me he used to go to the apothecary on Baumschulweg every Wednesday to get yours and your wife's medicine. He said that Mrs. Jaegermeister—agitated she was—couldn't fall asleep on her own and needed sleeping aids. He would also get some kind of a lotion for you, but he didn't know what it was, since it always came very well-wrapped; he could tell it was a lotion 'cause of the "glub" noise it made when shaken on the ride back. Hans was struck dumb when I proposed to save him the next trip to the apothecary; not that it made a great difference with him—you see, there's hardly a time when he's not dumb—but it was the first time someone ever offered to take over one of his chores. I'll tell you this: We usually don't trade chores amongst us, and even less so for nothing in exchange.

So I told Hans that Wednesday was market day and that I had to go run errands on Elterlein Platz, which is only a block away from Baumschulweg. I also told him I could speak to the apothecary about my rheumatisms. Not that I have any, my body is healthy as a heifer's. Still, I needed to find something for Hans to masticate; I couldn't tell him I did it out of good-heartedness, like it would make any sense.

So I left Hans to his mastication and his Schnapps, and the Wednesday following our conversation, I was on my way to the apothecary. Well, I'd never been to one of these places before, and believe me, I don't think I'd ever go back for the life of me.

Really, do you honestly believe you can get anything good out of a place like that? Anything to make you feel better? I know you never go there yourself, but I have to tell you this: That place is a plague. As I walked into Baumschulweg that Wednesday, I saw something wasn't quite right. People on that street, as they get closer to the apothecary, they don't walk. No, no, no, they don't walk; they just crawl in and out of the place, making sure no one is looking at them. Men lower their hats on their heads, and women hide their noses and mouths behind their scarves and gloves. The place stinks, and you just pray that the smell won't stick to you too long. I've been around cows a lot, and the worst manure is Heaven's bliss compared to this. When Uncle Heinrich died back there in Tyrol, they let him rest three days on his deathbed at the farm; well, the smell of the apothecary is like Heinrich on his third day, only stronger.

Anyway, Mr. Jaegermeister, I'm no coward, and even good-for-nothing Hans went in there once a week.

So I went in past the doorstep, despite the whiff—crossing myself twice just in case—and waited to be greeted. Well, absolutely no one was to be seen at first. After a while I noticed the ring on the counter. So that was that: They expected me to ring the doomed thing to drag them out of their vault—a bell that's been touched by dozens of unhealthy Viennese. God grant me protection. So with one index finger carefully wrapped in my sleeve, I rang. You should thank me, for remember that I cook your Kaiserschmarrn on Wednesdays, and you wouldn't want it smeared in Viennese muck.

I thought the worst of it was behind, but that was without planning for the Devil himself: Mr. Bluzenstricker—the apothecary. You wonder how I know his name? Well, how do you think he christened the hellish place? After his own name, in bold white letters on his storefront. Some people are just without shame.

I swear, it took me a good minute and a lot of effort to see a man behind the obese toad with a pair of stained glasses hiding God knows what.

Mr. Bluzenstricker doesn't just look like a toad, he croaks and moves like one. I'd never seen anyone walking quite like that, if that can be called walking. He hops in slow motion and plants himself just inches from your face, with your own reflection in his greasy glasses reminding you of how fast you want to get out of there. And then he opens his mouth and you wish you'd been born deaf.

It is no human sound that comes out of his jaws—rather the howling of some unearthly creature transmuted into German—and it is a wonder that one could make out what it is that the Apothecary Bluzenstricker, has to say. I was so shaken upon hearing his "Grüß Gott, how can I help you?" that I must have stayed silent and motionless for quite a while before he was at it again: "Grüß Gott, gnädige Fräulein, would you have a prescription that you need to pick up or an order for a preparation?"—Oh, God. Just one more of his "Grüß Gott" and I swear I would have lifted the cross from around my neck to guard myself from such a diabolical beast. How could this swine address me as "gnädige Fräulein" as if I was some youngster with freckles? I couldn't take any more of his questions, for the sound of his voice was coming up on my nerves like the sharp side of a knife on a milk bottle. You know me, I don't usually talk a lot—only what is necessary for the kitchen staff to know how long to roast the schweinsbraten or when to take the semmelknödel out of the boiling water—but this time I spoke more than I had in months, for I would do anything to avoid having to listen to the growling of the Apothecary Bluzenstricker. I explained that I was coming instead of Hans to pick up your and your wife's prescriptions; that this was because Hans was unavailable that day, which, even though he would never admit it, was because he had had too much Schnapps the day before, and that the mere sight of the sun would feel like an axe planted into his already feeble brains; that I wouldn't have usually given a hand to a drunken idiot like Hans, but that we had had a recent outburst of rats in the neighborhood, and that I had spotted a couple in the hallway in the attic where we have our quarters, and that, above all, I wanted to avoid the good kitchen of Mr. and Mrs. Jaegermeister being infested by the pests. In short, I needed the prescriptions, but also something powerful enough to make sure we got rid of the nuisance once and for all before it had any health consequences for the good Jaegermeister house.

I was getting ready to call upon some memory of my cows in Tyrol so as to be able to bear the next sentence from the Apothecary Bluzenstricker when what he said surprised me so much that I almost forgot the nauseating gurgle he made as he was talking. He said he would just double the amount of corrosive sublimate used for your prescription, and that if I only added a few drops on whatever could be used as bait, it would be enough to decimate an entire army of vermin—" Just a few minutes and I'll get this for you, gnädige Fräulein."

And so I watched the obese and dark-goggled Apothecary Bluzenstricker pivot slowly upon himself and hop back into the darkness of his back-store, and I waited.

Corrosive sublimate … so this was your prescription. The name sounded honorable, and I could have sworn I had heard or seen it before, but I couldn't place where. You see, the only thing I've had to remember in my entire life were recipes; from each ingredient and quantity to the exact amount of time they need to be roasted, braised, seared, or boiled to perfection. This requires great focus, and I cannot waste my effort on memorizing pointless details along the way. Anyhow, I would soon have the prescription in my hands and, with some patience; I could probably make out what was on the label. I know this will surprise you, Mr. Jaegermeister, but I can read. Back there in Tyrol, our priest, Herr Gruber, taught us the alphabet. You shouldn't undervalue me.

After a while, Bluzenstricker came back out of his hole and handed me both prescriptions from under his claws. I rushed out without asking for more, and believe me, I ran four blocks before I sat under a porch and caught my breath while I read the label. So S-Y-P-H-I-L-I-S is what you have. Even ignorant people like me know what it is and where it's from; we call it "the French disease" because only the filthy French could have brought this upon us and other good nations. I thought of Annemarie for a minute. I wondered if you'd let her know, if you'd shared your prescription with her. Anyway, these concerns are way beyond me and way beneath you. I know where I belong, and it's not for me to say. Schnitzels are what I do, and I leave sentencing to the judges.

That day, when I came back to your house, Hans the Schmock told me you were to leave for Klagenfurt for two days, and so I knew the time had come. You see, like I can tell a cherry when it's ripe at the Naschmarkt, I just know when there's no need to wait any longer.

So I had gotten her ready, or so I thought, for I had seasoned her night chicken broth with a good measure of sleeping aids. Well, guess what, your wife probably had one of her stomach episodes and didn't touch any of it, 'cause I found Klemens, your arrogant butler, down her doorway with the empty bowl still in hand and snoring like a wild boar with a cold. I had no choice but to carry bigheaded Klemens up two flights of stairs to his room, and trust me, not only the head is big in Klemens. I tripped and sweated and let the animal drop once or twice, but I made it all the way up and, believe me, it was no small undertaking. As I got back down, I knew Mrs. Jaegermeister would still be asleep at this hour, but I'd have to do without the sleeping aids, for I hate to postpone the task for tomorrow that I can do today. After all, I had done the Blümchen at the barn, and it probably required more muscle. I was also lightheaded some from carrying big Klemens around; you see, anything looked effortless after that.

Your wife, Mr. Jaegermeister, she was lying on her bed, tucked under three layers of quilted covers as if the weather permitted. Pillows were everywhere, and I had a variety of choices: from the bratwurstlike bolster to the tiny, square, embroidered cushion to the round and rectangular cotton ones; for every angle in her—and God knows she was full of them—she'd have a specific pillow shape. I always slept on straw back in Tyrol, and I didn't know of pillows before I came to service in your house. I can see now how she needed those, for her skin was flaky and her bones rachitic. She wasn't built for this life, and this was really a favor I did for her too. I chose the one she'd propped herself onto for breakfast, the deep-blue one with golden fringe, and flattened it against her face. She struggled, all right, and I didn't expect such resistance. Anyway, I meant no disrespect, but I had to sit on her. I sat on the blue pillow on top of her face to free my hands and hold her arms. I sat and sat and sat until her jerky moves faded and her muffled cries receded. I sat until my own stiffness dropped along with hers and I started feeling good. I can hear you wondering and questioning, but trust me, there was something soothing in that moment, like there had been with the Blümchen. Right when life left their bodies, something hung around for a while, and the sweetness of that seasoned everything near. I felt it with the Blümchen and again with your wife, so I know it's no accident. New death is like fresh-fallen snow, Mr. Jaegermeister. I don't want to think, or talk about this too much, for you might get the wrong idea. After all, I did it for your sake only, and that's that.

It was bigheaded Klemens who found her late-morning that day. Fat Klemens who had finally emerged from the sleeping aids broth all dressed up in his room, pretending that nothing had happened (he never struck me as the honest type). You see, your wife had always insisted that we let her sleep for as long as she needed. They say the world belongs to those who rise early, but they have it upside down—you rise early because you have to, and you rise late because the world already belongs to you.

Anyway, he found her, and so they called Dr. Obermoser, and his diagnosis was formal. It was a sudden death like you see in infants who stop breathing in their sleep. Only she had brought it upon herself by using a different prescription for sleeping aids than the one he had approved. No one questioned it, for why would you question a well-established doctor like Dr. Obermoser? After all, he was the archduke's doctor as well. God bless Dr. Obermoser and his diagnosis. That her nose was broken, as fat Klemens pointed out (as if anyone would be interested in Klemens' comments), Dr. Obermoser attributed to a sudden collapse of the paranasal sinuses.

As for you, Mr. Jaegermeister, you got back from Klagenfurt a day early, since Hans had gone to get you there. And when you came home that day, agitated you were.

Instead of getting back into your old habits, you started pacing around the house like a dog with rabies. I couldn't keep up with you, and I'd never know where to serve your dinner or supper. Not that you'd eat any of my dishes anyway; they'd bring me your plates, untouched, back to the kitchen, cold; even the Erdäpfel Salat that you used to like so much, a sore sight for the eyes, potatoes and red onions macerated in vinegar for too long, sometimes a midge or two drowned in the sauce.

I really tried, you see. I massaged the beef with butter before roasting, I added extra egg yolk in the Nockerln, I even sent Annemarie for bitter chocolate at the delicatessen on Leichtweg so I could make a Sachertorte.

All of it came back to the kitchen only to be gulped down by Hans the Schmock and Fat Klemens, who, for one thing, hadn't lost their appetites.

And then you were just out of sight. The house had become silent, and you were in hiding somewhere in it for five long days after her death. I spent those days by the oven, listening to the murmured jabber of Hans and the like. Believe me, the murmuring made them self-important, as if talking in a low voice made them more articulate. But it was all jabber.

You didn't say goodbye, Mr. Jaegermeister. No, you didn't. You just decided to go, and off you did; and that only three days after the funeral, which they rushed like her body brought too much pestilence—like they pretended she didn't stink before—and breathe they could without her there. Still, they needed to make sure, real sure. With her six feet under, and even if she attempted to, she'd be confined, and they'd be safe and sound, and so would you. You see, deads tend to be resilient, and you don't want them hanging around too long, so to speak. God bless good coffins with strong bolts.

And you? A change of scenery, they kept saying. Like you'd need to recover from the loss. Salzburg, they'd say. I was good with Salzburg; I was all for it. I came all the way from Tyrol to cook in your house, and they say travel is good for you. Like the geese that flew above the farm back there, you need to keep it going; a goose that stops traveling is only as good as her liver and the leberwurst you make with it.

Only you had other plans. And so you didn't say goodbye. I found out from Liesl as she came back to pack her luggage. Liesl the chambermaid, loudmouthed as a squealing sow. And squealed she did as she went on and on about how they were all getting ready for the four o'clock train on Friday at the Westbahnhof, how the house in Salzburg was just on the Salzach River, with more service rooms to accommodate all of them independently—and this she repeated three times before she could pronounce it correctly—how the air was so much better than in Vienna because of the mountains, how they'd come tomorrow to shut the house for good since God knows when, or if, they would be back, and so on and so forth, until she got tired from so much squealing. That's how I found out, and it got me real quiet.

Anyway, you took them all with you, Mr. Jaegermeister, and that's that—even good-for-nothing Hans; fat, arrogant Klemens; stupid, loudmouthed Liesl; 14-year-old Annemarie. They all shared the same compartment on the four o'clock Friday train, and I wasn't in the wagon. You didn't ask me there, and I know how to read the signs.

So I stayed, and they didn't see me when they boarded up the windows and locked up all the doors from the outside. Believe me, they didn't inspect anything in the house, and a Prussian army might have settled there for all I know, and they still wouldn't have noticed. I sat by the oven and waited for them to be done.

So now I have your house all to myself, although I just stay in the kitchen, for where else would I go? You didn't send for the cookware or the silverware before you left, and I've always stocked up to make sure we didn't miss anything around your house, and so I have plenty for a while.

I'm a cook, like you've always known me, and this is what I do. I peel and clean round white potatoes and boil them. I shred cabbage and ferment it in your pots. I cook apples and pears with brown sugar for winter conserves. I make great strudels too, although I now have little coal left for the stove. I stuff sausages into their casings and sear them gently in sour butter (the fresh one is long gone) until they snap and spritz their juices in little fountains up to my apron and my hair.

I started using lots of onions, for onions do not rot, and there is never too much of them in a good dish. I peel them and cry a great deal and fry them slowly until they turn transparent and then yellow and then end up all sweet, like marmalade. Patience is what pays off with onions—they start rough and end up sweet.

You see, I am nowhere near short of good food, and I eat it all too, 'cause I hate to waste. I can hear the bench crack when I sit, and the table too as I lay on it to rest.

It's pretty hot now, even with everything boarded up, and I take it that it must be summer outside. More things have started to decay, and I'm using them as bait for the rats. They're just everywhere, and I've followed the Apothecary Bluzenstricker's advice and use some of your corrosive sublimate to slay the vermin. This thing comes in handy; you'd never have guessed. I pile their small bodies in the cellar, for I can close the door on them and let them rest in peace.

Patience, Mr. Jaegermeister, patience is what pays off, and I'm in no hurry.

Blue Nun

Kathleen Gunton

Father Killian arrives for dinner
and offers me the slender
neck of a wine bottle.
Blue Nun. On its label
a woman in white veil blue habit
safeguards grapes in a basket.

In reverie I travel the vineyards of my past.
NYC 1965. Cardinal Spellman has invited
nuns and postulants (like myself at seventeen)
to attend the movie opening of Sound of Music.
I see women in habits of brown and black
cream and gray, long skirts swishing,
rosary beads heavy-hitting doors.
In that holy throng one nun
appears like grace in cobalt blue.
A Morpho butterfly who suddenly disappears.

Father Killian and I sip & converse.
In Liverpool the Beatles are also drinking *Blue Nun.*
Their bottle vibrates on an organ played by Paul McCartney.
Ciphered notes react to pedal, pipes and speaker.
You can hear it in their song, "Long, Long, Long."

O clean, sweet wine you taste like my spirit
when I was a Bride of Christ.
How could I ever have lost you?

All the Beautiful Ladies

Toti O'Brien

Charity called all of us Tramp and in her voice it sounded good. You almost felt proud about it. It established the ambiance: down to earth and no frills—though we dealt with frills, didn't we? Charity was a costumer for large-scale period movies: huge productions, featuring stars, and loads of extras.

"Come here, Tramp," she'd say while snapping her fingers and we felt at home in her bullshit-proof realm. Very impartial, she addressed all the same way: assistants, seamstresses, and extras—both women and men. She didn't treat producers, directors, or principals any better. She only added a smile and a kind of mellowness to signify she was kidding. She was famous; she could afford liberty. No one was outraged. All knew, all played along.

With us, she didn't bother to soften the tone. Sharp, matter-of-fact, and supported by a twitch of her hooked index finger: "Come here, Tramp, I need you." If the moment weren't stressful or tense, there would be a hint of laughter, humor under the surface. Most of time, none was detectable. We did not imitate her, of course. We had not earned the special immunity due to her incommensurable talent. Had we tried, we would have won a slap in the face.

She called everyone Tramp. It was true, and wasn't. The noun came with an adjective—for those, her imagination had no limits. She found one for each individual in seconds. You could see it happen: a stare, an insight, and then her fantasy took fire.

"Call me that Mousy-Tramp who just entered, will you?"

"Who?"

"Come on, you Dumb-Tramp, I need Mousy-Tramp, the one whose shoes squeak, don't you hear?"

Booby-Tramp, Skinny-Tramp, Fringy-Tramp.

You'd quickly get tuned and need no more explanations. But the game lightened the gloom of the four a.m. call, the twelve p.m. overtime. It affirmed we were part of a comedy, whatever the present script. We were all characters whether cast or not.

The "tramp" thing leveled us in spite of the gap on our weekly checks. We all responded to a same label. First, a colorful attribute and then the suffix: short and final, a gunshot. Tramp. We all ended that way, Stingy-Tramp or Sweet-Tramp, Scared-Tramp, Giggly-Tramp.

I said "we" but I shouldn't have for I happened to be the exception. Why, I never figured out. I could think out of love although I was not sure it applied. After Charity staggered for a few minutes on Tiny-Tramp, Weeny-Tramp, Mini-Tramp because of my small frame, she called me Trampoline. It stuck and I adored it. Such tenderness. I felt special, precious: a pearl of a tramp.

Now let me describe Charity, for the sake of it, in hope you'd remember her as I did. She was striking. Square-faced with small features and a slight strabismus—a subtle asymmetry, alas, causing her young self to think she was ugly. She had tossed marriage and such over her shoulder without looking back. Her choice must have unburdened her, at least career wise.

Tall, built like the mountaineer she was, and endowed with a practicality as well as genius, she had her hair cut at chin level, straight as rain, and untimely white. Candid, in contrast with her juvenile appearance, such color kept us at bay—it conferred her the right to blabber whatever vulgarity she wanted, which she did as a stress management policy. It worked.

She had given up marriage, but not romance. Uncommitted, free of ties: why not? She was stylish, witty, fun—she attracted men by the dozen. She enjoyed her relationships. Yet, at fifty, she cut them short with the quickness she would use to nip a curl or to open cleavage, impromptu, even with cameras on. She was used to interrupting a scene because this or that needed fixing. I have seen her do it more than once. No director ever stopped her. She was overly talented, as I said.

That she was a lesbian was a current rumor. I knew it to be false because she had admitted me into her confidence and I had met her lovers. Otherwise, she kept her privacy private, so to speak, uncaring of what others thought. The intimacy she reserved for me as her first assistant, especially my nickname that she incessantly shouted, had created the gossip. I wasn't sure it bothered me. Maybe it did early on when I still believed truth was for all, but soon it became a comfy shield. A façade—no confirmation, no denial—that earned me freedom of action and slowed down curiosity like a steak thrown to a pack of famished jaws.

Charity wasn't closeted. She had secrets though. The main one was her shyness: her lonely nature and the horror the entertainment bunch inspired in her. She came from a valley secluded by mountain chains. Her folks were poor farmers. She had shown a talent for drawing that wasn't ignored. Maybe, a schoolteacher had been particularly stubborn, especially wise. Her sister, a bit older, left school, went to work, and saved for Charity's college. Charity, of course, never forgot.

When her parents died, Charity took her sibling with her. In their home, they reproduced the simplicity of their peasant habits though they lived in the suburbs of town. Between that peaceful island and the industry glamour, Charity wanted to cut the bridges. She only left a tiny causeway for me. She trusted Trampoline could understand for Trampoline was like her. I understood her.

I understood that, for Charity, getting out of her lair in the morning, throwing herself in the cinematic bazaar, required supreme effort. I was not sure where she found the courage: her stylish clothes helped, and the music she blasted in her car as soon as she started driving. Her collection of tapes boosted her mood. Glorious, great symphonies collected her spirits.

Her shoes counted as well. She told me all about it, since the start, though initially I didn't get it. "Your feet, Trampoline. You have no idea how important they are if you want to keep standing." There was also earthy food, good wine, daily laughter.

Once, after an exhausting ball scene that had lasted twelve hours, we were undressing the ladies. Taking off layers of silk, velvet, brocades, unfastening a nonsensical number of snaps, untying busts and petticoats, unbuttoning boots. We, the assistants, took off a zillion bobby pins and handed out tissues to remove makeup while Charity stormed about for the task she had reserved: rapaciously collecting gloves, laces, fans, and all period jewelry—though entirely fake, it was worth a fortune.

She was as exhausted as we were. It appeared in the increasing sharpness of her voice, up in pitch and volume with every call. Her eyes scanned the surrounding chaos, searching for females bending besides hangers, crouching down to take off their socks, heading to the restrooms, still bedecked with some glamorous spark they had forgot or, indeed, wanted to sneak away.

One-by-one, she would check them; index finger fishing her victims and then frantically fumbling among catches and clips with lessening gentleness while the hour went by.

"Tramp? You, Ruby-Tramp, come on darling …"

"Turtle-Tramp! Give me those turtle combs of yours, I need them for Carmen, you're not going to sleep in those, are you?"

"Bony-Tramp, where are you going? Those pearls have to come off before you can pee."

That was when the husband arrived. Not Charity's; she didn't have one. This husband must have heard Charity's shout from downstairs and had gone purple. When he appeared on the landing, his face had such color. Charity still yelled at the lady—tall, dark haired, with large sculpted features. Very kind in spite of her strong looks. "Princess-Tramp," Charity had shouted. "I'm not done. You can't leave."

Alas, right as Princess-Tramp smiled, either by habit or weariness, her husband had caught her.

He lunged forward with mad eyes. We scattered out of his way. He pulled Princess-Tramp by her arm while Charity was extracting a peacock-feathered comb from her bun. For a moment the lady's neck tilted, the hair contraption still holding as her man yanked her towards the door. It must have hurt: her eyes popped in astonishment. Charity's jaw dropped. It took us a while to realize what was happening.

Spouses never came to pick up extras after the shooting, since they were always occurring in weirdly remote locations where you wouldn't drive if you didn't have to. There was nothing special at being an extra, in spite of definitions. It was sort of a nine-to-five routine yet, in this case, exhaustingly lingering after hours. It was so late the lady must have been concerned. Maybe she had missed the last metro and she called her husband, perhaps waking him up or disturbing the match on TV.

We heard him yell down the stairs, stopping every two steps to hammer his point, surely squeezing her arm, if he didn't slap her. We hoped not. At each stop, one of us—assistants and seamstress, sympathetic supernumeraries and actors—dared a peek from the landing, wishing to intervene.

"I heard what the lady told you," he was shouting. "I heard what she said … you smiled, why did you? Those words meant what they meant. Slut! As I turn around, don't you take advantage? What did you do, all day? Tell me."

Her voice was conciliatory. "Stop, please. I'll explain. Let me."

From the landing came our chirping chorus: "Sir, listen up, please. She always does it. She calls everyone Tramp. We are all Tramps, here. Ask, if you don't believe it."

Believe? Of course he didn't.

Charity disappointed me, for she didn't step in, though she had caused the trouble. Either fatigue numbed her or the jewelry she worriedly counted was her only care. Or she, in fact, thought the extras were irrelevant bodies she could … tramp. While the quarrel continued to the main hall, I felt increasingly sad. For the first time the thought occurred to me that not everything was a comedy. A thin slice of drama could sneak in, trip us. Even Charity.

After that, we spent several months on a remote island for another period movie. There were forests, villages, and a rural feel my boss found refreshing. Charity befriended a robust guy, who took care of carpentry and props. Sometimes they left the set to attend village balls, country dinners, hunting parties, or mountain hikes. She told me about those diversions for I still was her faithful Trampoline. In fact, she was giving me more responsibilities with the hidden intention, I guessed, to make me her professional heiress when she'd finally retire.

I received some male visitors on the island. A number of them: it was quite a long stay in a remote location. I didn't hide my adventures from Charity. It would have been hard. She listened, gladly, eager to give advice. Her aesthetic skills had sharpened her understanding of physical appearance. So she said: she could tell what features, body structures, clothing styles signified. After carefully studying my flings, she spitted few sibylline sentences, then concluded: "Those eyes have no pity. They will make you cry." Although it sounded probable, in most cases, I got weary of listening to the same verdict. I guess she wasn't aware of the pattern. Her formula must have surfaced by itself, floating up a geyser of ancient pain. Something must have happened before marriage was thrown over her shoulder.

I did marry after another movie or two. When I did, Charity gave me a special present along with her wishes, a bittersweet congrats. My spouse and I were to move abroad, I was leaving the industry, and wouldn't be honoring her legacy. That must have been more of a blow than I understood in my juvenile blindness. Trampoline—her flexibility, her soft pliability notwithstanding—wouldn't allow Charity to leap out, leave the world of stress, competition, and fake gold to retire in the world of earned simple pleasures. Trampoline, bewitched by a pair of male eyes, no doubt harbingers of future hurt, had jumped away.

Still, she gave me a present. Something she had cherished for years, she said. Something special that I had to keep it with me at all times. It was a small sewing set. A tradition from the valley where she was born, she explained, given from mother to daughter. A golden tube, maybe brass, partially painted red, one end rounded, the other closed by a thimble. Inside were two small wooden spools, one filled with black thread, the other with white, and a sheath containing a needle. It all looked pretty sexual to me, but that was why people married, after all. Was the charm passed down by Charity's mom? She didn't say.

I kept it, forever, way after my divorce. The red paint came off, but the gold remained.

Carmen Walks the Camino de Santiago

Tobi Alfier

Monday through Saturday Carmen
watches out her window, mother-of-pearl
cleavage at rest on the peeling husk of the frame.
A small gold cross, and smaller earrings

complete a pastoral still-life
against the faint piss-smell and detritus
of an alley off Bourbon Street
known for its women of all hours.

If her window is closed, she is busy.
If her window is closed, it is Sunday,
a day for Vieux Carre Baptist Church—
where they know she is broken

but do not care. Carmen keeps two
cigar boxes from her beloved grandfather
in which to save money—
one for Sundays, one for her dream

to walk the Camino, to walk with undiluted faith,
trek with the other pilgrims, all damaged
in some way, all searching for blessing, sense
of connection, some way out of unspoken grief.

Carmen counted the bunched-up bills in that box
like a child counts the hours until bedtime.
She stopped one day after church, took a modest
passport photo, and bought her ticket to all the hopes

her years amounted to. She paid her rent,
latched her window for at least two months,
and began her journey the way a blind woman
remembers the way through her house.

The House on Blix Street

Brandon French

It was a bright white, one-story, stucco building in Sherman Oaks with a fire engine red sign that read Moorpark Title—the last stop in a process that had begun in January and dragged on, because of the sluggish real estate market, into the nervy Santa Ana winds of October. Today, Marisa and Alex would sign the property title documents that ended their ownership of the house on Blix Street—the first house either of them had ever owned, the 61st one they had looked at when they were house hunting two years earlier, and the only one they had fallen in love with, driving up and down the streets of North Hollywood together in 1981. It was a Spanish style, one-story, stucco model built with small variations throughout Los Angeles and the San Fernando Valley in the 1920's with beam ceilings and unspoiled hardwood floors beneath the mildewed, snake green shag carpet that some misguided 1950's housewife had deemed *de rigueur.* It had a formal dining room designed for dinner parties of eight to twelve, and a snug second bedroom for Marisa's daughter Lizzie, which Alex had spent an entire weekend painting "Fandango Blue," a boisterous lavender that tilted toward purple, to celebrate her twelfth birthday. There was also a two-car garage, which Alex converted into his office, adding three rectangular skylights and plush beige carpeting that invited bare feet. And outside the Moorish arch of the living room window was a grassy lawn where they planted flowering trees—white crepe myrtle, purple jacaranda, and a fat-budded fuchsia Chinese orchid that would eventually camouflage the chain link fence that separated 2019 Blix, owned by a blustery, dog-hating, retired TV actor with two heart attacks under his belt, from his dog-owning neighbors at 2021.

Marisa parked her navy blue Toyota Corolla at a meter on Ventura Boulevard at 3:50 in the afternoon, a little later than she'd expected because her UCLA graduate seminar on *Gravity's Rainbow* had run over by at least ten minutes due to one student's impassioned diatribe against Thomas Pynchon. She checked herself out in the side mirror, fluffing her auburn bangs and powdering the shine from her nose. *Tired*, she thought, scanning her face as if it belonged to someone else—strained, gaunt—and something else, something unsettling. *Old.*

Alex was standing out front waiting for her, smiling. He looked the way he always looked, like a big friendly Labrador retriever who wagged his tail and bounced around on large, clumsy paws. He was holding a grease-stained bag of chicken parts from the Lucky Cluck barbecue stand across the street. Its contagious aromas of poultry fat, molasses, garlic and charred wood made Marisa queasy.

"Hi," she said, walking quickly past him into the office.

"Hi," he said, following her.

They hadn't had much to say to each other once the house sold at a $20,000 loss.

"We must be the only people in California who lost money on real estate," she had said, wanting him to know that his infidelity had cost her more than just emotional pain. Hadn't some writer observed that in Los Angeles all love stories involved real estate?

Not that theirs was really a love story.

Oh, Christ. She didn't want to think about the relationship. She only had to live through the next hour, sign the papers, and it was *adios, amigo.*

Alex sat down in one of the imitation Eames leather chairs and opened his chicken bag, pulling out a drumstick.

"I had to grab a late lunch. Want some?"

"No, thank you," Marisa said, sitting down on the faux leather love seat across from him. "Better wash the grease off your hands before we sign the docs," she said, looking around at the pictures on the walls, a visual cliché of happy households with golf green lawns, white picket fences, backyard barbecues, smoking fireplaces, and sunlit kitchens with fruit pies cooling on the windowsills.

"I will when I'm done," he said, nearly spilling the container of barbecue sauce onto his khaki pants.

Marisa reached for the October issue of *House and Garden* on the rectangular glass coffee table and started thumbing through the pages.

"Look. There's our lamp," she said, holding up the magazine so Alex could see the furniture ad.

He leaned forward and peered at it. "Almost," he said, reaching into the bag and pulling out a thigh. "But the shade is a little different."

Marisa looked at it again. Then it struck her how absurd it was to be discussing their furniture as if they were still living together. But after seven years, back East at Brown and then in Los Angeles, she found it bewildering that they were no longer a couple.

She and Lizzie would have to move out by the end of the month—poor Lizzie, who had loved the house and her Fandango Blue bedroom, loved their Basset Hound Eleanor Roosevelt, loved Alex more than her real father, loved inviting her friends over and introducing them to him. "My stepfather," she called him, even though Marisa and Alex weren't married. "He's a math genius," she announced proudly.

A week earlier, Marisa had finally found an apartment she didn't despise. It was on Laurelgrove and Riverside, small compared to the house, but sunny with two bedrooms and a second half-bath. And it was within walking distance of Lizzie's high school, so Marisa wouldn't have to drive her each morning. She had actually started looking around even before Alex told her about Lidia, sensing that their relationship was in jeopardy when he began to dress up each morning before he left for his teaching job at Pepperdine, carefully pressing his pants and shirts with the iron, trimming his beard, and finally using the Hugo Boss cologne she had bought him for Christmas.

The big announcement came on the night of her fortieth birthday, as they were preparing to go out for a celebratory dinner. Alex burst into tears and said he was in love with a student at Pepperdine. He said her name was Lidia. He said he had only stayed with Marisa this long because of Lizzie.

Marisa tossed the magazine back onto the table and sighed. "Are you done eating yet?"

Alex crumpled the Lucky Cluck bag and stood up, looking around for somewhere to toss it. He wiped the barbecue sauce off his face and hands with the unused part of his napkin.

"Ask the receptionist what's holding up the show," Marisa said. "Tell her we had a four o'clock appointment and it's already 4:15."

"So you think romantic love lasts forever, is that it?" she had demanded after he told her about Lidia.

"We think it might," he had said.

"Oh, we do, do we? How old is she, nineteen? An expert in the duration of love, no doubt. What a stroke of genius to turn to a teenager for wisdom, Alex. She must really have fucked your brains out."

"By the way," Marisa said to Alex, who was now grading trigonometry quizzes, "we had to move the Chinese orchid."

"How come?" Alex asked without looking up.

"It grew into the chain link fence, and the buyers wanted us to fix it before escrow closed. The gardener and I had to amputate part of the trunk to get it loose and then uproot the poor thing."

"Did you toss it?"

"No, we replanted it by the front window. They'll be able to see the flowers from the living room now. Assuming it doesn't die."

At 4:30 the receptionist finally came over and escorted them into one of the offices. There was a long table with chairs on each side rather than a desk. Behind the table was a credenza with another happy home pictured above it, the husband watering the grass of a craftsman-style house while his smiling wife gathered pink tulips into a basket.

Alex and Marisa sat down across from a plump young woman with a round, pretty face, expertly made up like the salesgirls who peddled cosmetics in the department stores. She introduced herself as Miss Jacobson and handed them each a thick set of documents. Marisa noticed that Miss Jacobson's bright coral suit was wool rather than polyester and that she was wearing an impressively large engagement ring. *Won't be "Miss" for too much longer*, Marisa thought.

"Do you need pens?" Miss Jacobson asked.

"I have this," Alex said, holding up the red pen he'd used to grade the math quizzes.

"No, it has to be black," Miss Jacobson said. She reached over to a large mug stuffed with Moorpark Title pens, took out two and handed them to the couple. Marisa examined the pen, assessing its weight and girth, and then set it down.

"I'd rather use my own," she said, taking out her treasured Mont Blanc ballpoint. It was the gift Alex had given her for their first Christmas together after they'd met at a holiday party in Providence. A real writer's pen, he had said, back when he was crazy about her and wanted to read everything she'd written, the stories and plays and even the novel. Back when he thought she was beautiful and smart and talented and he could hardly believe that she liked him. But that was the problem, of course. She *liked* him. And what she liked most was the way he was crazy about her.

"I know he's not someone you'd expect me to choose," she had said to her grad school mentor and former lover Stephen, out from Brown to deliver a lecture on Shakespeare's "problem" sonnets.

"He's a little goofy," Stephen had said, swirling the cabernet in his glass. "Kind of a lightweight, don't you think?"

"Lizzie loves him," Marisa said defensively. "And I wanted her to have a real father, not another wacko genius. Or a married man, like you, my dear Stephen. I wanted a family."

But there had been too many nights when she turned away from Alex, longing for someone sophisticated, who adored literature and poetry (Alex preferred music, which he said was aural math). She desired a man with elegance, who enjoyed gourmet restaurants, expensive wines and liked his meat rare instead of well done the way his mother had cooked it.

Marisa's eyes watered as she was scanning the documents and her nose began to run. *Oh my God, no.* Why was she crying, for heaven's sake?

Several years earlier, Alex had asked Marisa to marry him while they were visiting her Aunt Sylvia in Cincinnati. He had waited to propose until after he'd charmed the aunt (and all the other Cincinnati relatives) by sitting down at the grand piano and performing a little song he'd composed about Sylvia's multiple marriages:

Sylvia Hattis Maltz Solway Wasserman
Three lucky men have loved you in your life
Your cooking and your smile
so many men beguiled
No wonder you've so often been a wife.
(Now let's all sing it together . . .)

Sylvia had cornered Marisa against the refrigerator door later that evening and whispered, "I'll pay for the wedding."

"But I don't love him," Marisa protested.

"You're a damn fool," her aunt said fiercely.

"Do you need a tissue?" Miss Jacobson asked.

"No," Marisa said, keeping her head down and trying to focus on the documents.

"I just got over a summer cold. It took forever," Miss Jacobson commiserated.

"I don't have a cold," Marisa said.

"Then it must be allergies. Aren't they a bitch?"

"Where do I sign this one?" Alex asked, remaining doggedly on task. "This page doesn't have any place to sign."

Two years ago, he had wept after they signed the papers to purchase the

Blix Street house, terrified of the risks and responsibilities of being a first-time homeowner. She had been frightened, too, but she quickly pulled herself together.

"There's nothing to be afraid of, Alex," she said with authority. "Stop being a wimp."

Now it was her turn to cry.

She fumbled in her purse for a tissue, pushing aside the books (*Lost in the Funhouse* and *Grendel*), keys, wallet, cough drops, safety pins and paper clips, a half-empty bottle of Ativan, and a tattered address book. Everything but Kleenex.

"Shit," she said, wiping her nose on the sleeve of her Liz Claiborne suit jacket like a three-year-old.

"Do you need …" Miss Jacobson started to ask.

"No," Marisa said with more irritation than she intended. Alex continued to sign documents, not looking over at her.

"Do you know why I hate you?" he had said as they were driving home a year earlier, cutting her off as she pontificated about *Atlantic City*, Louie Malle's film about a love triangle.

"You hate me?" she repeated, shocked.

He did not continue, instead turning on the radio to a classical music station. They drove the rest of the way without speaking; their emotions drowned out by the dramatic chords of Rachmaninov's Prelude No. 2.

Marisa moved the documents back a little to keep her tears from falling onto the paper. Biting her lip hard to distract herself, she pushed on, page after page, as if she were slogging through mud. Even after she'd signed the last page, there was no relief. This is it, she realized, feeling as though she had just signed a divorce decree. As soon as she and Alex stood up to go, the bond would be severed, the family dismantled, the marriage ended.

But when had she married Alex? When in the last seven years had her heart done something without telling her head? Had there been a wedding somewhere that she had not attended, had not even been invited to? *Oh my God, my God.*

She pushed her chair back and stood up, feeling disoriented and dizzy. She tried to steady herself but everything had begun to spin and blur as if she were on a Tilt-A-Whirl. She could feel her pulse racing and realized that she was having a full-blown panic attack. Grabbing her purse, she rushed out of Miss Jacobson's office, bumping hard into the coffee table in the waiting room, which sent the magazines tumbling onto the carpet. She pushed open the entry door with all her force and nearly fell into the street, gasping for breath, the sobs she had barely suppressed bursting out and convulsing her body so violently that she had to grab hold of a parking meter to remain on her feet.

People drove past her, staring, but she was beyond embarrassment. She wanted to cry out to them, "You lousy motherfuckers, here's what a loser looks like. Feast your eyes."

A few moments later, Alex came after her with two Moorpark Title folders.

"Marisa, you forgot your copy," he said, holding it out to her.

She looked up at him, her face red, swollen, and distorted, mucus spilling from her nostrils down past her lips and dripping off her chin.

"Here," he said, handing her the folder.

She took it with her free hand, still gripping the parking meter for balance. He grinned at her idiotically.

"Well, see you," he said and turned quickly away.

She watched him cross Ventura Boulevard and walk to his car, a little bronze Triumph convertible they had bought together, his first automobile. He had loved driving it recklessly through the twists and turns of Laurel Canyon, enjoying the exhilaration of delayed adolescence and adult privilege.

Marisa noticed that the little rose-colored ribbon was still attached to the Triumph's radio aerial, billowing in the early evening breeze like a taunt. Lidia had taken it from her hair, Alex told Marisa, and given it to him after they began their affair. He seemed to relish every opportunity for cruelty during their last days together.

"You know why I hate you?" he had said, and then left her hanging.

A year later, Lizzie went to their wedding, held in the backyard of Lidia's parents' Brentwood home. Afterward, Marisa pumped her for details, but Lizzie was evasive, saying only that there were about fifty people in attendance, mostly Lidia's friends and relatives, and a lot of shrimp on ice.

"I just want to know how she looked," Marisa said. "Did she wear a bridal gown?"

"Why do you want to hurt yourself, mom?" Lizzie asked.

Marisa didn't know how to answer.

After the wedding, the new couple moved to a house in Los Feliz, Spanish like the one on Blix Street, only larger, with a children's swing in front. Several years later, there were baby pictures on line, first of Abel and then Emma. They took vacation trips to Greece, Ireland and Costa Rica, mugging for the camera in indigenous hats and tee-shirts.

Marisa mentioned to Lizzie during one of their nightly phone calls that Lidia looked heavier in the pictures.

"She's got a belly now, and her face has filled out."

"Are you gloating, mom?"

"Possibly."

A decade passed before Alex called.

"Eleanor Roosevelt died last night in her sleep," he said without identifying himself. "I thought you'd want to know."

Marisa groped for a response. "Oh," she said. "Oh, dear."

"She was a great lady," he said and his voice quavered. "Fifteen years old."

"I remember the day we bought her," Marisa mumbled, feeling as if her organs were shifting around and pressing against her diaphragm. She had treated the dog miserably during their last days together, despising Eleanor for continuing to love her when Alex no longer did.

"By the way," he said, trying to recover his composure, "I went by the Blix Street house a couple of weeks ago. I just happened to be in the valley, so I thought, what the hell."

"I can't go near there," she said. The idea of seeing the house again, even after all this time, was unbearable.

"Everything looked pretty much the same. The trees are bigger, of course, higher than the roof now. Our hanging baskets of geraniums are still out front."

"Geraniums are hard to kill, I guess."

"The orchid tree you replanted is in full bloom. There must be a thousand pink flowers," he said.

It had survived after all, she thought. Survived the amputation, the uprooting and the new placement. Her eyes filled with tears.

"Thank you for telling me," she said, struggling to keep her voice steady. She pictured the front of the house as Alex had described it—the bushy crepe myrtle and the fern-leafed jacaranda, a spill of red and purple geraniums and a riotous panorama of pink Chinese orchid blossoms stretched out across the sky. "Our babies," she had called them once, fondling the tree's heart-shaped leaves.

Both of them were silent for several seconds, as if they were standing together on a ridge and moving forward might be fatal. Marisa's refrigerator gurgled and whirred. A window in the next condo unit shut with a muffled thud.

"Lizzie's doing well," Alex said with determined cheer. "Don't you think? We email each other all the time. Did she tell you?"

"No, she didn't." *Maybe it was Lizzie he had really loved.*

"I – I just wanted to say that I'm sorry," Alex said. "I know I said some … bad things."

"You said you hated me," Marisa said. The memory was as searing as a fresh burn.

"I'm really sorry. I don't know why I said that."

But Marisa knew. She had held her heart back from him for seven years, like a miser, finding little favor and critiquing every imperfection, as if he were a graduate student's lame dissertation. She had cheated him at every turn, cheated herself, too, until she drove him to look elsewhere.

"I don't blame you for leaving," she blurted out. "You did the right thing."

Marisa's throat was parched after she hung up, as if her words had shriveled into little claws that scraped the tissue raw. She sat quietly in the kitchen with her hands in her lap, watching the daylight leak through the windows until the night enshrouded her. She finally stood up, her neck cramped and her legs stiff and unruly, and moved slowly through the condo, turning on each lamp and light switch she passed until all the rooms were ablaze. But she knew—in the same way we know after a lengthy search that the car key or wallet or diamond earring we've lost is lost for good—that there would never be enough lumens to penetrate the darkness.

For Glover Davis

Cindy Maresic

I cross the lawn in a thin shirt and slippers
toward the darkening trees
that stretch their heads like saints
into the quiet night.
Leaves flutter their sounds of foliage,
and because I am a poet,
I feel I should know the names of these trees,
and what species they were born from,
but as I stand there alone,
waiting for a spark of scientific memory,
I realize I have nothing to offer
these holy daughters of the earth.
Again, I've disappointed the man who taught me
Philip Levine and Wallace Stevens;
the man who believed I could harness
the melody of black dust and roses
and set whole cities on fire.
His words are hungry lions
as I consider the gardener, who, with gloveless hands,
lifted these young roots into the ground,
arching her back over the stunned earth,
until only the damp bark could be seen
quivering into life.

Three Houses

Sharon Goldberg

The Town House

A brand new home to shelter our brand new marriage, nestled in a San Francisco suburb, near a lagoon dotted with windsurfers and rowboats and ducks. We knew nothing of loans and points, APRs and ARMs. Could we afford it? Together, we stepped into a question mark. The town house felt so big: three levels, 1,210 square feet, two bedrooms, two bathrooms. It was warrantied for a year, nothing to worry about. We appreciated things then we took for granted later: a walk-in closet, a washer and dryer, a candlelight dinner, a cuddle on the couch.

In the living room, we watched *Thirty Something*—Hope and Michael, Nancy and Elliot—and we shed tears when their marriages faltered. We're not like that, we said. Are we? And we're not like our friends, the Campbells, either, her nasty comments, their constant bickering. We don't treat each other unkindly.

In the bedroom, furnished in low-grade lacquer, we made love. A lot.

In the kitchen, he injected me with Pergonal, a fertility drug; we were trying to make a baby. The shots left me bruised and sore. Later, we talked about adoption, but only I made inquiries and investigated.

When I turned 40, he surprised me with a party, friends waiting in the living room, lasagna and birthday cake and gifts in the dining room.

The tub in the master bathroom leaked and seepage turned the white flooring grey. We paid to fix the plumbing and replace the floor. The warranty had expired.

On October 17, 1989, the Loma Prieta earthquake struck Northern California toppling 40 buildings in Santa Cruz, demolishing homes in San Francisco's Marina District, and collapsing a section of the Nimitz Freeway crushing 41 people in their cars. I drove home from San Francisco that evening down spooky, silent streets lined with shops and offices exploded with debris and broken glass. He drove home from San Jose crossing fissures in the 280 freeway. I remember my relief when he rushed in the door. We were both safe. So was our home; the only damage a broken Asian vase, a wedding gift.

The Tree House

Seven years married and itchy for change, we moved to Seattle. Our money bought more there and we had more of it. We settled into a three-level house on a hogback surrounded by trees, a view of Lake Sammamish reigning glorious from our deck. Our nest was bigger and better feathered: 1,700 more square feet, two more bedrooms, one more bathroom, hot tub, floor-to-ceiling windows in the living and dining rooms, and a front door 20 feet high to match our expectations. We bought the seller's teak bedroom furniture and relegated our old stuff to the guestroom. We made love in our master suite but less often than before.

At ten years, we renewed our vows. We decided we were happy without children.

We battled mice, carpet beetles, carpenter ants, and woodpeckers that pecked at our shingles instead of the trees. Our roof leaked and leaked and leaked and we replaced and replaced and replaced cedar planks in the ceilings. Birds crashed into our windows and landed dead on the driveway, the danger invisible to them. We heard trees crack in windstorms, but we were lucky—none ever hit the house.

In the living room, on his 40th birthday, I threw a party with games and gifts and guests from out of town, including our friends the Hoebers. We're not like them, we said. She's angry. He's self-involved. We thought *we* knew how to communicate. And we never ran out of conversation.

In 1995, a zealot assassinated Israeli Prime Minister Yitzchak Rabin, and two former soldiers bombed the federal building in Oklahoma City killing 168 people. In 1997, Princess Diana died in a car crash. In 1999, two alienated teenage boys massacred thirteen at Columbine High School. Life can change in an instant, I knew, and there's no way to prepare.

The Dream House

The stock option house. The "we've made it" house. The house I thought we'd live in the rest of our lives: waterfront on Lake Sammamish, 3,500 square feet, three levels (of course), the lower floor ready for overnight guests and parties on the lake, a dock with a great blue heron perched on the end, a security system to protect us and our property. We'd been married thirteen years.

We knew going in that the builder had used the wrong nails (not anodized) when constructing the house; they would rust through and corrode the shingles if we didn't fix the problem. We hired a painter to seal every nail and repaint the house—danger averted.

We bought high gloss lacquer furniture for our bedroom and made love there sometimes: I went to sleep late. He got up early. He rarely initiated.

The shower in the master bathroom leaked—botched insulation. We replaced sheet rock and glass bricks and tile and marble on the floor. Canadian geese pooped and pooped and pooped on our deck. Nothing we could do about it but sweep away the poop.

On my 50th birthday, he surprised me with a masked ball in our backyard. Twinkle lights flickered on the deck. A caterer served dinner and wine. My parents flew in from Ohio.

I was happy. He said he was happy. But he had secrets; I learned that later. And we argued. About Bush vs. Gore. About money. About taking risks. About taking vacations. Don't all couples argue? Don't all relationships cycle through ups and downs?

He became hard-edged, more restless, less kind. What had I become?

On Sept. 11, 2001, he woke me, anxious and shaky. A plane had crashed into the Twin Towers in New York City. We turned on the TV and watched together as the impossible happened again. The world will never be the same, he said.

One Sunday three years later, the morning after we'd argued about investing money in a new business venture—we'll sleep on it, we decided—I awoke, the sun gleaming on the lake outside our bedroom window, and he, already awake next to me, was waiting to share his epiphany. I don't love you anymore, he said. Our marriage is over. And, by the way, I might want to have a child.

What is said. What isn't said. What is hinted at. What is missed. What is ignored. What is allowed to fester. What stings. What stuns you to the bones. What lives inside four walls. What dies there.

He moved out. We separated. Don't you dare bring her here, I said. We sold the house. We divorced. We never spoke again.

Bachelor Pads

Ryan Boyd

They frighten me, the old men.
Not the corner drunks or the bus-bench heaps,
Not the wobblers with walkers
Nor mumblers on the train,
But the men in my building
With its brass elevator and roach traps,
Its odor of meat and paint,
The ones who kept a liver-spotted grip
On the lower rungs of an orderly life,
Mailmen, cab drivers, dental techs,
Close to retirement checks and Medicare gaps.
They order small pizzas and keep succulents
And fold slow in the laundry room.
"I'm good, real good," one tells me.
He has a cat that sometimes slips into the hall,
A tabby with a woman's name.
Flu shot, bar tab, wristband, Keds,
Weak smiles worse than any glare.
Once, a terrible scene: I came downstairs
For the mail and some old boy's Hefty had torn
En route to the recycling bin,
Spilling empties—Rite Aid vodka,
Tonic bottles, jugs of Yellow Tail
Appalling in the lobby. He stood looking.
I turned upstairs two steps at a time
To my kitchen, boiled water,
Ground coffee, washed a mug.
It must have been 2 p.m. The light
Humiliated every surface,
Having shown another man
Useless in his bachelorhood,
Unlabeled wreck, an uncle, a shabby double
In a city as broad as forever
And small as a loosening button.

Impermanence

Paul Gacioch

In the shower, he found three new tattoos. On his left forearm was a Maori pattern, on his right pec was something Celtic, and ringing his right ankle were interlocking Stars of David. He belonged to no tribe or religion. His tattoos had never imparted messages, but now he could imagine their advice: *seek solace by joining a group.* He knew he wouldn't.

He shut off the water and heard his phone, its ringtone like an old pay phone's chiming. He knew he couldn't reach it in time—was this the start or end of its ringing?—and dried himself and went to check for a voice mail. There was no voice mail, just a missed call alert and the number. Naked, he called the caller back.

How long till all women on the phone stopped sounding like Stephanie? The woman said hello three times before he said he'd just missed a call from this number.

"Sorry, I didn't call anyone. You must have the—"

"Who is this?"

An adjustment in her voice. "This is Spring Mortuary. Can I help you?"

He'd dealt with these people almost a year ago, for the cremation. He feared there may be, after all this time, a problem with his payment.

"No, you can't." He hung up.

He put on mismatching clothes and forgot to eat breakfast and drove to work in silence along the beachside highway and realized only as he parked that he had no memory of the drive. He pretended he was texting someone as he entered the office and passed some coworkers and got to his cube where he booted up his machine and got lost—he liked getting lost, hiding, being forgotten—in so much data.

It was dark when he got home. The refrigerator's inside's brightness shocked him, he felt as if he and a liter of two-percent were on the moon's surface, and he shut the fridge to return to Earth. He drifted to the bedroom, the fridge-moon still burned into his vision, and shed his work clothes and put on jeans and a t-shirt, still in the dark, and then sneakers and a jacket—which wasn't enough, he knew he'd be cold—and grabbed his wallet and keys and was just out the door when a streetlamp, moths orbiting drunkenly, revealed a new tattoo on the back of his right hand.

A bar code. As if he could swipe his hand over a checkout scanner to see how much he'd cost. He judged it a smartass teenager's tattoo, yet wondered if his cost might rise if he did something with his life. Went back to school. Went to the gym for the first time in a year. Went out for more than dinners in waxed cardboard boxes from Earthfoods.

Where office professionals scooped *arroz con pollo* out from under heat lamps.

Medallions of pork. Cranberry walnut salads. Sushi in plastic boxes in the cold case; cubes of artisanal cheeses impaled by toothpicks, to sample. He chose the cold konese noodles and a local microbrew and saw as he went to pay that the bar code tattoo was gone.

And that the checkout girl's dimpley smile was like Stephanie's. Long ago he'd have smiled a certain way at her, made some conversation, some eye contact. Now he told himself she was just doing her job; perfunctory greeting, bland pleasantries, don't look again, don't read her name badge, just swipe your card.

He didn't want to start walking yet, he found a free weekly abandoned in the dining area, its front page stained by someone else's spills, and sat near a floor-to-ceiling window and checked himself in the dark glass—like seeing your reflection through sunglasses—and noticed a teardrop tattoo had shown up below the outer corner of his left eye.

He heard his name like it was a question. He turned. Ruth from HR. She'd always looked happy to see him—something was there, something he'd have once pursued—and now her smile looked real but also like it concealed something. They talked about how it felt odd to run into a co-worker outside of work, like, oh so this is how you really dress. She also had a thing of konese noodles, which he remarked on and ha ha too bad she didn't have the same microbrew. She had a bottled water. He thought maybe he should invite her to sit, but instead he acknowledged what sat beneath her smile, he had to act like he'd always had the teardrop tattoo.

"I cover it with makeup at work."

"Huh."

"Yeah. Don't get a tattoo on your face. Or your neck. Is my advice."

"But I like yours," she said. Then she said she had to go and feed her dog, and as she walked off she added, "I'd like to see your other tattoos sometime."

Which he didn't know how to take. Women no longer spoke to him like that, but was it really that? Or was he a fool for even thinking that, when really it was a friendly parting, a topic they could talk about if and when this happened again?

People came and went and the scent of their meals affected the taste of his own. He drank his microbrew and thought about how he couldn't name most kinds of trees, or say what make a car was unless he saw the logo on its trunk, and how he possessed only a basic vocabulary for different styles of clothing. He couldn't quite tell what Ruth's ethnicity was. The noodles felt gluey in his mouth and the beer tasted like summertime, the wrong season, and he sat there a while after he'd finished.

He rolled down his sock and saw the Stars of David had faded, almost vanished now. Sometimes he could feel a new tattoo forming, it was like a tickle, or a ladybug crawling on your arm before you see it. He couldn't stop it by scratching or pressing on the spot, or by rubber-banding above it to cut off his circulation, or by holding ice or a flame to it, and if he cut his skin where the tattoo was coming up it would be there when the scab retreated. Now he felt one emerging on his right shoulder blade, a big fast dramatic busy one, one he might photograph before it disappeared. They could take their time in forming, some took days, and could fade over weeks or vanish in a blink.

A woman pushing a shopping cart carried the same purse Stephanie had carried. Or one similar. Or he could be wrong.

Three hundred sixty-three nights ago, Stephanie began going through her papers, shoes, purses, her old photos and letters, and more, arranging things in piles to be thrown out or donated. Some piles got to knee-high; he thought of trail markers in a forest. She was a clutterer, he liked things Spartan, it was a source of tension. She refused his help so he sat and read and looked up sometimes to gauge her progress. Eventually he put the book down and watched her, and he knew she knew he was watching, she'd been an actress, and he hoped she'd talk about the things she cleared away, but she only went to the bedroom. He figured she was cleaning there also, but when he got tired of his book he went and found her asleep.

She looked peaceful asleep—unselfconscious, at least. Their bedroom curtains fought the moonlight, and lost. Her mouth was open, her face was slack, and he saw none of the lies her expressions often told, none of the firm suspicion she often met the world with. He didn't know which bothered him more, that she'd gone to bed without even saying so, or that that firmness returned when he slipped in beside her.

He left Earthfoods and walked by downtown bars and restaurants where mounted TVs usually broadcast sporting events, but he saw through the windows that tonight they showed footage of devastation in some faraway place. He entered a bar and stood watching, hands in pockets, as shots of fire filled one of the screens, so much fire that he couldn't tell what kind of structure was burning. Then came images of the victims. He feared seeing one that looked like Stephanie, he hurried to a men's room the size of an elevator and locked the door and took off his jacket and t-shirt for a preview of the tattoo starting on his shoulder blade. But the angle was bad, the mirror scratched and dull, and he could make out nothing.

Sharpied onto the door, inches away, was the equation *F=ma*. He put his shirt and jacket back on and looked for more. Names, profanity, non-words like "wuzza" and "enjymz." Profile of a flaccid penis on the wall beside the toilet. In an upper corner, where you'd almost expect a security camera, he saw:

You have my permission.

—and then he looked away and looked back and saw just dingy drywall there and wondered if he could trust his own senses.

Someone shook the door handle hard, and for longer than it should've taken the person to realize it was locked. He stood still and held his breath while it was happening, this other man's urgency, till he heard footsteps leaving. Scratched finely into the doorframe, as if done with a pushpin, syringe needle, or dentist's scraper—either look close or overlook it—was a phone number. He used the toilet. He washed and dried his hands and wiped his mouth and the teardrop tattoo had faded. He got out his phone and punched in the number, the buttons sounded like clacking typewriter keys, and hit *dial* at the same time he opened the door.

"Hello?" The man's voice sounded old, patient.

"Yes, who is this?"

"You called me."

"Do you have any tattoos?" Expecting the old man would hang up at this.

Instead, a silence. An adjustment in the man's voice. "The body is a temple."

"You must be religious."

"*Pax vobicum*, my son."

He admitted he wasn't Catholic and then asked if he could ask for advice anyway, if they could talk about Stephanie, and the priest said yes. He left the bar and walked as he spoke and the priest replied with grunts and *mm-hmms* and an "I see." He said more than he wanted to say, he said things you shouldn't say about the dead. That she was fragile, flighty, distant; a bad actress, a worse waitress. People had been surprised she ever married; they didn't seem as surprised at her memorial. He told the priest about marriage, he said it took years to know someone, and by then she'd have changed. He talked about things a year ago. He spoke of giving her cremains to the ocean and then decided he was done, he wouldn't talk about the tattoos starting up a week later.

He noticed he'd wandered into a construction zone. Orange cones and barricades with reflective silver stripes, two lanes closed. A long trench was cut through the road to some broken pipes; no one was near enough to stop him, he could just fall into it and maybe keep falling till he met Stephanie far below. The priest told him that God had meant for this phone call to happen, there are no accidents, and he should come to confession. Now.

"At the least, it will clear tonight's tragedy from your mind."

"I wouldn't know what to say."

The priest gave him an address. "You'll know what to say when you hear yourself saying it."

Three hundred sixty-two mornings ago, he awoke to a house filled with fog. She'd risen early and thrown wide all the doors and windows and shut off the heat. His first thought was *fire*, but then there was the cold, and the calm, and the scent of the nearby ocean. He stayed in bed. That was the last time he saw her alive, but she seemed even then like just a fragment, a sketch, her figure barefooting through the rooms, scooping up her piles of possessions and taking them to the dumpster outside or out to her car to donate. The fog got thinner with his every breath, but was thick enough yet to swirl in her wake, and when the fog was gone, she was gone, and he left the bed and found things she'd dropped from her armfuls, things now strewn about the floor like detritus washed up on a beach.

There'd been tattoos of the sun and moon and constellations, of scripts in dead languages, of logos of products he wasn't sure existed. Tattoos of flags of faraway nations, music staffs he couldn't read, names of women he didn't know. Tattoos of things people didn't get tattoos of: a chair, a pigeon, a taco. Census data. And ones people only used to get: a U.S. Navy anchor on one forearm, an Auschwitz number on the other, a naked woman who danced when he flexed his bicep. Whales and muscle cars, fleurs-de-lis and lipstick kiss marks and religious iconography and bears. Tattoos looking like bullet holes, needle tracks, puncture wounds in his palms. Tattoos *in memoriam* of long-gone strangers. One he liked: a green octagon with "GO" in white letters. Another he liked, knowing it was temporary: a closed zipper running from one ankle up to the notch between his collarbones, where the zipper's pull tab was.

Tattoos resembling ordinary moles and birthmarks and body hair that lay flat. Tattoos that looked like socks on his feet. Tattoos on his tongue delineating which parts tasted sweet, sour, salty, bitter, and umami flavors. Tattoos of lines and words indicating his body's cuts of meat: sirloin, shank, flank, brisket, chuck, round, rib. Iridescent tattoos: you wouldn't notice them till they caught the light. Transparent tattoos: all you saw was their sheen. Tattoos, he suspected, inside him, on his organs, lining his lungs and tubes, rolling microscopically—like the seeds of tattoos?—through his blood vessels.

He supposed no doctor would believe these just appeared on him, they'd ask him to leave or refer him to a psychiatrist. Friends and family, already worried, would make things worse and worry more—he changed his phone number and wouldn't give out the new one, he wrote no more than a sentence in his email replies. At work, he took on strictly data-centric projects, letting his colleagues handle clients while he worked measurements and dollar figures into elaborate tables, charts, and graphs: see the information this way, now that way, now from over here, now there, review it, project it, and do you really *see* it yet? Before leaving his cube, he'd peer into a pocket mirror for new tattoos on his face and neck, and if one had surfaced he'd cover it with stage makeup that Stephanie had neglected to throw out. He feared someone would notice and ask about it. He could think of no plausible lie, but it didn't matter, no one was looking, no one said a thing.

He walked through a place he didn't know well. In a year, he'd seen almost every block, every street, mostly at night—a neighborhood's feel could change from one intersection to the next. After many months, he'd seen the same people enough to recognize that the city had other wanderers, ones who likely also walked not to think but to avoid thinking, ones who too had become noticers.

Here, lights were off in most apartments above stores. The wind tasted somehow metallic, which brought to mind sucking on pennies as a child, and how they'd knocked against his molars. A sunken freeway ran beside the road, and commercial billboards stood in a neat row like giant, lurid gravestones. Gas stations, liquor stores, a payday loan center, a convenience mart, a collision repair shop, a used car lot fenced off with tall chain link.

A famous actress who didn't resemble Stephanie looked almost feline on the billboard ahead. She was in a movie, out soon, that involved humans taking sides in an alien species' civil war. In his mind, he told the actress he'd been a bad husband. He didn't want to say how.

"And so," the actress didn't say, "you took it like an accusation."

"And one I couldn't answer."

"As if: 'You weren't enough to keep me here.'"

"Which I couldn't answer because it was true."

He remembered seeing a trailer for the movie coming out soon. The trailer gave away that the actress's character was such a skilled assassin—less a person than a devastating weapon—that leaders on each side of the aliens' civil war courted her by offering humans more advanced technology than we could likely handle. He was curious about the ending, but not so curious, he knew, that he could sit for two hours and watch it.

A man and a dog approached him on the sidewalk. The man was smoking a cigarette. The dog, he could tell from afar, was a German Shepherd, one of the few breeds he easily recognized. No other people were out, and both the street and freeway carried sparse traffic, and he couldn't tell if there was no moon tonight or if clouds concealed it, and he felt anxious about having to pass the man and the dog, they were still a ways off, and he wished that he too smoked so he'd have something to do with his hands. He began to think about how he was walking, which made his gait feel and perhaps look awkward, which made him think even more about how he was walking.

What he'd thought were regular glasses on the man turned out to be sunglasses, and what he'd thought was a leash was really a harness. He decided that the dog was not only the man's eyes but also his personal assistant, motivational coach, life manager—a guru, a sage, an oracle. The dog had been a companion, and had kept the man alive, yes, but also had, just by being there, kept him going late at night as he read cases in Braille, had fetched him matching suits and ties each weekday morning, had lit his cigarettes—enabled him—and listened as the man rehearsed courtroom arguments, responding in Morse code with tail thumps against the wall.

He passed the man and dog now. "I fucked other women," he didn't tell the dog, "but I don't think she ever knew."

"She knew about one woman," the dog didn't say, "but that's not a good enough reason."

"It's an act that runs in her family. She was a loyal daughter. That was her reason."

"Or is that just the story you tell yourself?" The man and dog were well past him now; maybe it was the trailing smoke that hadn't spoken.

He found the intersection he wanted and turned and looked at addresses to see which side of the street he should be on, and whether the numbers were rising or falling, and what it might be like to live in this or that place—he knew he should move, but had taken no steps. Again, apartments above stores were mostly dark; in many, TVs flashed blue on the windows and walls. Orange would burst amid the blue, as if people were all watching the same show, one with explosions and fire. The tattoo forming on his shoulder blade tingled like a foot that had fallen asleep, and the wind's metallic taste was strong now: snow was coming. It hadn't snowed here for years.

He found the address. This was no church, this was an apartment building almost Soviet in its featurelessness; it seemed as if it had always been here, and the world had risen around it. Beside the building was a driveway, bumpy with the roots of trees that had since been cut down, leading to covered parking in the back. The priest had given him no apartment number. He tried the phone number and no one answered and the call didn't go to voice mail. He studied the windows for one that might look Catholic but he saw no crucifix, no votive candles, no hanging rosaries or statuettes of Mary or the saints. In the dark windows were only billowing curtains: heaters were blowing. He went to the cars parked in the back, maybe one would look like a priest's.

Finger marks in the dust on their trunk doors. Dents and scrapes not worth repairing. Would Stephanie look any different at just a year older? The covered parking structure was made of corrugated iron with naked fluorescent tube lights on the ceiling, where moths flew fast and wild and he didn't know how they didn't collide. One veered off near a support column and got caught in a spider web and he didn't know a spider could move so swiftly; like a bird hopping from branch to branch, it got to the struggling moth. It had done well, surely it was bigger than most of its kind, whatever its kind was, and had more food than it could ever eat, and was usually complacent and sanguine but sometimes wondered if this was all there was. Was it lucky or smart, or both, to weave its webs here? It began wrapping its newest kill in spider thread, for later.

"I was gonna leave her," he didn't say, "as soon as I found a better woman."

"But you didn't?" the spider didn't say.

"No. She died."

"Did you eat her?"

He'd picked the wrong creature to not confess to. He went to the building's front entrance and shook the door handle longer than he needed to to confirm it was locked. A snowflake kissed the side of his neck. He buzzed an apartment, unsure what he'd say if a hello came through the intercom. Instead, the door buzzed in reply, someone must've been expecting someone, and he opened the door and stepped inside.

Three hundred fifty-nine nights ago, a policewoman called asking him to come to the hospital. There, he was escorted to a basement morgue where they hoped he might identify a body as that of the missing woman. The room as cold as their language. All was shades of blue. God wanted to apologize, but could find no words. Someone folded the sheet down to her collarbones. That was how her hair looked when she woke up each morning. That was her shoulder, its skin now eggshell white. That was her tattoo, now drained of color. He couldn't look at her face. They asked questions and he heard himself talking. Was told something about the beach, a jogger, an estimate of *when*. There were papers to sign if you could, sir.

Inside, mailboxes were on his left, a laundry room on his right. A bare concrete floor, a smell like dog food, a stairway ahead. Somewhere on the second floor, a bird sang. Lights far above shone on a glaze of grease on the stairway's handrails. The steps were made of old, dingy granite, and his every footstep made a scuffing noise. On the third floor, he smelled someone's cooking; he couldn't place what kind of food it was, or what those spices were, but he sensed it was eaten alone. Where two or three people were behind a door, little was said. He heard maybe a sentence in a language he couldn't identify. Water ran, toilets were flushed, people were alive. On the fourth floor, in a corner, an umbrella lay open and long since dried. The final flight of stairs led to a door he figured would open to the roof. He wanted to see snow from up there. Flakes in the beams of cars' headlamps, flakes sticking to bridges as if painting them white. Flakes melting the instant they hit water.

Up there, the door was locked. He gave up and walked down a few steps when he heard the door open behind him. He turned. Ruth from HR—how? Surely it was no coincidence, but he hadn't sought her, and she hadn't led him, and how could he trust his own senses? She must have been frightened, she'd take him for a stalker, or worse, so he held up his open palms.

"I'm sorry," he said. "I'll go."

But he didn't move.

"Don't go," she said. "I need someone now, too."

He entered into her living room where a very old dog slept in a corner. The TV was on and they stood watching scenes of devastation, explosions caught on security cameras replaying in slow motion, making it seem like they happened over and over, at the odd pace of a dream. Quotes and unconfirmed numbers crawled at the bottom of the screen, and news anchors kept repeating the little they knew, they interviewed experts who could only speculate, they repeated officials' cautious statements, they never cut to commercials. When their words ran out, there were live helicopter shots, aerial views of flames, the helicopter's whirring the only sound from the TV. He heard, then, a stutter to Ruth's breathing and looked and saw her cheeks were wet.

And she studied him back. "You don't need to cover it around me, OK?"

The teardrop tattoo must've vanished. He nodded and picked up the remote control from her coffee table and pressed the *power* button and the devastation, at least for a while, was gone. He went and unplugged the TV and moved it to a corner where it wouldn't be the focal point. She slid the coffee table away and pulled out one end of the couch and he got the other end and they moved it to a new spot and she took out the vacuum for the dustbunnies and crumbs and soon they were moving the rug, the bookshelves, the recliner to new places and adjusting their angles and vacuuming those spots the furniture had covered.

She began filling a white plastic trash bag with things she'd accumulated and must have wanted no more of—old literary journals, a brittle-brown house plant, spent batteries, mail addressed to *Resident*, souvenir trinkets from long-ago trips, outdated work documents, doggie chew toys, a flattened box, a postcard from Lima, a broken necklace that lay coiled on her end table. A candle that had melted down and hardened flat atop a glass dish.

He couldn't help her, he stood watching not just her choices but also her beauty—her cinnamon skin, her black hair in big, loose ringlets. The ways she moved, the looks she gave to things she kept and things she got rid of. Daunting books on her shelves, an impressive diploma in a frame—he wondered how she'd come here, and how she might change over time. He said something to himself about becoming a good man.

The room was hot from all their work, it had happened slowly, and snow was falling at a slant outside, and she peeled off her longsleeve shirt to a tank top beneath, and he realized he was sweating and had been for a while and took off his jacket with more suddenness than he intended. She gave him a look and went to the bedroom.

Where he'd have been OK with rearranging more furniture, more cleaning, more of this moment. They could do her kitchen, her bathroom; they could do his place tomorrow. He laughed. They could start a business where they did this for other people—people who'd just as soon set their past on fire. She laughed back, and he knew that neither knew what the other was laughing about.

"So: your other tattoos?"

He took off his shirt and turned his shoulder blade to her. He still didn't know what was there, or if it was even finished. He didn't know where this was going, if they were about to fall into bed, or what, and he didn't know if he was ready—what would being ready be like?

She came close and ran her fingernails down his spine. "It's amazing," she whispered. Her breath was hot and sweet. "I've never seen anything like it." Snow was striking the bedroom window and sticking. Soon the whole window would be covered.

Our Kisses, Lately

Michael Mark

I

Dried fruit, stingily
offered, the heat sealed
    from our lips' parched lands.

      No peeling back of breathy
layers, teasing, diving in again
                                and again.

            Lolo,
you must remember sucking
the ridges of my tongue smooth.
 The huntress you, hunting.

II

Now, we dole out antiseptic
            medicine cabinet kisses.
One in the morning.
One upon leaving the house.
One at bedtime.

III

When a river runs out
of what makes it a river
can a withered spring
still rise from its memory?
Does it lose its instinct – its river self?

IV

A broken man on his flat
noon walk sees a hose in a yard.
As a boy, he would shamelessly
    turn a stranger's spigot – cold
        rushing, spraying,
            falling
          on his bare feet.
The scrape of metal against his teeth, tongue
                swimming against the current.

V

Tonight, we set our books
on our tables, lights off,
and instead of tasting
another day's tiredness,
may our mouths meet memory—
            bring our river back
                for us to drink and drink
                    and drink and drink more.

How Do You Go On?

Lauren Paredes

March 21st

Pearl asked Calvin to move her into the parlor for some fresh air. Calvin obliged her—of course he would—and carried her faster than you'd imagine moving a dying spouse, which is to say at a brisk pace with no time for eye contact or conversation. Her white shawl, once cocooned around her thin frame, had come undone and flapped with every step he took. It wasn't that he meant to be brusque, she was sure of that. At the side of the settee, he sat her down and just as soon as her legs were level, their calico cat, Kitty, climbed aboard Pearl's feet.

Outside the parlor windows, it was an overcast morning. Pearl had hoped the neighborhood children, just recently released into the wilds of spring vacation, would be outside playing tag around the azalea bushes at the front of the house. She kept these windows unobstructed in all seasons in order to enjoy the sounds, smells, and abundance of natural light that came in, but today, the streets were quiet except for the recycling truck groaning up and down them.

Calvin left and entered the room, while Pearl peeked out, trying to appear as though she was resting. He had to check the kettle; he had to dust the rooms on the upper floor; he had to step outside for air although a breeze was presently smoothing back Pearl's hair every few minutes. The truth was that she pitied him—she had already come to terms with the disease inside her body, and she had left literature on various tables inside the home, but they would never have a conversation about any of it. Meanwhile, Kitty remained a constant pulse most days, getting up only to inch further up Pearl's body, toward her torso.

Later that same afternoon it began to rain and bits of precipitation spat in to the room, landing at the foot of the settee. Pearl shivered and rocked in place but did not call out to Calvin who had begun to iron shirts in the hall. Soon, it would not matter how cold or wet she was. On his next trip in, Calvin noticed the beads of rain collected on her forehead, and he went to the nearest window and closed it with a jittered force. By the time he turned back to ask her if she wanted some sugar in her tea today he saw that she had died.

March 22nd

Oh, God. Something *happened.*

First: I was propped up, every nook and cranny of my body tired, and watching Calvin run around like he was the one afflicted. And then, suddenly, I too was in motion; I was part of the breeze, but I couldn't find a way out of the room. The windows were closed, so I moved towards the closest breathing thing near me, Kitty. She took me in with a yawn, and I moved on, or in. The transition felt soft and seamless. I can't tell you why or where the old Kitty went, only that now I feel no pain in my abdomen.

Second: I lay on the wreckage of my own former body until Calvin moved me, looking horrified and desperate for comfort. He pressed his face into my side until this body was also covered in moisture, and all of me felt sticky and matted down. Every part of me wishes not to be touched, to be clutched in this way.

<u>April 1st</u>

I tried to sleep through the aftermath. Sleeping is just as easy now, in this skin, as it was before.

Family came and went; my parents arrived separately. Seems they were able to come together if only to bury their 40-year-old daughter. There were quiet accusations over whose side of the family had compromised genetics, whose female ancestors might have had uterine cancer. People from the neighborhood had come carrying casseroles, and it took everything in my power not to devour the tuna fish while their backs were turned in mourning. I don't even *like* seafood. I don't recall meeting some of the visitors before. Perhaps they are Calvin's colleagues.

So I tried to seek out the furthest, darkest corners of the house, away from the *situation*. The attic and basement worked best. Calvin didn't try to find me, nor did he remember to refill my food and water bowls.

<u>April 15th</u>

Some sounds travel further or maybe just differently to these ears that are in every way foreign to the ones I used to have—they are raised high and delicate. I can now hear the bed creaking when he turns over and over, from any place in the house. I fear this will get old very soon.

And that compressor in the refrigerator—it's getting louder. I wonder if he'll think to call for service, or a replacement, now that I'm no longer there to do it for him.

In the kitchen, I nudge his calves with my head, pushing him toward whatever I think needs fixing, doing, cleaning. Each time he taps me, says *Not now, Kitty*, and walks in the opposite direction holding a glass of bourbon.

Not much has changed. Only before, I would use my voice and he wouldn't drink.

<u>May 1st</u>

Small mounds of laundry, like tiny graves, have cropped up all over the house, and he still hasn't removed an ivory slip of mine on the bath rack. No one is watering the roses. We all feel sorry for ourselves in our own ways.

<u>May 16th</u>

The desire to stand on two legs has me practicing my balance on the sides of chairs and boxes. I wish I was tall enough to reach door handles and cabinets. Part of me wonders if that is my own unique thought, or if that is something Kitty dreamed of also. If only I could make Calvin a cup of tea, or at least help with the dishes. They sit in the sink in murky tubs of water until a visitor washes them when Calvin isn't looking. I'd rather not think of these things.

So, instead, I remind myself of these new pleasures:

One: I have discovered the comfort of hiding under the dining room table, sleeping against the leftover scent of him on the chair cushions. Kitty never took to these spots, and I can't imagine why. The fabric is the softest cotton that I can't burrow into far enough.

Two: I've started to see things that perhaps I didn't have the time to notice before when I was busy at the library, planning the monthly poetry readings and writing the newsletter. Now I see what Calvin looks like when he is panicked (his jaw drops, and new lines appear), and the way the air conditioner moves the aloe plant in the bathroom (in a hypnotic motion).

June 2nd

I've taken to sleeping next to him, in my old spot, on the right side of our bed. I find the essence of my former body still on the pillow—the smell of Pantene—a little less every day. I linger there as long as I can; I watch him sleep a little better every day.

Does he notice this strange behavior from "Kitty?" She could never stand to sleep in our bed. She was afraid of his snoring and waited for the nights I slept alone to even come into the room. Now, sometimes he wakes up from a dream and caresses my back. Does he see me in here? Does he feel me?

June 14th

The only way I know that time is passing is by staring out the windows at the trees, flowers, and the outfits on the neighbors. I regret, now, the decision not to have installed a cat door at the back of our house. Kitty was once a stray, so we kept her inside to keep her from the troubles of her past. We wanted to coddle her, give her a safe home, and reprogram her to be only ours.

I'm ready to go outside; I'm ready to breathe fresh, new air. I've started meowing and scratching at the door while he makes his meals (both of these movements feel more natural than you'd think), but he only responds with *tsssk*.

Did I mention that I feel ornerier now than I ever have before?

I try to catch Calvin entering and exiting the house at just the right time, just so I can leave for a little while, but he spends long hours away. I noticed this yesterday morning, as I attempted to rub my face against his while he slept, whisker to whisker. I didn't feel anything—only smooth skin. I think he's gone back to work. He is finally grooming himself for a future life.

June 29th

Some days I fear there is nothing beyond these cyclical parts of living. Waking, eating, waiting, sleeping.

July 5th

This evening when I stretch and rise from a deep nap by the fan in the parlor, I am surrounded by the smell of coffee. Kahve, from our favorite local roasters. I would know it from any other brand, regardless of the body that I am in. We drink their anniversary blend on our anniversary. Today is not that day.

I am spooked walking through our narrow hall to the kitchen. The lights are dimmer than usual, creating a shade of gold I don't typically see from our wallpaper. Calvin is there. He looks at me with two mugs in his hands and says "Hi Sweetie."

And then I see a purse on the counter, and then a woman. A stranger in a pale silk shift with fringe.

She takes the mugs from him. She is pouring him a cup of our coffee. She drops a sugar cube, and it hits my paw. She blushes and apologizes to *him*.

I *feel the need* to spill their drinks. I feel the need to grow five feet tall. I feel the need to tear the fringe off her dress with my teeth.

<u>July 24th</u>

The woman with fringe has been invited back three more times. For dinner, for drinks, to hear Calvin play the piano that has been covered by a sheet since my death.

<u>August 1st</u>

Marguerite.

She is willowy, is younger than me, can speak three different languages. Romance languages.

<u>September 1st</u>

It is time to devise a plan of communication with Calvin. There must be some way to tell him (show him?) that I never left and that there is no need to bring her back here ever again.

I crawl up the stairs, as soft on my padded feet as I can, with a pencil in my mouth. I will try to write something on the notepad on his nightstand. He will read my message and never feel alone again.

But upstairs, the pocket doors to our bedroom are pulled from the wall and meet at the center of the doorway. I forgot this was even possible; we've had no reason to use them for years.

I angle the pencil to fit into the small space between the doors, and the lead cracks, the tip breaks.

And then, soft music can be heard. It comes out from underneath the doors, followed by the scent of tangerines. A French record, something old and melancholy. The song ends and then plays again. The song plays over the hushed sounds of a woman's breath.

<u>September 3rd</u>

All I can do to express my utter dissatisfaction is to create trouble for her, for them.

First: I began with her red scarf. She wears it often; I'm hoping it's her favorite. Once she left it on my settee, draped over the very spot where I died as if to say, look, *X marks the spot; this too is* mine. So I did what was necessary. I attacked it. I wrestled it down to the floor and scratched out tiny holes. It must have looked like a tornado of calico and brocade. I exerted more energy than I have in years, more than Kitty ever had.

I then took the scarf up the stairs (teeth work best moving everything around) and left it underneath the most unused guest bed, in the dustiest corner.

Of course she noticed it was missing, and Calvin could see how upset it made her. So he purchased a yellow one, a green one, and so on. One for every time I made the previous one disappear.

So I work harder; sometimes joy comes from taking it away from others.

Second: At every chance I get, I drink every drop of water in my aluminum bowl as soon as it is put out and hold onto my liquids until they have left the house. The pair of moccasins she bought him for his birthday are now kept in the mudroom; her pair of imported gardening clogs she left here have the soil from my former garden stuck in the grooves on the bottom. So I imagine a thunderstorm crossing our town's borders, bringing a tremendous rain to our backyard. I find my balance, squat down, and release all of my anger. The warmth pours out of me and onto their treasures.

I hide on a kitchen chair one Saturday morning, when she arrives dressed in an apron and jeans. She slides her slender feet into her gardening shoes and pulls them out with a scream. "Oh no, she never does this," Calvin says, stomping around the house in horror.

I scamper upstairs to my study, find a patch of floor with sunlight, and stretch out as far as my new limbs will take me.

September 11th

I wonder if this is all my motivation or if there are traces of Kitty in this, too. Is vengeance only a human emotion?

October 4th

Calvin is home less and less on his own. Marguerite has taken up spending time here while he is away. She offers to tidy-up for him as she rubs his shoulders.

I hear her talk to her girlfriends on the phone as she lounges on my couch with her laptop computer. "This place is so *Holly Hobbie*," she says each time as she picks at my crocheted throws and pokes at my collection of antique embroidered artwork. Most of these things I've kept because they are heirlooms—meaningful to our family. She does not seem to pay any mind to history. Every day she seems to think of herself as a more permanent fixture than what came before her.

October 31st

It must be Halloween, as I can see tiny angels, demons, and superheroes run down the street tonight. She is over and helping Calvin give out candy to the neighborhood children.

This is something we never did, for some reason. I would host trick-or-treaters in the children's room at work and he would take the opportunity to stay late at the lab. But he looks like a natural. He is happy to interact with every Superman and Elsa that comes to our door.

When all of the candy in our basket is gone, Marguerite pulls out a small box. *The* small box, and inside it, a familiar ring. *No, please no.* I run into the nearest closet and vomit.

October 31st (later)

He tried to put it on my finger when we were just out of college, but it didn't fit. His grandmother's. My finger was too thick, and the ring was too delicate to be resized. So he went to a store downtown and bought something pretty and generic. A ring with no story to tell. I had no idea that he'd kept this other one.

It fits her. In every way it compliments her, somehow. This ring an antique, and her just a pretty and generic girl. For Halloween she is dressed as the Bride of Frankenstein, and now she is glowing and glowing. And he, Frankenstein, looks like he is giving it to someone for the first time.

November 15th

I've not felt well in weeks. How could I?

She is preparing to officially move in now. She says she will help clear some of the clutter from the upstairs. I hear a lot of the phrase, "Don't worry, dear," but it's never directed towards me. I have made myself scarce.

Today, I heard rustling from inside my study. Marguerite was there going through my stack of manuscripts—poetry criticism I had started writing before I died. She gave them the once over and put them in a closet. Next, she brought out a box labeled Goodwill and in went my first edition encyclopedias, literary magazines, and my secret collection of romance novels. I paced around and around the box, trying to push it over with my body. Somehow a journal of mine gets thrown in. I dive in to rescue it, but I lose my footing and crash into the box. She hears this and laughs. "Time for you to go, too, huh?" she says, pretending to close the flaps over my head. I claw my way out and cut her ring finger in the process.

The journal is too heavy and too thick for me to retrieve. I realize now that being *this* way with *these* thoughts is a lot like writing in a journal knowing no one will ever read it.

November 29th

Sometimes I wonder if karma exists. I never gave it much thought before now—never had to because nothing ever changed.

On Thanksgiving, Calvin and Marguerite spent the day preparing the meal for his and her family. They bought the largest turkey they could find; they roasted butternut squash; they baked a lemon almond tart. I won't lie; I had plans to ruin it all. Pick bones clean, kick the tart to the floor with my hind legs. I had all of this energy I *wanted* to exert. But I wasn't able to make it on to the counter—I couldn't even make it up on to the chair. I collapsed at Marguerite's feet, and that was the last thing I remember.

I woke up in a sterile white room, on a padded table, much like a human doctor's office. Someone in a lab coat was taking blood, while I lay there anesthetized. And Calvin was there, stroking my head and looking concerned. Finally, after all of this time, his eyes locked on me. Familiar? Yes. Comforting? Yes.

December 24th

It is Christmas Eve, and she and he sit by the fire admiring the tree they have decorated together. He tells her that he's worried about Kitty. He says the words *kidney failure*. They talk about mortality until it is Christmas morning. She says, "There, there, I am here now." There are multiple fires inside my body; all of them burn hot.

January 1st

They had a New Year's Eve wedding. Something small and intimate, I hear them say. I paced the halls every hour before midnight, each jaunt exhausting me. I imagined Calvin arriving home before midnight to scoop me up and proclaim that he just couldn't go through with it. I would nuzzle his chest in understanding, and we'd go on living our lives together.

But that will never be the case; he came home around 1 A.M. carrying his new bride into the New Year.

January 14th

She has offered to administer my medications. I would rather be ill than have her try to cure me.

Nevertheless, she has named me "poor sick Kitty-dear" and force-feeds me bitter liquids and large tablets. Sometimes she tells me that she is gaining practice for motherhood. If only my anti-nausea pills weren't working so well.

February 3rd

Marguerite's nurse skills are pitiful; I don't feel any better. To my dismay, Calvin's behavior towards me now is very much the same as it was a year ago. There is no careful attention. There is no looking at me in the eyes for long periods of time so we can both acknowledge the saddest parts of life. There are no attempts at starting a goodbye. What kind of love did we have before, and where did it live inside of us?

February 14th

Marguerite's been planning a "reimagining" of a guest room upstairs and is revealing the finished space to Calvin for Valentine's Day. She's kept the room locked, kept it a secret from me, even. After their dinner together (candle-lit, home-cooked French comfort food made from her memory) she led him upstairs and revealed a modern nursery. Gray tones, white beadboard, crown molding. Easily the most polished room in the house, like something alien. I looked for any trace of my former life inside and found she had salvaged an antique rocking horse I had picked up in Brimfield years ago, when I thought we might try to expand our family, before my body was compromised.

"Congratulations, Cal," she said. "We're going to have a baby."

Surely this is hell. He found me underneath the rocking horse, and while her back was turned he winced. That was my sign; that was all I needed tonight.

March 4th

It feels like I've been asleep for weeks; the medication I'm on now feels stronger than anything they gave my human self. It's as if my current doctors are urging me to give up on this life of isolation and incontinence. What will that mean for me this time? Will there be seven more lives beyond the two I'm conscious of?

The brighter side is that I slept through most of the phone calls Marguerite has been making to friends, families, and co-workers about their news. There is no mention of me.

So I've spent most of my time in the parlor, watching the neighborhood kids get off the school bus each afternoon, while I still can. When their baby is all grown, and I'm gone, who will watch from the window?

March 14th

I no longer worry about paying attention to anything but the most basic things such as color, the daily increase of sunlight, and the quieter sounds of the new refrigerator. Some things cannot be fixed, so you do what you have to do and replace them instead.

March 18th

I dream in double-vision. Sometimes I'll wake from a dream of Kitty's memories paired with my own: a moment of love with her on my lap while I read Mary Oliver— I feel Kitty's peace and my own. I know she felt things deeply. These mornings I know that she's halfway still inside me, and I am halfway out.

March 21st

It is the first day of spring. I know because Marguerite is singing an upbeat song in French and opening up all the windows to let new air touch everything. She picks me up carefully, like a baby, and brings me to the settee in the parlor.

It is not raining today. Calvin is outside watering the plants and collecting some flowers to place on the mantel.

"There, there," she says, holding me now against her heartbeat, against my will. Maybe our souls are the secrets our bodies are keeping from us all along. I wait for the breeze.

Made in Italy

Janice Westerling

A morning of shopping on the Via Tornabuoni shattered my dream of buying an Italian handbag. I didn't have enough lira for a wallet. With these prices, it hardly mattered that my travel companion, Kathy, had forgotten to pack an English/Italian dictionary, despite her two overstuffed suitcases to my modest one. I studied my map of Florence, but when it came to affordable leather, I was lost.

Frustrated from shopping and confused by the language barrier, I boarded a sightseeing bus with Kathy in tow. While waiting for our English-speaking guide, I struck up a conversation with a sleek blond Texan named Ceci. When I admired her chic alligator handbag, she lowered her voice and glanced around. "I bought this for practically nothing at the San Lorenzo Market," she drawled. "A man named Tony sells designer bags *under the table*. Go to stall number ten and tell him I sent you." Handing me her card she added, "But don't spread it around."

After our tour had ended, Kathy and I headed to the outdoor marketplace, eager to experience a Florence that less savvy tourists wouldn't see. In a wide semicircle, dozens of vendors shouldered together under peaked white tents. I located stall number ten, where tooled belts, colorful canvas totes, and T-shirts silk-screened with the *David* filled the racks. My spirits sank. Had I gotten the address wrong?

When I asked for Tony, a slender man of about thirty with hazel eyes and dark hair curling above his ears stepped forward. A sickle-shaped scar near his mouth accentuated his generous lips and strong nose.

"We're looking for designer handbags," I said. He shrugged and shook his head. I shot Kathy a withering look: *If you'd remembered the dictionary, I could ask for designer bags in Italian.* She ignored me, but I pressed on.

Like a mime, I waved my purse in front of Tony, unzipped it, and tapped my finger on the label. No response. Barely moving my lips, I played my ace. "Ceci sent us." I slid her card across the counter and gazed into middle space, cool as a secret agent.

Tony hesitated a moment before speaking to his partner in rapid Italian. With a sweep of his arm he directed us, and we followed him out of the marketplace. Two blocks later he veered off the tourist-clotted Via dell'Ariento, and we snaked through cobblestone backstreets. The walkways narrowed and the crowds thinned. Then disappeared.

Growing uneasy, I grabbed Kathy's arm and jerked my head toward the marketplace, signaling we should turn back. She brushed me off and charged ahead into the shadowy alleyway. Still nervous, I trotted behind her.

Tony stopped in front of a stone building and joggled a key into its thick wooden door. He motioned us in. With a dull clank, the door shut. We stepped into the elevator, an iron birdcage, and clattered up three floors with our shoulders touching. I smelled gamy sweat: Was it his or mine?

After trailing him up a flight of narrow stairs, we waited while he opened an office door. I walked into a room, eight feet square, with no windows. Kathy followed. Hearing a click, I snapped my head around: Tony had locked the door behind us.

There wasn't a handbag in sight.

Tony stepped to the wall opposite the door, where gold necklaces hung from particleboard. He pulled a jackknife from his pocket and unfolded a blade. Terrified now, I gasped for air; the room swayed; darkness hovered at the edge of my vision.

Flashing his knife, Tony parted an invisible seam in the board. The wall pivoted and swung open.

Behind the false wall, dozens of designer handbags filled a secret space. I recognized Gucci and Valentino. In my lust for leather, my fear dropped away.

I'd wanted an Italian bag until I saw a classic navy Chanel. I pointed to the quilted model, which Tony handed me. I looped the chain-link strap over my shoulder.

"How much?" I asked.

Tony named a number. I mentally calculated in lira and countered. Shrugging his shoulders in defeat, he accepted my bargain-basement offer of eighty dollars.

Kathy, as usual, was less measured than I. She chose a woven-leather Bottega Veneta, a black Ferragamo shoulder bag, an oxblood Prada … and more. As her pile of bags swelled to six and then eight, Tony's English seemed to sharpen. Was he flirting with her? When her resistance was at its weakest, he unlocked a wall-safe. Slowly he lifted out his trophy piece: a Louis Vuitton briefcase with caramel leather bindings and gold clasps, which retailed for forty-five hundred dollars. Reluctantly, he let it go for four hundred. He even threw in a nylon athletic tote to carry her purchases.

Before we parted, Tony invited us to meet him for drinks later that evening. Kathy was eager to accept, but I'd had enough intrigue. I put my foot down and we declined.

While Kathy dressed for dinner, I removed the paper stuffing from my bag to admire its lining. Inside a zippered compartment, I found a small tag that read *Made in Italy*. Wasn't Chanel manufactured in France? Now that I looked closely, the brass zipper seemed a bit coarse for a fifteen-hundred-dollar purse. I made excuses to myself and said nothing, wanting so badly to believe in my secret Italian discovery.

Our last evening in Florence, Kathy and I walked the streets, searching for a restaurant. Too early for a proper Italian dinner, we couldn't agree on the few eateries that were open. I felt a raindrop on my arm, and another. Rain pattered and then poured. Caught without umbrellas, we bought pizza from a street vendor and ran back to our hotel. By the time we reached the room, water dripped from my hair. Even my underclothes were damp.

Kathy pitched her boxed pizza and newly purchased Ferragamo bag onto her bed. Smoky stains covered the front of her white sweater. Dark streaks ran down its arm.

"Oh no," I cried. "What happened to your clothes?"

I looked at the bed. Black polish bled off her new Ferragamo, exposing the smooth synthetic underneath.

"Dammit." Kathy tore off her stained sweater and hurled it into the bathroom sink. "What a piece of crap."

I didn't ask if she meant her bag or Tony.

Twenty-five years have passed since I bought my Italian-made handbag. Bargain shopping, I'd found, transcended language barriers. Tony, fluent in salesmanship, had spotted a willing mark, lured me with the promise of hidden treasure, and surrendered to my "superior" negotiating skills. No one ever questioned the authenticity of my Chanel bag, so I wore it for years, when the weather was good.

Last Cherry

Jeff Ewing

The hiss of the chainsaw works its way in, through
the squawks of jays and blackbirds, the boom of the gas
cannon, even through the crash and rip of the splitter.
This is no idle music. The orchard is run out.

Last year it couldn't fill a dozen lugs, now it's falling
under our hands—branches snap at the joint, stubs plunge
into dry ground. Row after row succumbs. Fell, buck,
haul and split. Our eyes sting, our sweat's half sap.

At lunch we sit in the broken shade of the last cherry,
loosen our boots and file our worn teeth sharp. We'll take
this final tree only after the others are gone, hauled off
to Marin where we get better money, one-sixty a cord.

We drink its shade greedily. When we do drop it, we
show our gratitude by posing with beers held high on the
wound-knobbed trunk, uprooted in the unopposed sun,
leaning confidently into the wind already stirring the topsoil.

Matanuska Thunderfuck

Max Talley

Matanuska Thunderfuck. How did those two words lead Gary Marder sixteen hundred miles from his Oregon couch to a rural valley in Alaska? A childish whim launched him on a quest for a stoner's Holy Grail, sending him up against dangerous bikers, Eskimo fishing guides tweaking on crystal meth, and bar maids with faces like a twelve-car pileup. Not to mention a variety of people-hating, meat-eating creatures that roamed the northern wilderness with impunity.

For seven years, Gary had worked at Powell's Books in Portland. As he approached his fiftieth birthday in August, Gary realized he had become a cliché: the dude in a button-down shirt with a graying ponytail and glasses employed as a bookstore clerk.

Life changed when he met Spright, two years back, at a Rumi book club gathering.

She was fortyish, a second-generation hippie like Gary. "You need to make a life choice," she said, after seeing him for a month. "You should be on the path by fifty. We should be living together or married by then." Which meant cleaning out his ramshackle, cluttered two-bedroom house on South Hawthorne Street, so Spright could move in at the end of summer.

Gary denied he was a hoarder. He simply cataloged his life through reading material. His closets and second bedroom teemed with piles of magazines and books. Starting with his childhood comic collection, then moving to horror mags, *National Lampoon*, and *Rolling Stone*, then *Playboy*, and eventually to science fiction paperbacks. It took weeks to review the stuff before he sold it in bulk to Future Dreams Collectibles on East Burnside. Once Gary removed ninety percent of the accumulated mass, he tucked the remaining treasures in a single closet.

During that last phase, he unearthed a *High Times* magazine from 1980, the year he became a serious smoker. Gary opened to the centerfold chart of the exotic weeds of that time. Just before seedless sinsemilla buds took over the American pot market. Next to the images of Colombian Brown, Acapulco Gold, Panama Red, Thai Stick, Senegalese Black, and Lebanese hash oil were check marks in blue pen. His own teenage writing.

Gary smiled with pride. *I've sampled all those.* He looked to the bottom of the centerfold and saw Matanuska Thunderfuck, the infamous Alaskan super-weed. But no check mark.

He had never smoked it.

Normally, this wouldn't have meant a thing, but Spright said, "According to your Vedic charts, fifty is the age to give up smoking." Spright wasn't a ball-buster, she just asked, "Don't you think after thirty-five years, you might take a break, for your lungs?"

"Sure," Gary said. "No problem." Pot didn't even get him high anymore. It just took the edge off of a reality that had long since lost its edge. Christ, he lived in

Portland, not Syria, or New Jersey.

Staring at a calendar, Gary realized September was looming. When Spright moved in, he'd become responsible, learn to share, build a life, and listen to a woman's thoughts long into the night. It just seemed a crime that he never smoked Matanuska Thunderfuck. What should have faded from his middle-aged memory in a couple of days; instead, infested his dreams until he became obsessed.

Gary contacted a stoner friend on Facebook who lived in Alaska.

"Yeah, it still exists," Tom messaged back. "Very small quantities though, and the real stuff is grown by bikers who keep it to themselves. You or me getting a taste is the equivalent of Biblical scholars touching the Shroud of Turin. It's possible, but pretty damn unlikely."

Somehow, that didn't dissuade Gary. With two weeks of vacation coming at Powell's, a quick jaunt up to Alaska to cross off the final entry of his teenage "to-smoke list" felt necessary.

Closure.

What was the worst that could happen? A final moment of youthful madness to celebrate whatever first made him grow his hair long, listen to deafening music, and treat his body like a chemical testing lab. Gary decided to make his travel plans secretly. He would notify Spright later.

Gary white-knuckled the bumpy three-hour flight. He tried not to think of the horrific Alaskan plane crash in the movie *The Grey*, but saw it vividly whenever turbulence or a wind shear jolted the aircraft.

After landing at Ted Stevens Anchorage International Airport, Gary rented a Subaru Outback station wagon and was pleased to get a dull blue model instead of the ubiquitous green ones that snarky Portland locals called "Lesbarus." While waiting for his travel bag, Gary tapped an Oregon number on his phone.

"Beads and Crystals. It's a beautiful day," said a hoarse male voice.

"Hey, Moonjava, can I speak to Spright?"

"Gary?" Spright soon said. "Is something wrong? You never call me at work."

"I took a trip to Anchorage. I needed a break from Powell's and it's sort of a quest."

"A vision quest?"

"No, I, uh, came after some rare weed, since I'm about to give it up forever."

A long silence followed.

"Gary," Spright said. "I've always wanted you to follow your bliss." She paused. "I guess I just hoped that your bliss was me."

"It definitely is, Spright. I'll just be up here a couple days, two weeks at most, then we'll proceed with your plans. I mean, our plans."

"My co-worker, Moss, is four percent Shoshone, so she's pretty psychic. She says you're not evolving, Gary, that you have past-life shit to deal with."

"That's why I came up here, to put the past behind me for good." Gary felt guilty since Spright's parents Mason and Janis named her after the elves and wood fairies, but every time he said Spright, Gary thought of carbonated soda. "I'll be back soon. Call you tomorrow."

"Love and light," she said in a cold, brittle tone.

"You know I love you," Gary attempted. No reply.
"I guess I love you too, brother," Moonjava finally said before disconnecting.

Because Gary felt as though he'd left America, he had no qualms about hiring a tour guide.

Len was half-Native American and looked a boyish thirty. After Gary picked him up outside the airport, Len relaxed once he slumped into the passenger seat and saw Gary's gray ponytail.

"Oh, good," he said, "you're not another retired general on a fishing trip. Boring." Len was so relaxed, he began rolling a joint minutes into their journey out of the airport.

"Hey, man … what about security, the TSA, or Anchorage police?"

Len laughed, then pressed his black shiny hair behind his ears and concentrated on the task at hand. "Dude, are you up on current events?"

Gary looked sideways. "Uh, decriminalization?"

"Not even. Since February, 2015, total legalization." Len licked the sticky strip, then carefully tightened the rolling paper around it. "I can have up to one ounce on my person, as well as be growing six plants in my house."

Gary felt like an idiot, utterly oblivious of Alaskan law. "You can?"

"No, I do," Len said before lighting the joint. "To follow the letter of the law."

Gary nodded while driving north along the coastal lowlands.

"I'm guessing you're a weed tourist." Len smiled. "Up here to sample our finest. May as well start now." He passed the joint, but Gary shook his head.

"No, thanks." It seemed unnecessary, the interior of the car fogged with pungent smoke. Every breath Gary took exhilarated him and simultaneously brought on paranoia, but his restraint was born of snobbery. Gary had made this sudden venture with the intent to sample only the best. Gourmet, not gourmand. "I'm up here on a mission," he said, as if reading a movie script. "I've come to smoke … Matanuska Thunderfuck."

Len inhaled a deep hit then froze, his face reddening, body trembling. Gary feared he might keel over and die. Finally, Len exhaled in a convulsive mixture of coughing and laughter. "Matanuska?" he said in the thin voice of an ancient wise man sitting atop the airless peaks of the Himalayas. "You mean a pharmacy strain grown from those seeds, right?"

Gary shook his head.

"Dude, you may as well try to find Bigfoot or the Baby Jesus in his manger." Len let air play through his nostrils. "That's the dankest of the dank, the rarest weed in Alaska. If you'd come up twenty years ago, maybe. But now?" He tamped out the joint, as if matters had gotten too serious for getting stoned. "For real? That's why you hired me?"

"Look," Gary said, feeling vexed. He pointed to the half-folded map lying between them. "The Matanuska Valley is an hour or so northeast from here, just across the river, or strait. You're saying you can't get me there?"

"Sure, sure," Len said. "I can guide you to Abbey Road but I can't find you the freaking Beatles. It's complicated." He pressed a hand to his forehead. "Take the next exit. We'll hit up my friend Gad. His parents farmed the Mat-Su Valley back in the Seventies. He'll set you straight."

Fifteen minutes later, they entered the Chum Bucket on the 700 block of West 4th Avenue. The dive bar was populated by a mixture of Eskimos, Asians, pale hipsters, Scandinavian sailors, fiftyish bikers, and heavily made-up middle-aged women still dressed in their teenage skank-wear. Somewhere through the nicotine haze wafting in from the street, alley, and bathrooms, Gary heard the clack of billiard balls and twangy outlaw country music emanating from the back room.

"Gad's a bus boy," Len said. "He cleans tables, mops up puke, and takes drink orders whenever that waitress with purple hair and fishnets topples off her pumps." He pointed.

As soon as Gad spotted Len, he threw his bar rag down to take a break. They moved into an alley behind the open kitchen door. Gad and Len ignored the rats on the dumpster and the chundering Norwegian at the end of the alley, so Gary did too.

"This guy came up here looking for Thunderfuck," Len said.

Gad nodded. "Some try to climb Everest, and some want to skydive from space. Others dream of smoking Matanuska." Gad wore a headband over a face that looked really young and extremely old at the same time.

Gary pegged him as a tweaker from the pock-marks, skin discolorations, and his sunken eyes.

"We'd all like to blaze some MT," Gad said. "I certainly partook when I was twelve." He paused. "Hippie families used to grow it through the Seventies and the Eighties, but now it's a biker gang thing. The Devil's Saints." Gad gazed inside the bar and lowered his voice. "They cultivate it, police it, smoke it, and sell it amongst themselves."

"Like Hell's Angels? Like Altamont, killing hippies and such in San Francisco?"

"I don't know anyone named Altamont," Gad said, "but the Devil's Saints are mostly here in Anchorage. They grow weed up there."

"Out in the Valley, that pristine, beautiful place?"

"Indoors, in blacked-out greenhouses. Their grows are all about light-deprivation. Our summer sun is relentless."

"I'll pay you just to lead me there." Gary sighed when neither man responded. "These are modern bikers, family men, my age or older. If I offer them cash, I'm sure they'll sell me enough for a taste."

They drove up Glenn Highway to Palmer late the following morning, then veered west toward Wasilla, past farms and lush fields with huge pumpkins, cabbages, and oversized cucumbers.

"Back when your parents grew outdoors, Gad. Where did they plant?"

Gad pointed. "In those overgrown fields beyond the farms and crops."

Gary handed them fifteen dollars. "You two get lunch while I take a walk and look around." Gary slowed then turned into the general store's lot.

"Nothing out there but moose and deer scat, but suit yourself." Gad and Len got out.

Gary parked on a dirt road at the edge of a cabbage field, before walking into the high grass and weeds. Brush raked at his clothes as he advanced in the direction of the tree line. The marshy land sloped toward pine trees on hilly ground, while in the distance, foothills rose to eventually merge with the icy Talkeetna Mountains. Finally, at the edge of the grasslands, Gary reached an elevation where he could stare down over the rough terrain he just navigated. Putting a hand over his eyes to deflect the glare, he gazed west and squinted. It looked as if a quarter mile away, a section of the hardscrabble land had been manicured and flattened. *Could it be a secret harvest area?*

Gary heard a horn-like sound coming from the dense forest of hemlocks and spruce pines, followed by heavy clomping. He retreated and watched antlers protrude from between two trees. Then he saw it. A large bull elk with his head low as he slowly emerged. Five-hundred-pounds, at least, antlers pointing south, pointing toward Gary. Unlike moose, who were nasty bastards, elk were usually spooked by humans. Except during rutting season and, oh shit, Gary had somehow intruded into the middle of this bull's booty call. He jerked his neck to gaze around but couldn't spot a cow elk anywhere in the vicinity. A new horror trembled through him. What if this bull elk was myopic and Gary in his brown clothing vaguely resembled an unsightly female two-legged elk?

He sprinted toward the farmlands in a panic. Halfway across the field, his shoelaces caught on a dead branch and Gary face-planted on hard dirt. He remained, paralyzed in fear. When he finally lifted himself, the elk had disappeared back into the curtain of forest.

Gary picked up Gad and Len waiting on the porch at the general store. His face was dirty, one of his sunglasses lenses had popped out, and his long hair hung wild and tangled after his ponytail band snapped.

Len laughed from the back seat, leaning forward to study Gary as if he was a scientific curiosity.

"What happened to you, nature boy?" Gad smiled. "Did a moose stomp you?"

"Just a run-in with an elk."

"Dude, elks are scared of people." Gad shook his head.

"We're going back to Plan A." After Gary cleaned himself up, they continued west through a fairy tale world of giant vegetables, lush fields, and snow-capped mountains, until they reached the far end of the Valley. Vegetation grew sparse as they merged onto a rock-strewn and muddy road. Gary passed through an open fence with skull and crossbones flags. A sign read: *Private Property. Trespassers will be shot, then eaten by pit bulls.*

"You sure about this idea, bro?"

Gary felt nervous, but Len's apprehension annoyed him. "I'm just going to ask. No tensions."

He motored toward an aluminum-sided warehouse near a greenhouse whose glass had been covered in black plastic sheets. Two large men standing by a row of motorcycles came lumbering toward the car and waved Gary to stop.

"Did you read the signs, or were you drop-kicked in the head at birth?" The first biker asked, tapping a shovel lightly against the Subaru hood. He wore faded jeans and a black leather vest over a hairy chest and protruding stomach. His graying brown hair stuck up in the air and looked like it was held in place by dried dirt.

The second man gripped a baseball bat.

"No disrespect," Gary said. "I'd just like to buy a taste of your Matanuska, then we'll leave and never trouble you again."

The two bikers looked at each other, perhaps mulling over whether they felt like getting violent so early in the day. The second began giggling.

Gary extended a hand with three twenties in it. "Whatever amount you think is fair."

"Oh, sure," the first one said. He went inside the warehouse and returned almost immediately. Two more men trailed behind with dumbfounded expressions. "Here you go." The burly biker handed a tiny bag of green over. Gary's face must have shown disappointment. "Okay, you and your dick-head friends, get the hell out of here—now."

Gary turned to retreat up the gouged and pitted road, the three bikers hustling after them.

The leader slammed his shovel against the back of the car with a clang. "And don't ever come back, or we'll kill you, you coffee-guzzling Seattle pussy."

Gary didn't see the sense in correcting him. He kept driving until his heartbeat slowed down fifteen miles later at the east end of the Valley. He pulled over to examine the bag. It was potent weed but, "That's not Thunderfuck," he announced.

"Well, no shit," Gad said. "But you got a good deal. You're still alive."

"Forget about the Matanuska," Len said. "Hang with us in Anchorage. We'll hook you up with serious green bud. Literally."

"Yeah, maybe."

Gary dropped them down in the City, then made his own plans. He drove back northeast to Palmer and checked in at Mountain View Lodge by the mouth of the Valley. From the shared deck on the second floor, he noted that the sun set at ten p.m., and twilight faded to dark by eleven. Retired men in windbreakers and baseball caps smoked cigars outside and spoke with enthusiasm about a possible Trump presidency. Gary guessed they had come north on fishing trips.

The following morning, the desk clerk informed Gary that the local's breakfast hangout was the Busy Bee Cafe two miles west. So he hunkered down at the cafe counter to search for an original resident leftover from the Seventies. He might resemble Willie Nelson, or he could be a bald, grizzled old coot in overalls. Working at Powell's had made him an expert at reading people. Around eleven a.m., a friendly, rangy man sat on the swivel stool next to Gary. He showed a wrinkled, sunburned face, and stringy gray hair hung down to his chin.

"California?" the man asked, looking Gary over.

"Yeah, no, Oregon."

"Portland was my second guess," he said. "You're not a hunter or a fisherman, so what brings you to our fair valley?" His smile went wide with knowing.

"I'm looking to find someone who's lived here thirty or forty years."

"Bingo. I moved here to farm in 1975 when I was twenty."

"Can I buy you breakfast and pick your brain?"

"Sounds like a deal," he said, "for me." Jesse led Gary away from the counter and they sank into a back booth. After their waitress Darlene brought him biscuits and gravy, Jesse said, "Ask me anything, son."

"I'm on a quest to smoke Matanuska Thunderfuck," Gary whispered. "I know it's controlled by bikers now, but it used to be grown right out there." He gestured toward the crop fields. "Does anyone still cultivate it outdoors? I only want a little."

Jesse seemed oblivious, digging into a platter of scrambled eggs and bacon.

"I took a walk yesterday," Gary continued. "Thought I saw a possible grow area way out in the wild grasslands, northwest of here. I didn't come to cause trouble or give away secrets. I'll pay for whatever can be spared, then head home to Oregon." Gary waited as Jesse ate his hash browns.

"Here's the deal," Jesse finally said. "There are maybe six of the old-time hippie farmers still around. We don't get high much anymore. Our thing is growing organic, having enough food to eat and selling the rest." He craned his neck to take in the customers at neighboring booths. "All of us grow several plants at that spot you mentioned from the original Thunderfuck seeds. It's for good juju." Jesse waved to Darlene. "We do it for the spirits who live atop Matanuska Mountain, and so those spirits protect our food crops every year."

Darlene deposited a steak and a stack of pancakes in front of Jesse.

Gary swallowed his cynicism. Spright held many wacky spiritual beliefs and he had learned the value of not laughing at them. "How do you know it's working?"

"When the weed flowers, the animal spirits eat the plants and not our fruits or vegetables."

"Animal spirits?" Gary waited while Jesse sliced into the steak.

"Well, deer for one. Maybe elk and critters too." Jesse extended his hands, palms up. "Who knows why, but it's worked for ten years, so what the hell?" He propped a fist under his chin. "Listen, if you stay to the end of the week, I'll get you a taste." He dug a card from his pocket that read: *Jesse Hargrove: organic farmer & compost whisperer.* "Give me a call. Don't try it on your own." He forked a chunk of pancakes into his mouth.

"Do bikers patrol those fields?"

"Our pot isn't as strong as their super-weed." Jesse smiled. "But nature is kind of wild up here. If a moose stomps you, you'll wish you were dead." He rose from the welter of empty plates.

Gary called Spright back at the Lodge. She didn't answer her cell, so he tried the bead store.

"Hey, Moonjava, it's Gary."

"Spright can't talk to you," Moonjava said.

"Will you put her on the line?"

"She's with Topaz, Angelica, and Jasmine, off the grid."

"Is it their monthly getaway already?"

"Yeah, they all synchronized their cycles, so they camp out."

"Sure," Gary said. "On Cannon Beach."

"She'll be back Thursday night for our yoga session."

"Can you tell Spright I'll be coming home by the end of the week?"

"I'd get back sooner," Moonjava said. "You don't realize how close you are to losing her."

"You don't sound very evolved, Moonjava." Gary remembered that the dude was interested in Spright, and often acted possessive. "Take some Ujjayi breaths and count to twenty, bro."

There was an interstice of silence.

"Namaste, motherfucker." Moonjava hung up the store phone.

Gary stretched out on his bed. Maybe he should return to Portland. He'd never been suspicious of Spright's nude Bikram yoga class before when he thought it was for women only. Who knew what the hell went on when everyone was sweaty and delirious? Not to mention the petting orgies at the end of the sessions they called cuddle puddles. Spright definitely admired the thirty-two-year-old Moonjava with his nose piercings, smelly Crocs, and egregious man-bun.

Gary needed to get his sample tonight, then leave Alaska tomorrow.

At Outdoor Sports World, he loaded up on equipment. Trekking poles were mandatory, basically repurposed ski poles that made people on weekend walks feel like mountaineers. Gary also bought a flashlight, matches, greasy, stinking lotion to ward off wild animals, and a whistle.

"You racing in the Iditarod?" the female manager asked.

"Night hiking."

"Sure, okay, Jack London."

When the sun set at ten p.m., Gary walked by the fishermen on the Lodge's porch and drove through the still bright Alaskan twilight. He parked as near the farmers hidden field as possible. Then he put on hiking boots, slathered on some Backwoods Funk lotion, and gripped his trekking poles. It took twenty minutes to locate the patch. Gary clambered over low fencing and headed for the nearest flowering plant. In the twilight, and with a full moon just rising into the sky, he could see the pale blue-green buds with snowy white hairs threading them. Gary pulled off a tiny bud, barely enough for three hits on a pipe, and tucked it into his breast pocket. He ambled his way toward the center of the patch, spying the largest plant.

Two or three sizable buds, that's all I need.

A sound came from nearby. Something on four legs, quietly munching. *Probably a deer*, Gary thought, and continued toward his objective. He crouched down to examine the big plant. When the sky darkened, Gary assumed a cloud had covered the moon. He looked up and almost experienced a heart seizure. What had been on four legs, now stood on two: a bear, nearly seven feet in height. Gary had never walked backward in a squatting position over uneven terrain, but he learned quickly. Park rangers said one shouldn't appear small to wild animals, so he rose up and waved his arms. He read that singing in a low-pitched voice scared bears away, so he bellowed like Jim Morrison. "I went to the roadhouse and got myself a beer."

The bear neither advanced nor retreated. Its head shuddered as if enduring something unpleasant, then it growled.

Gary tried to think logically. It was a black bear. Generally shy and eager to avoid people. The Nature Channel claimed they were much less likely to attack or eat humans than a ferocious grizzly. Maybe Gary had startled him. If he walked away singing "Everybody Knows" by Leonard Cohen, some day, many years from now, Gary could laugh about this incident. Since he had backtracked to the border of the patch, he reached for a small plant to bring along.

The bear growled loudly and moved forward, still standing tall.

Bad idea, Gary thought. Maybe this bear had not viewed the recent Nature Channel special and was unaware how he should behave. Then Gary recalled than many animals were colorblind. Perhaps this one didn't know he was a black bear. What if he identified as a grizzly bear? Gary continued to edge away. He had always hated the term *disemboweled*. First, the word bowels made him wonder how long until he voided his own, but worse, the literal meaning reminded Gary that bears didn't operate under an animal form of Geneva Convention. They basically ripped your entrails out while you were still alive. Among "worst death scenarios," this was in Gary's perpetual top three, and he hadn't even seen *The Revenant*.

The bear staggered onward and Gary started jogging backwards. When his boot heel hit a jagged rock, Gary fell, his weight snapping a trekking pole in two. His ankle hurt and getting up proved difficult. So he waited for the bear to loom over him, resigned to his fate. The injustice of it all. Gary planned to stab the remaining trekking pole deep into the beast's chest. It wouldn't stop the monster, but would help the authorities hunt and kill the bear later on. Poor Spright. He imagined her, forced to identify Gary in the morgue, his body resembling raw flayed strips of bacon draped over a skeleton. The final insult to a vegan like her.

He pictured Moonjava telling Spright, "Breathe into your pain. Exhale your sorrow."

The bear didn't come, but Gary heard distant snuffling and grunting. What was the protocol? Was Gary supposed to surrender himself to the creature? Eventually, he got up on his knees. From there, he spotted the bear sitting on the perimeter of the grow area munching. The full moon had risen to its zenith and Gary noticed the bear's eyes. The fucking beast was stoned out of its gourd. He didn't want to devour Gary. No, like the elk before, he just wanted to guard the flowering plants.

Gary crawled south for several minutes, then hobbled along on his twisted ankle. He made it back to the Subaru, with face scratched, pants torn, leaves and small branches attached to his clothing. Exhausted, he collapsed fully-dressed on his bed at Mountain View Lodge.

Upon waking, Gary didn't shave or shower, just checked-out and drove to Anchorage International Airport to purchase an expensive ticket back home. For whatever reason, Gary got pulled aside for a random TSA screening. It didn't matter. He had escaped with his life last night; he could deal with this minor hassle.

"You really got into the backwoods, didn't you?" The middle-aged TSA agent chuckled.

The man brushed twigs and dirt off Gary as he patted him down, but stopped when he reached his chest. He tapped Gary's breast pocket. "There's a bump here." With a gloved hand, the agent extricated a tiny bud. Forming a pinched face, he examined it closely before shaking his head.

"You're not going to ..." Gary said. "I mean, with it being legal."

"No," the agent said. "But you can't transport this from state to state." He crushed the bud into dust and smelled his latex glove. "Hot damn, that's Matanuska Thunderfuck." His eyes went young and watered for an instant, then the TSA agent pointed Gary toward the departure gates.

Lost & Found (For My Hometown, Portland, Oregon)

Dylan D. Debelis

i.

Under the 'Made in Oregon' billboard and strung up Christmas Lights
the Burnside Bridge bends itself like a crescent moon towards the river.

We are standing in the rain where the waterfront meets the homeless
shelter, pale bodies shivering in their donated sleeping bags
and us in our North Face fleeces drinking gin from the handle.

Under your shirt I move my cold hand against your hot back and the steam
from your mouth forms ghosts that threaten to jump the railing.

There is a barge passing, displacing the syringes in the surf
with an ice breaker and a life boat that has come free. Your singing
pawing at the night like the snow coating the esplanade.

The science museum submarine flicks its spotlights off
and it is too late for our own good. A fog rolls
over the mood ring I bought you for your birthday.
Somewhere upriver the footsteps of a runner and her dog,
while from the church a piano begins to crack its knuckles.

On nights like this I wonder if the city thinks of me,
I wonder if Old Town still creaks with the weight of our footprints on its mud,
if the armory theater seats still retain
some of the water damage from our raincoats,
or if the Crystal Ballroom still has a bit of our love lodged deep in its floorboards.

ii.

I am writing this on a placemat in a diner
somewhere after Boise. With a crayon
I am tracing the map of the United States. I am
a radio losing its rhythm between time zones.

For all our talk of symmetry
the heart always shuts down one ventricle at a time.
Frostbitten toes fall off one by one until the knee is sawn off.
Young Adult novels talk about Chinese railroad labor
placing chopsticks between their teeth during amputation.

We gnaw our cheeks again tonight
and the rivulets of our blood fill the cracks between the Mt. Hood and St. Helen's
until the storm plains flood with Dogwoods blooming

crimson topography. I wonder, from that far off

did your breath witness the factory blowout
by shivering slightly, enough for you to rise from your mattress
and ease the window closed, enough to stare out at the Louisiana live oak
just for a moment
and wonder how far down the roots reach.

Or did your brain think better of stirring, instead
turning into your pillow
and waking a few hours later to the sounds of meadowlarks ushering in a late
February dawn.

For my part, I kept driving

until the snow melted to reveal the carcasses
of creatures who went missing months ago.

iii.

I was awake when you came in,
though I pretended to be sleeping
so that you would come closer. This winter has been
lonely, but still I wrap my scarf and shuffle daily
to the hospice down the road. I am
not the sick one, I tell you
even though I am not sure if your ears are
open yet. My arrhythmia has a cadence
like high heels crashing on a vestibule tile.
This winter has been
the resting place of too many children
I knew well enough to love like my own.
At midnight my stomach holds the space
of the month-long dashes on their headstones. Why
do I hold the bundles so tightly
when I bring their wrappings from the NICU to the morgue?
They keep me company I suppose,
like you,
who came in,
though I pretended to be sleeping
so that you would come closer. I am
not the sick one,
but I am keeping the stint
on my heart valve wide open. I am
cradling this winter like your favorite quilt,
or the quilt that would have been your favorite
if you had been given time to know it
like it knew you. Like I knew you
in my stomach kicking,
when I would sing and you would dance
and leave imprints of your shadow
like snowy footprints sidling through an open bedroom door.

The Good Life

J.K. Frerichs

The official slogan of Nebraska used to be "The Good Life." A few years ago the Department of Tourism decided to change it. According to urban legend in the Panhandle, some bureaucratic mucky-muck accidentally wandered into this part of his state. He supposedly took one look at the land and the people who dwelled upon it and hastened back to Lincoln. A short while later the slogan was changed. For those of us who live out here, this apocryphal story is totally credible.

The Land. It's everything and nothingness. Cheyenne County. The High Plains. Short-grass country. Where I grew up, in Dalton, Nebraska, the land stretches to the horizon—unbroken sight lines to the Earth's end. It's cattle and winter wheat, blizzards and drought, gravel roads through a nullarbor. And the wind—always the wind.

The place where I lived as a young girl lies about 150 miles west of the hundredth meridian. This invisible north-south line bisects the state like a barbed fence, and is often reckoned as the boundary between Middle America and the West. As one travels westward across the state, the prairie succumbs to the plains, and the land becomes increasingly dry (a mere 16 inches of rainfall in the Panhandle), higher (nearly a mile), and less populated.

Once, not that long ago, Columbian mammoths roamed this desolation seeking food and refuge. Western Nebraska is littered with the ungathered bones of these great beasts that tried, but failed, to survive here. In a nearby natural history museum can be found the interlocked tusks of two gigantic herbivores that fought each other to death. They were, perhaps, the more fortunate ones; the stoic farmers and ranchers who work this land swear the others died from despair and the wretchedness of their lives.

Following an exploration of the High Plains during 1820, Major Stephen H. Long drew a map showing a "Great Desert," which bordered the North Fork of the Platte River, extending south to the Arkansas River in Colorado and Kansas, and west of the 101st meridian to the Rocky Mountains. An arid wasteland of uninhabited solitude and, according to the chronicler of the expedition, a "dreary plain, wholly unfit for cultivation." Long wrote on his map that "The Great Desert is frequented by roving bands of Indians who have no fixed places of residence but roam from place to place in quest of game."

Anxious to populate this area with its own citizens, and in accord with the Manifest Destiny to expand westward, Congress sent Lieutenant John C. Fremont on a survey of the area with instructions for a more upbeat report. So, during the summer of 1842, Fremont passed just north of where I once lived on his journey of re-discovery. With Kit Carson as his guide, Fremont described in detail the geology, animals and plants on the nascent Oregon Trail, and mapped the way for the emigrants, which were to follow in his steps.

He traced the North Fork of the Platte River to Fort Laramie in what is now Wyoming. Wary of hostile Indians and suffering from oppressive heat and illness, Fremont tried to put a good face on his expedition, romanticizing the "utmost magnificence and grandeur" of this new territory. He was more restrained in his evaluation of the Panhandle, however, describing the area as a "vast expanse of uninteresting prairie."

Soon after, lured by the apparent ease by which they could reach the Oregon Territory, thousands of pioneers followed his route. Near the western border of the Panhandle there is a peculiar geologic formation known as Chimney Rock.

Fremont camped near here and, later, so did multitudes of emigrants in their prairie schooners. This rock was a monolithic exit sign, signaling the end of the travails they had suffered while crossing the "Great Desert." They were now well advanced on their journey to the rich, inviting farmlands of the Willamette Valley, but behind them on the trail lay the broken wagons and the broken men.

Cheyenne County is defined by straight borders, a result of the Land Ordinance of 1785. This rectangular survey system and public land laws allowed the settling of new territory by granting quarter sections to homesteaders, all neatly plotted and marked. A hundred and sixty acres of free soil in Nebraska, treeless and sere—barely enough to graze four steers, and utterly incapable of supporting a pioneer and his family (much later, in 1904, Congress, recognizing the realities in this arid country, granted a full section, or 640 acres, to new homesteaders in Western Nebraska).

There are five centers of civilization in the 1,196 square miles of the county: Dalton, Gurley, Lodgepole, Potter, and Sidney. The county seat and only city is Sidney, about twenty miles south of Dalton down Federal Highway 385. Sidney once had a colorful, but turbulent past. During the late 1800s, hardy and foolhardy men gathered at this railroad stop (named for Sidney Dillon of the Union Pacific Railroad) on their way to moil for gold in the Black Hills of South Dakota. These men sought respite from their quest. In Sidney, they found certain pleasures, which the numerous bordellos and saloons provided. Having relinquished their money and their morals to the enterprising citizens of Sidney, these intrepid miners continued their trek to the gold fields, vowing never again to return to this frontier outpost. But the city remains, a legacy of that golden age.

Dalton was founded in 1907. The village was established as a work station during the building of the Nebraska, Wyoming, and Western Railroad. Later, it became a depot with a section house, water tank, and stock pens, after which came alternating periods of growth and decline. At the time of my birth in 1964, the population was about three hundred, and has remained stable to this day, the births pacing the burials in the town cemetery.

My father migrated to Dalton from Raton, New Mexico, fleeing a boyhood of toil in the coal mines, met my mom, and opened a machine repair shop in town. My mother stayed home and raised her three children. I was the middle child, a girl, with two brothers. My grandparents also lived in Dalton. Unlike the majority of

Daltonites, however, our family lineage was short—we were relative newcomers to the area. My friends' families were similar to mine in that their dads worked, their mothers remained at home, and there was rarely an only child.

Highway 385 was the only paved road in Dalton. It was intersected by a "main street" fronted by a restaurant, post office, library, bank, dress shop, beauty shop, tavern, a barber, and repair shop (my dad's). There was a grain elevator nearby. There was also a gas station and grocery store. Dalton had a school, four churches, an American Legion hall, and its own telephone company. If you crossed the railroad tracks to the west, you were "out in the country."

As a girl growing up in Dalton, everyone knew my name. They watched out for me as I rode my bike up and down the dusty streets. I kept my horse in an empty lot behind my house. I was welcomed into almost everyone's home. The neighbors were my parents' "eyes," and you knew it, but didn't seem to mind. As a child I felt like a princess in that idyllic place.

Later, as I became older, I liked to help my dad at his work. My assigned tasks consisted mostly of keeping out of his way and keeping the place clean. But for me it had a secondary gain. During the summer, in my shorts and halter-top, and with my broom in hand, I'd attract the glances and invitations from the young men who worked the combines during their northward chase of the wheat harvest.

My mother played the piano and she desired that her children also play. She wished to teach us some measure of refinement in our rural backwater. So, every day, my brothers and I hammered away on that machine while learning our fingering and notes. I took quickly to the piano and later played organ in our church. My favorite hymn remains "For the Beauty of the Earth." I earned spending money playing at weddings; I would musically escort the bride down the aisle with Frank Mills' "Sunday Morning Suite."

Being a "girl from town," spending weekends with my friends who "lived on the farm" was something I tried to do as often as I could. The girl that I was couldn't understand why they complained about having to do chores and having to ride the bus to school. I envied their lives. I wanted to become a farm girl. I graduated high school as the top student, but eschewed college for marriage and a chance to live on a farm. So, at age eighteen, and against my father's wishes, I became a farmer's wife.

We lived north of Dalton several miles down a straight, dirt road, then around several curves, across a sand draw (impassable during wet weather), and up a hillock. It was an old house built with sod—"Nebraska marble." The walls were constructed of straw and dirt, and were very thick. I could fit my five-foot, two-inch self in the windowsill, either standing up or lying down, with room to spare.

The outside walls were plastered and whitewashed; the interior was roomy and neat. The sod insulation kept my house toasty in the winter, heated by two freestanding wall units, and comfortable during the hot summers. We paid fifty-dollars rent for our two-bedroom "soddy," complete with indoor plumbing, and with outbuildings and corrals that would soon be bustling with our farm animals.

My house had a fine view of the land, the topography being more variegated and hummocky here. I could look west across the open fields, watch the approaching weather, and mark the day's end as the last rays of the sun sunk below the distant horizon. At night the Milky Way became my diamond necklace, as shooting stars arced across the sky to the yip-howls of the coyotes. This was my home sweet home.

We had a windmill adjacent to the house, so water was easily available to us. Such was not the situation for the early settlers of the Panhandle. They cursed this place not so much for the wind, the cold, or the suffocating heat, but for the lack of accessible water. In their ignorance they did not realize that a few feet below their dry wells lay a vast underground reservoir, the Ogallala Aquifer.

The Land. There were years of unusually heavy rainfall during the 1870s and early 1880s when the short grass grew lush and fertile, and homesteaders rushed to settle the Panhandle. These years coincided with a theory of climatology widely embraced at the time: that cultivation exposed the soil's moisture to the sky with a consequent increase in rainfall—"rain follows the plow." Consecutive drought years beginning in 1886 debunked this myth and resulted in numerous "homestead busts." The land had returned to its normal aridity.

Nelson Horatio Darton worked for the United States Geological Survey and he explored in detail the western portion of Cheyenne County and the surrounding counties of the southern Panhandle during 1897. In his "Preliminary Report on the Geology and Water Resources of Nebraska West of the One Hundred and Third Meridian," he describes "a calcareous formation of late Tertiary age to which I wish to apply the distinctive name *Ogalalla formation*." Named for a nearby town, the spelling has changed over the years.

The Ogallala Formation consists of an assorted collection of clay, silt, sand, and gravel eroded from the Rocky Mountains and transported by wind and water and deposited upon the ancient landscape about 10 million years ago. These sediments soak up water from rain and melted snow over the eons, forming an aquifer, which covers 174,000 square miles and extends over eight states. Most of this water lies beneath Nebraska soil. In Cheyenne County the depth to the aquifer as measured by Darton varies from one- to three-hundred feet. It was only after the development of deep-water pumps and center-pivot sprinklers (which later allowed the growth of industrial farming and cattle feed lots in the area) that farmers could at last ignore the scarcity of rain.

I wasted no time getting my farm up and running. First things first, I thought. We needed a cat. We must have a cat because all my friends had cats on their farms. And why the need for cats? To keep down the mouse population, of course. So, Sam the cat joined Cinder the dog in our sod house. I never did see Sam catch a mouse—it seemed Friskies was his preference.

With our domesticated animals now in place, I forged ahead with my dream. I told my husband I wanted some bottle calves, those that for one reason or another had lost their mothers and needed to be fed from a bottle. He obliged, and soon I was the proud caretaker of ten hungry calves. We bought some milk substitute and bottles, and I was in business. Mornings and evenings I fed my bottle babies their milk, and they eventually gravitated to more substantial food. I was not an expert on when to wean calves, so I deferred to my husband who said it would be soon.

I would certainly miss our moments together, the calves and I—having my feet stepped on, getting pushed around by the ten noses, having my person sniffed and licked—but I was excited about the next phase of their development.

I painfully awakened to the reality of farm life when, shortly thereafter, my husband pulled up with a cattle trailer behind his pickup. I didn't think anything of this as he was always hauling something as part of his job. This time, however, he backed up to the pen that had been home to my calves and began loading them into the trailer. I was a bit confused, but thought maybe they all had to go to the vet for a checkup. But my husband told me they were going to another farm to be "fattened up." When I was a child and my dad told me one of our pet animals had "gone to the farm," I didn't get a good feeling about that. Once again, I wasn't getting a good feeling.

"Why do they need to be fattened up," I wailed, "and why can't they stay on this farm? I will fatten them up, but I think they look fine the way they are. They're healthy."

My husband tried to explain. "They are not your pets. They did not come here to live until they die of old age. We will fatten them up and sell them, hopefully make a profit, and keep one for our freezer. That is the way things are."

There are moments in life when a person must step back (and perhaps hold onto something to keep from falling) and reconsider a previous decision. As I watched the pickup and the trailer with my calves disappear down the road on their way to "the farm," I decided that I didn't want to be a farm girl anymore.

And so I became estranged from the farm and, later, from my husband. But with three children and debts to pay, we hunkered, battling the land and each other. For a long while my life became as immutable as the drab, treeless landscape. I often reflected on the fictional lives of Per Hansa and his wife, Beret, in Rolvaag's "Giants in the Earth." These immigrants struggled against a hostile environment and their own strained relationship. Per, like my spouse, devoted himself to working the land, while Beret and I raised the children and endured the desperation. The desolate plains became a metaphor for my own life.

Many years later I re-claimed my town-girl life and began a personal odyssey, working at my profession in various locales of the outside world. I collected boyfriends and moonstones while journeying to Atlantic sunrises and Alaskan auroras. But now, after my time as a vagabond, I've returned to the High Plains, not so distant from my girlhood home.

The Land. My sod house on the hillock is now a ramshackle. Lingering on the edge of forever, it shrinks within the circumference of the vast expanse. Shadowed by the lowering clouds and beneath a sky of lead tinged with zinc, this ancient brown landscape shrouds itself in a somber aspect, not unlike Hardy's Egdon Heath at winter's twilight. The wind—the breath of the plains—blows easily, sometimes a susurrus, often a banshee wail or chthonic roar. The grasses grow thick and wild on the hilltop, with an occasional black-eyed Susan or prairie wild rose to color the scene.

I stand in the broken doorway and remember a time when a young wife lived here, suffused with hope and anticipation, until the day her childhood ended.

Once there was me, and there were the stars, my nearest neighbors. There were noons of such pitiless sun that the air ceased to breathe, and mornings when drifts of lambent snow covered the land so that the world seemed dead with the cold. I watched indigo-dark clouds approach with muffled thunder and wild lights; blue fire danced on the horizon as darkness collapsed around me. There were pellucid days of refulgent light when the sky was the texture of porcelain and the world became soft and benign. Sometimes the sky annealed to the earth in monochrome gray, the day becoming a diluted solution of night.

Mostly though, I remember the immensity of the land and the feeling of being in the presence of something that's been here since time's beginning.

I've returned to the farm life. I live on eight acres with a tree windbreak on the west and northwest property lines. Horizontal fields of wheat, millet, and chickpeas surround me—and the great domed sky. I don't grow much, just a few flowers—I only grow older. As a young girl I used to run wild in the fields, but now they encompass me. I am possessed by the land. When old friends ask me why I've returned, I have no adequate reply. Perhaps my life needed nature's balancing, or maybe my roots burrow deep into the soil, like those of the tough plains grasses, tethering me to this land.

Sometimes I am asked to play the organ during services at our community church. The congregation is much older than I remember and smaller in number. I play at more funerals now, in my own way helping those born on the soil to return to it.

As I drive my pickup along the section lines to my place, I'll often stop on the roadside and let the dogs run free. They'll bolt from the truck and dash pell-mell, trailing dust clouds. Barking and chasing small rodents, they exhaust themselves.

Afterward, sitting and resting, they will look around and must wonder in their dogs' minds, what is this place? Then, with their tails wagging, they lope back to me and we continue homeward.

When suitors come to visit, I will show them the straight-as-an-arrow roads leading to nowhere in particular, the houses and other places for which I have singular memories, and then we will drive into town to dine and have conversation.

But mostly, I will show them the land, so that when my mood darkens and I become, like the land, bleak and stubborn, they will understand.

I often rise early, brew my coffee, and allow myself time to reflect on my rare joys and exquisite sorrows. I'll hear the low moan of a distant locomotive and note the beginning of the day. Soon I will go and tend the flowers, my pastel rainbow shimmering with the morning's dew. Then I may sit and listen to the breeze rustling the poplars, like the sound of soft rain. Perhaps I will venture further and walk the land of which I am so aware. But now, with the promise of the day and the expectancy of wondrous tomorrows, I am content.

"Blessed is my life," I say. "Blessed is my life."

The Good Life.

Dancing with a Stranger

David K. Slay

Franklin first noticed her off in the distance, a solitary figure in motion, in the mostly empty parking lot. He'd look up from his newspaper and see her gliding in great circles around the few cars there. He'd lose track of her, return to his reading, and then she'd flash by in his mirrors behind his parked car. Then he'd see her farther away again. It was unusual to see a girl skateboarding alone. She wore vintage-looking plaid shirts and a gray knit cap pulled low over her ears. Strands of long brown hair escaped from the back of her cap and trailed behind her.

New to southern California—SoCal, as he learned it was called—several times a week he would bring morning coffee and a newspaper to a nearby park. Although not that old, he had taken an offer from Uncle Sam to retire early. He had been a postal worker, a mail carrier, mostly in the Beacon Hill area of Seattle. When the offer came down, at first it didn't interest him much. Being a mailman suited him well. He liked routines and structure, and preferred being on the periphery of things. Younger co-workers were incredulous he needed to give it any thought whatsoever. It's a no-brainer, they said. Nice package with great bennies. He had to admit—to himself at least—years of walking hilly routes in cold, damp weather had taken a toll. His knees were wearing out. It seemed he always had a runny nose. While mulling over the offer, he recalled an unhappy stint in the Army after high school in California, just south of Monterey. He had enlisted to get some sort of job training, but couldn't adjust to the noisy close quarters of barracks life. But at least the weather there had been very nice: sunny, warm and mostly dry, even during the winter months.

At the park he had a favorite parking spot, overlooking a putting green and duck pond, half-encircled by a stand of bamboo and a variety of palm trees. Palms everywhere were the first thing he noticed after relocating. He would bring the *Los Angeles Times*, turn a soft-rock station on low, and slowly page through the various sections of the paper, reading whatever looked interesting. Then he would finish off with "Ask Abby" and the comic strips. Sometimes the comics reminded him of the cartoons he used to study in *The New Yorker* when he was at work. After getting back from his route, he would sit in the substation toilet—"the library" it was called—with several of the undelivered weeklies, going from one cartoon to another. Although he didn't get most of the humor, he liked how each one was a glimpse into the lives of others—at work, on dates, in their houses, even in their bedrooms.

One morning after reading a while, he was leaning back in his seat, resting his eyes, and the skateboard girl spoke to him through the passenger door window.

"Hello in there, are you alright?"

He was startled. "What? Yes—why?"

She stood a few steps from the side of the car, leaning in slightly and holding the skateboard under crossed arms, wheels out.

"I thought maybe you were homeless or something, because you're here a lot."

"Homeless?" Franklin was still flustered by her sudden appearance. Could he look homeless?

"In this car?" he said. With the morning sun behind her, he couldn't see her face very well.

"A lot of homeless people live in their cars."

"Yeah, but not this kind of car. They usually have old wrecks, and all their belongings in them."

She leaned back slightly and appraised Franklin's silver Buick Century.

"Yeah, you're right. Plus, it's real clean."

"Thank you," he said.

She placed the skateboard on the ground, cast a sidelong "See ya," and pushed off. He watched her coast down to a lower parking lot, crouching slightly with arms extended to manage the speed.

The following week while parked in his usual spot, a patrol car came into the mostly empty lot and backed into a stall several rows behind him. At first Franklin didn't pay much attention, but then he remembered what the skateboard girl had said about seeing him there often and about thinking perhaps he was homeless. He adjusted a side mirror a few degrees, so he could covertly watch the black and white car. The policeman lit a cigarette and smoked it slowly, hanging his arm out the window. He wore wraparound sunglasses. Franklin's chest tightened when it occurred to him the cop might be watching him at the same time. After a while, he dropped the cigarette out the window, rolled it up, and drove away.

Franklin looked around the parking lot at the few other cars there. All were empty. Everyone else must be doing something—taking walks, picnicking, playing with their kids. He tapped one finger idly on the steering wheel. Maybe he should skip a few days or park somewhere else for a while. After all, there were other parking areas throughout the park, connected by a winding, two-lane road. Then he thought of the skateboard girl again. His finger stopped tapping. Maybe she had complained.

He stayed away for a week but then returned to his favorite place. He was paging through the Calendar section of the *Times* when the girl coasted around the lot and then stopped by his car, this time on the driver's side. She stepped on the back end of the board, making it stand up smartly, and then held it against her chest under crossed arms.

"Haven't seen you around," she said.

"Oh really? Well, I've had other things to do." He wanted to sound indifferent, but he was glad she still was friendly. It meant she probably hadn't complained about him.

"Don't you have a job?" she said.

"Not anymore. I'm retired, actually."

"Retired? You don't look *that* old."

"Well, actually I did retire early. From the Postal Service. I was a mailman. How come you're here so much?" he asked. "Shouldn't you be in school or something?"

"I am in school. I go to City College," she said. "And I work part-time. Retail."

"Really. What's your major?"

"Don't know yet. I'm interested in art and fashion." She pushed a few strands of hair back behind her ear and under her cap.

"Fashion. I bet you like that antique stuff. You always wear those older kind of clothes."

"I do?" She looked down at her shirt, a mostly red and black plaid. It reminded Franklin of a hunting shirt. "Spying on me, huh?" She gave a quick smile to show she wasn't serious.

"Wait," she said. "*You're* into fashion?"

"No way. But I used to see those shirts a lot in Seattle. At one time they were everywhere. Never thought I'd see them down here, though, in So-Cal."

"Yeah, that was grunge."

"Grunge?" He thought about the word. "You mean like *grungy*?"

"It was just a look. You know, flannel shirts, work boots, stocking caps—and usually from thrift shops. It was popular down here too for a while."

"Well, that's easy to do in Washington."

"I wasn't into grunge, but I do like vintage clothes and stuff."

Just then he had an idea. "You won't believe this," he said, "but I was just about to give away some of those shirts and things to Goodwill. I need to get rid of more stuff since I moved here. Maybe you'd be interested in them."

She cocked her head slightly and squinted at him. "Oh sure. You just happen to have this great stuff you're giving away, like, right now. How likely is that?"

"What? No, wait …" Franklin was stunned. She didn't believe him. He remembered something a coworker used to say: No good deed goes unpunished.

She looked over toward the putting green. Two older-looking men were practicing putting and chipping.

"Well," she said. "Maybe I'm being a little unfair. How about you bring it here with you sometime."

That evening Franklin went through the closets in his condo, gathering together winter shirts and clothes he no longer had any use for. While sitting on the edge of his bed and carefully folding them, he thought about the girl possibly wearing his shirts. There was something both casual and intimate about it, like dancing with a stranger. He had a daydream about slow dancing with the girl with her in one of his shirts. The image was vaguely arousing but mostly disquieting. He had never danced with a girl. Growing up, he always had been painfully shy around girls and more so with young women. A counselor in high school said he would grow out of it, but that hope had faded long ago. Before bagging the shirts, he smelled some of them and checked their collars to make sure they were clean. In the morning, he loaded into his trunk four brown paper bags of flannel shirts and a few wool scarves.

Several days passed without the girl coming to the parking area and it seemed her absence was longer than usual. He caught himself leafing through the same newspaper section several times. He told himself he had wanted to take the clothes in the trunk to Goodwill anyway, so he could do that any time now. Then on a Thursday morning, she coasted into the lot. When Franklin spotted her, he got out and stood with the car door open, almost waving to her, but then he felt self-conscious. For the first time in years, he was giving some thought to his appearance, how he looked, what clothes to wear. This morning, he had put on a salmon-colored polo shirt, tucked into khaki walking shorts, and a Titleist golf cap. The shirt and cap, along with a putter and package of four golf balls had been a retirement gift from some co-workers.

"Hey," she said, coasting to a stop. "Fancy seeing you here." She was wearing another plaid shirt, this time green and black over black leggings.

"Yes. Well. You see, I was serious about the Goodwill stuff—it's all back here, in the trunk."

"Cool."

They moved to the back of the car and he squeezed the key remote to open the trunk lid. The latch released with a thump, and at the same time a police car turned onto the road below, leading up to the parking lot where they were standing.

"You know what?" she said. "Maybe this looks a little weird."

"It does?" But then he followed her gaze toward the slowly approaching cruiser.

"Oh my." He leaned an elbow on the trunk lid until the latch clicked shut.

"Let's just get in and leave," she said, "you know, like, casually?"

They got into the car and Franklin's pulse was racing. She removed the knit cap, shook her hair loose, and sat looking straight ahead with the skateboard between her knees. The police car entered the parking lot, drove slowly by and parked somewhere behind them. He fumbled with the keys, almost dropped them, but got the car started. As he released the brake and glanced over his shoulder to back up, she suddenly seemed so close. He could smell a fresh shampoo fragrance. It was difficult to believe she was there, in his car, her elbow casually propped in the window, waiting for him to drive off with her.

On the road leading away from the lot, Franklin watched the police car recede in his mirror. He exhaled. "Well, that was exciting. What shall we do next, rob a gas station?"

She gave him a puzzled look. "It's not like we were doing anything wrong," she said. "It's just I know that guy and it's best to avoid him."

"You *know* him? What does that mean?"

"He's hassled me in the past. He's a creep."

"Good grief," Franklin whispered.

She leaned back against the headrest and looked out her window. A breeze lifted loose strands of hair. She seemed lost in thought, but Franklin didn't know where they were going. He passed another parking area and was nearing the exit to the main highway.

"Maybe we need to stop somewhere so I can show you the clothes," he said.

"Oh. Right," she said, sitting up. "How much is there, anyway?"

"Four shopping bags—there was more than I realized."

They came to the stoplight at the park exit. She looked into the middle distance beyond the windshield; he looked at the dashboard.

"What about this," he said. "I can take you to your place—if you don't mind, of course—I don't have to come in or anything ..."

She looked at him and smiled. "Sounds like *my place or yours ...*"

"What?"

"Just kidding."

Franklin jumped as the car behind them honked. The light had turned green.

"Turn left," she said.

Her street was lined with surprisingly tall, spindly palms, in an older neighborhood near the college. He parked and raised the trunk lid for her. After peering tentatively into several of the bags, she said, "Let's just take it all inside."

Her place was a converted garage apartment behind a small stucco house with faded canvas awnings. They carried the shopping bags up the narrow, cracked driveway—he with three bags embraced in his arms, she with one and the skateboard. She turned to him and whispered, "My landlady's going to freak about this. She always watches me come and go."

He glanced at a lace-curtained window on the side of the house as they went by, expecting to see a silhouette. At her door, she shifted the bag and skateboard to one arm, and fished in her shirt pocket for a key.

Inside the small room, she took his bags of clothes and put them on the bed, a twin-size doubling as a divan with a fitted corduroy cover. The room had been only a single garage to begin with, so a kitchenette and toilet had been added on the back. There was a waist-high half-wall with an opening in the middle, to give the impression of two rooms, and the musty smell of old linoleum. She had left the door partly open.

"Ok," she said, hands on hips, addressing the clothes on the bed. "Let's see what we have here." She began rummaging through the bags, taking items out, unfolding some to hold against her front. "Not bad," she said. "I like a lot of them. What I don't use I can probably sell."

Franklin shifted his weight from one leg to the other.

"Oh I'm sorry," she said. "Would you like to sit down? I'm not being a very good hostess."

"Maybe I should be going," he said. He glanced at the half-opened door. "Your landlady might be getting worried."

"Oh, it's ok. I can tell you're not a psycho-killer or something." She smiled and retrieved a chair from the kitchenette. "There," she said. She turned back to the heap of clothes on the daybed, and began sorting them into three piles.

Franklin sat with his hands in his lap, tapping the ends of his fingers together. His knees were white and bony and he wished he hadn't worn the shorts. He looked around the room a little but didn't want to pry. There was an old floor lamp next to an easy chair, for reading he supposed, and a turquoise clock radio on a worn chest of drawers. Some unframed posters were push-pinned to the wall behind the bed. In one, he thought he recognized John Lennon playing a white grand piano in a white room.

"You've got some interesting things," he ventured. "My mother had a clock radio like that. I think it was a Zenith, too."

"Yeah," she said, without looking up, "it still works. I use it all the time."

After a while, she turned to him. "Would you excuse me a minute?" Before he could respond, she stepped into the kitchenette and washed her hands in the sink.

"Would you like a drink?" she called over a shoulder, over the faucet's noisy plumbing.

"A drink?" Franklin called back. "I'm not sure about that."

She turned off the faucet and dried her hands on a paper towel. "I mean a soft drink," she said, smiling. "I think I've got some Dr. Pepper."

"Yes please," he said, suddenly aware of a dry mouth. He heard her open and close a refrigerator, and then the snap and fizz of two pop-tops. She returned holding a can in each hand.

She sat on the edge of the twin bed, crossed one leg over the other, rested forearms on knees and fixed her eyes on Franklin. Her soda can dangled from one hand.

"So," she said. "Can I give you something for all these things?"

"Oh no," Franklin murmured. "I was going to give it all to you—I mean Goodwill—anyway." His face was getting warm. "Please, keep whatever."

She sat looking at him and began to idly swing her leg.

"Well, it's not like I'm a charity case," she said. "There's a store I go to that buys stuff like this."

"No, please," he said. He covered his knees with his hands. A trickle of perspiration began to move down his side.

"Um, would it be ok if I used your restroom?" He made a little grimace, fearing he was being inappropriate, but he very much needed to relieve himself.

"Sure," she said. She took a sip from the can, suppressed a burp, and nodded toward the kitchenette. "Up the stairs, third door on your left."

"Excuse me?"

"Just *kidding*—it's very small, but it's right in there."

He stood and had to be careful because one foot had fallen asleep, but made it to the tiny john. He was afraid she might hear him so he sat to urinate. With the door closed, he found himself sitting in the dark because he hadn't seen the light switch was on the outside. He hoped she wouldn't notice. When he returned, she was standing next to the bed.

"Last chance," she said.

"Pardon?"

"How about twenty dollars for the lot?"

He looked at his shirts and things stacked on her bed, took a deep breath, and slowly let it out. "Would you dance with me?"

She stepped back slightly, but seemed more curious than offended. "Excuse me?"

"To the radio, maybe? Just one time?"

She looked at his face closely but he couldn't meet her eyes.

"Ok," she said. "It's a deal. But just one time."

She moved to the chest of drawers and turned on the clock radio. After it warmed up, she twisted the knob to sample several stations, and then settled on a slow country-western song.

"I think this one's just beginning," she said.

She straightened up, gathered her hair behind her ears and then let it go. She raised her right hand to take his left and placed the other lightly on his shoulder. As they came together, he closed his eyes and put his other hand on her side. After a moment of slowly circling to the rhythm, she put her cheek next to his, and softly hummed along to the tune.

The Skinny on Santa

Will George

"Ho ho, ho! Now grab onto the sleigh everyone. Hold on tight. We're heading into the clouds. Do you feel the cold wind? We're through the clouds now. Into the stars. Look, the moon. Over there, a shooting star. Alright, we don't want to tire the reindeer out. Let's head back to the shopping mall."

At 5'10" and 140 pounds, I was not your typical Santa. But I was a desperate out-of-work actor and Christmas was coming and I had nothing coming in. The Sunday Tribune ad read:

SANTAS
for Shopping Centers
in suburbs & Minneapolis.
Will train. Exc. pay.

Perfect. After mailing my resume in, I was soon sitting in a north suburban coffee shop with Don McGuire, owner of the Santa business, a nice guy who asked why I wanted to wear the red suit.

"It would be fun," I said. "I have a degree in recreation. I've directed and performed children's theater. I was in the Renaissance Festival as an Italian baker. I understand street theater and characterization. I've had training in improv."

Don listened calmly as he stirred his coffee. He liked my enthusiasm. Don didn't pursue the big malls; he had the lock on small indoor shopping centers that needed Santas to bring in extra business. It was the out of the way places where people went for haircuts, bought extension cords and ate Chinese food.

My day of Santa training began on a Saturday morning in the basement of Don's home with a lot of round, jolly guys. They had extra padding for me and I was soon off to a pizza shop in South Minneapolis greeting customers as they walked in the door, but my main gig was a strip mall just off Lake Street.

The typical Santa visit consisted of families coming into the display area and a photographer ushering them into the big red sleigh. Kids would climb up and I would greet them and tell them how proud I was that they had been so good. I repeated everything the kids wanted to the parents. "Well I can't promise, but we'll see what we can do." "We" would be the elves and I. Some kids asked for a hard to get items like a Nintendo set or a Little Miss Makeup. When I knew they were asking for too much, I always looked to the parent to see their reaction. Some parents were very clear. They would nod yes or shake their head no like a catcher behind the plate. Occasionally, I would tease the parents. "Jenny, you want a real horse. Of course we can do that. Ho Ho Ho." The parents' eyes would grow big with fear. Then I'd close with. "It will appear in your dreams. What color do you want it?"

Some parents were adamant about making sure I knew their kids were going to get everything. One father paced back and forth like a baseball manager and announced, "Santa, that's good. Do you hear me, Santa? We can do that. Everything is good."

I always responded with a "Ho Ho Ho," because the whole thing felt insane. Can people gain happiness from plastic?

When it was slow, I read children's books out loud, like *The Polar Express* or turned the set into a flying sleigh.

There were difficult moments. Unhappy babies. Particularly the ones that hated red, a beard, or a furry hat. They loved to rip the fake beard away from my face, which was attached with spirit gum, a theatrical glue. There were signs that it might not fair well. The kid's eyes would bug out like a muppet. Then the baby would lock every muscle and the face would go from fear to horror. The child would arch the back and launch into a loud banshee scream of torture in my right ear. Those pictures didn't sell.

The more difficult visitors were not the Santa hating babies, but adult women who got dressed for a picture with Santa. I said, "Now, you've been a good girl this year, right?" Most chuckled and said yes, but a small percentage would lean over and whisper, "I've been a bad girl, Santa." I turned as red as my suit and said a loud, "Ha. Oh no, you were a good girl."

"No I wasn't Santa. I was bad. Really, really bad. I don't deserve any gifts this year."

Some adults stated the obvious.

"Santa, you've lost a lot of weight this year. What happened?" Even with my fat padding, I was emaciated by Chris Kringle standards.

"Well, Mrs. Claus put me on a diet. Cuts down on draft and helps the reindeer. Every ounce counts. Ho, ho. ho."

The greatest challenge was the adults who saw me as St. Nick, the shamanic healer. They poured their soul out to me. It was as if once they reached my sleigh, they could release all of their holiday pain. Some adults didn't have enough money to buy gifts for their children; they were depressed or hated Christmas. I didn't offer solutions, but listened, genuinely. One evening, that did not work, for me or the visitor. It was a quiet weeknight. A tall, thin woman, about 30, walked in for a visit. Her gait was unsteady. She worked in the mall as a hair stylist. She told me she was diagnosed with multiple sclerosis. Due to her illness, she would have to give up cutting hair, and worse, her husband was giving up on her because of her health. I did everything I could to keep it together.

We both looked at each other, her brown eyes inches away. She waiting, me thinking. My chest tightened, a lump formed in my throat. I couldn't conjure one thing to say that would bring solace. I lost my Santa composure and took it personally. I broke character and said, "I am sorry. I am so sorry this is happening to you."

On Christmas Eve I worked the family circuit, visiting homes across the Twin Cities to parents who paid for Santa to deliver their packages. I had cue sheets for each house. I memorized names of all the kids, hobbies and favorite sports. The bag of gifts waited outside the house and I picked them up, shook some sleigh bells and went in and handed out gifts and then drove onto the next house. It was a blast, a little stressful getting all the names right, but it went well. Kids loved it and the look in their eyes when I said specific things about each of them made it worth memorizing all the information. "Elizabeth, I am so proud of how hard you worked in gymnastics this year. And I appreciate the way you helped your mother by washing the dishes and getting an A in history."

In the end, the responsibility that came with wearing the mask of Santa was more than I understood. Around the holidays some people become agitated, angry and depressed. Like offering a petition to a saint or a prayer wheel, visitors wanted Santa to help them. They carried wounds that need to be filled with light. I only hope by listening to their stories, I created the space for some to enter.

Magician's Assistant, Sawed in Half

Jon Boisvert

"Not much to think of up here, sitting in this box. Sometimes it feels like I'm at the gynecologist. Sometimes I wonder, what if? What if this time it works? How would I drive? What would I do with my legs? Maybe I want that. No blood, no pain, just real, irrevocable magic. My wounds smooth like cut geode. Maybe that's why people still show up, as if somewhere among them there's a real-life wizard just making ends meet by splitting women into tops & bottoms, breaking handkerchiefs into doves that go soaring away."

In the Valley of the Dry Bones

Frank Scozzari

They were killed to the last man despite the ingenious plans of Captain Branson. He had foretold their desperate scramble up the canyon, drawing it out in the sand; how they would make a valiant stand on the flats where they had killed half a dozen Taliban; how they would find refuge in the large rocks above the flats, giving them time to regroup and reload; how they would make that heart-thumping scramble up the steep, exposed slope with bullets zinging over their heads, and how, when they reached the small grove of pine trees at the top of the wash there with nothing behind them but high cliffs, and though it would seem they were trapped, they would find cover in the pines and would radio for air support. Then the jets would come in from the north from behind the tall mountains, flying so low they could not be seen until the last second, and the Taliban would be annihilated by their precision-guided missiles.

But they never made it to the pines, and now Sergeant Dax Garner lay alone at the highest outcropping of rocks with a bullet in his thigh, his mouth dry, his leg stiffening, and his gun barrel so hot from all the rounds he had fired that he thought it might jam if he needed to use it again. On a ledge below him, Captain Branson lay next to Corporal Donnelly, the radio not more than a yard away from his outstretched arm—the call for air-support having never been made.

Below, Garner could hear the Taliban shouting back and forth in Pashto. He pulled himself higher against the granite. There was a nice V-shape between two rocks through which he could see clear down to the bottom. Something blue stirred among the white boulders.

Yeah, he's the one, Garner thought. The one who ruined us. The one with the blue turban who out-flanked us in a place where we could not be out-flanked; who assembled his men against the canyon walls where there was no place to assemble; who made us easy prey for their guns. Garner sighed. That crazy, pack-laden, desperate rush up the slope that ruined us.

He turned and looked skyward, thinking of the jets that would never come. The bright, blue autumn sky was without clouds. He thought it might be the last time he saw such a sky. How was it that they had miscalculated their retreat so badly?

Scattered on the slopes below were several dead Marines. Of the five of them who had made it to this high place in the canyon, four of them now lay in the awkward positions of the dead; some small and crumbled up, others sprawled out with their arms and legs at odd angles.

Retreat was not an option, Captain Branson had said.

The last bravado words of a gung ho leader, Garner thought.

Well, his wish came true.

And now look at him. Of all of the dead, he was the most oddly positioned. His legs seemed to be peddling as if dancing on a roof-top and his head was twisted in the opposite direction, and still, that outstretched arm was reaching for the radio.

In addition to Captain Branson and Private Donnelly, there was Private Toby and Sweeney. Toby had been hit coming up the slope but somehow managed to reach the top and now he lay sprawled out like a five-pointed star with his arms stretched-out over his head. As Garner looked at him he thought of something he had said just yesterday on the way up the canyon. They had passed some old ruins. There are a lot of old ruins in the mountains of Afghanistan and sometimes they would go inside them and investigate and this time when they did Toby asked the group: "Do you ever think about the ghosts of these ruins? All the people who lived here, loved here, played here over time?"

No one replied but Sweeney.

"The lost and the forsaken," Sweeney said.

Sweeney now lay some ten yards to the Toby's right, crumbled-up with knees and arms tucked to his chest.

So what good was all that religious mumbo jumbo? Garner thought.

Not that Garner had a problem with all Sweeney's biblical sayings. In a faraway land, being shot at daily, religion was not a bad thing to have. But Sweeney drove it into the earth; quoting this little blue bible he toted around, preaching in a condescending way like the rest of them were nothing but mindless heathens. And when they had begun their climb up this wide valley from Kandahar, he started reciting Ezekiel:

"*The hand of the Lord was on me, and he brought me out by the Spirit of the Lord and set me in the middle of a valley; it was full of bones ... And I saw a great many bones on the floor of the valley, bones that were very dry.*"

The irony of it made Garner shiver. It was, and is, a damned dry valley, and now it was to be filled with bones of a dozen Marines and a shit load of Taliban.

"*I will make breath enter you,*" he recalled Sweeney quoting, "*and you will come to life. I will attach tendons to you and make flesh come upon you and cover you with skin ... and as he so prophesied, there was a noise, a rattling sound, and the bones came together, bone to bone, and tendons and flesh appeared on them and skin covered them.*"

Such volition, Garner thought. He should have been a preacher, not a Marine.

"*Come, breath, from the four winds and breathe into these slain, that they may live ... and breath entered them; they came to life and stood up on their feet—a vast army.*"

Garner's mouth was drier than the driest valley, and as he continued to cerebrally recite Sweeney's sermon he noticed Sweeney's canteen lying in the sand next to him, and it made him realize just how damned thirsty he was. It was the wound, he thought, and the heat and the fear, and that long scramble up the wash, that had dried his mouth out.

The canteen was laying on its side with the cap still on and Garner thought it had to have water inside since Sweeney hadn't the chance to drink from it.

He glanced down the wash. The Taliban with the blue turban hadn't advanced much. He was keeping his head low, carefully negotiating his way higher through the white boulders.

He was the smart one all right, Garner thought.

Garner began the long arduous journey down toward Sweeney's canteen.

Sweeney was a good ten feet in elevation below him and fifteen yards in distance, and Garner had to slither like a snake along a granite slab and in between two boulders, all the while dragging his rifle behind him. The gravity made it easier, he thought, leaning forward and pulling mightily with his arms. But each time he lurched forward, his leg began to ache again. Blood was oozing from the pant leg where the bullet had ripped it open.

When he reached Sweeney he had to reach over him to grab the canteen. He could not help but look at Sweeney's dead face.

"Mouthing off all that biblical shit?" Garner said. "A lot of good it did you. A lot of good it did us."

He grabbed the canteen, uncapped it, and guzzled down a mouthful of water. Then he rolled over and lay on his back, looked skyward, and took another long drink from his canteen.

"Where gone all ye Christian soldiers?"

He held the canteen above his mouth until the last drop trickled down his throat. Then he tossed it to the side.

"Let the four winds come breathe breath into you now," he said.

It was not long before he heard the Taliban voices again, louder and more confident. One was shouting in English.

"No need to die Marines." The voice echoed up the canyon.

Garner took hold of his rifle, checked the clip and, seeing he only had a few rounds left, took the spare clips from Sweeney's utility belt and stuffed them in the pockets of his cargo pants. He wiggled his way back to ledge of the rocks and peered down. The blue turban was higher, flashing bright in the sunlight between the boulders.

Garner lifted his rifle slowly over the top of the rock, aimed down-canyon, and put a bead directly on the blue turban.

Then it disappeared.

"No need to die Marines," the voice yelled again. "Surrender now and you will live."

"So you can trade me for a thousand of your friends?" Garner mumbled softly to himself. "No thanks."

Thirty seconds passed and Garner could see the Taliban standing higher, more boldly.

"Come on Americans, there is no place for you to go. Surrender and live."

"Come on you bastard …" was Garner's quiet reply "…just a little higher."

Then the blue turban came completely out from behind the rocks, fully exposing his torso. Garner looked on surprised.

He thinks we're all dead, he thought.

It had been some time since there had been any gunfire. The last follies from the bottom of the wash had gone answered. Garner looked over at Toby, who was sprawled on a down-sloping slab of granite, easily seen by those below. The other Marines who did not make it up the slope lay exposed below, and of the five who had made it, all had been hit and staggered before disappearing beyond the top ledge.

"We have food and water," the Taliban shouted. "You need water, no?"

Garner watched as the blue turban climbed higher. "Come on, just a little more. And bring some of your friends with you."

"Are you not warriors? You made a good fight but you lost. Realize that and you will live."

His English is very good, Garner thought. Too good. Bastard was probably educated in the States or England.

"If you are thirsty," the Taliban yelled. "We have water."

Wait for the perfect shot. Wait for the others to come out. Then you can take many.

Now the Taliban leader was a good ten yards beyond the cover of the last boulder.

"Come on you, Bastard. Come on." Garner kept his sight centered on the blue turban. "Not too smart now." Then another turban showed itself, a white one, and another white one. "Come on you, Bastards."

Garner could feel his trigger finger pulling downward. He had to do all he could to keep from pulling it all the way.

I'd love to finish it now, he thought. I'd love to finish him like he finished us. I'd love to put a bullet through that blue-shrouded cranium so that the pain would go away.

Garner glanced skyward.

But what good would that do?

Then what?

Then the parades would begin, that was what. And a public execution posted on YouTube for the entire world to see. He had seen how the Taliban handled their dead enemies. There was no honor in it. Their fallen foes were slaughtered like lambs. He had seen dead Marines dragged through the streets and Afghan soldiers beheaded. It was a grisly thought and he did not want it to happen to him now nor to his fallen comrades.

But it was their fate, he thought, because of their miscalculation and their bravado and that feeling of invincibility engrained in them by the Marine Corps.

We were done.

He looked skyward again. The blue sky was silent.

And worse yet, the bartering will begin. He knew he was worth more alive than dead. One Marine was worth many imprisoned combatants.

Unless of course there was an airstrike.

On the flat ledge below by Captain Branson and Private Donnelly the radio lay idle and waiting just beyond the Captain's outstretched arm. A laser-guided missile from the sky would finish it all, Garner knew. Then there would be no American bodies to be put on parade, no moral victories for the Taliban to celebrate, no high-value American soldier to be offered in a ten-fold trade for Taliban leaders, who would wreak a thousand-fold in terror.

Down at the bottom of the wash the Taliban leader climbed wantonly up the talus rocks with several turban-shrouded men following up behind him.

"Yes, a laser guided missile would finish it all nicely," Garner said to himself.

He checked the clip on his rifle; then swung it over his shoulder. Have to remain quiet, he thought. Have to lure them in close. Have to be certain they are close enough to kill them all.

Garner commenced a slow crawl to the ledge below—toward Captain Branson and the radio, sliding along the rocks. The pain in his leg increased with each long pull, but he did his best to shake it off. His newfound plan gave him strength.

There is no pain in death, he thought. And there will be no Taliban victories.

But as pleasing a thought as it was to destroy the Taliban, the notion of committing suicide was troublesome. He, who had always applauded life and despised suicide bombers, was about to join the ranks of the martyred dead. This sat uneasily in his gut.

And he thought of the sound of jets too—that glorious, thunderous roar that signaled the might of the virtuous imminently overhead. It was the modern-day equivalent of the cavalry horn: one that could even the odds in a desperate battle. He recalled a time when he had witnessed three hundred Taliban coming down on an isolated American outpost near Kamdesh. His team watched the whole spectacle from an observation post on a distant ridge. The Americans were vastly outnumbered. Every man among them was destined to die until the Observation Post Commander called in an airstrike. From beyond the hills, streaking in low like black hornets, two jets laid a hailstorm of destruction upon the Taliban, and after the jets passed they heard that beautiful roar of the F-A18s overhead. The tide of the battle was turned that quickly.

Recalling it now caused shivers to run through Garner's body. He wanted so much to hear that beautiful sound of jets again.

"Let them come," he said, "like Ezekiel's four winds to breathe life back into dry bones. We Christian soldiers will rise from the earth to fight again."

But he knew: this time he would not hear the jets. They would be long past, their ordinances detonated, before the roar of their engines would thunder overhead.

Such a pity, he thought.

It was better that way. Best not to know. Best for it be sudden.

He looked up at the blue sky.

It was a killer when death became the only way to get back home.

He crawled with greater volition toward the bodies of Captain Branson and Private Donnelly, climbing over rocks and dirt, biting his lip each time the pain in his leg became too terrible.

There was a moment he lost track of time. He looked forward and looked back realizing he had blacked-out, but for how long, two seconds or two minutes, he did not know. It was the wound, he thought. The pain of it, the loss of blood, and the damned heat. This placed a new urgency on his task. He could not loose consciousness again. He had to reach the radio. He tried to swallow, but his mouth had no moisture left in it. He hurried along, favoring his wounded leg and trying to keep focused and conscious.

But again he found himself motionless in the dirt, his cheek pressed against the hot sand. When he awoke this time he heard the sound of Taliban voices, much closer and louder.

Damn it. Stay focused.

By the third time it happened he awoke only a few yards away from Captain Branson. The radio, which was on the opposite side of Captain Branson, laid in the dirt just beyond the reach of the captain's dead hand. Garner crawled for it, stretching for it as one would stretch for a cup of water after a long desert journey.

But there was blackness again, and that dreadful sense of time-loss—waking and not knowing how many seconds or minutes had passed.

His eyes opened looking up at several gun barrels. Behind the gun barrels were several bearded faces in the center of which stood the Taliban leader with the blue turban.

"Well, Marine?" the Taliban leader asked. "You are the only one?"

Garner instinctively grasped for his rifle but it was not by his side. Then he saw it up in the arms of one of the Taliban soldiers. He glanced over to where the radio had been, but it was also gone; already up in the hands of another Taliban who looked at it inquisitively and played with its knobs.

"What is your company?" the Taliban leader asked.

Garner did not reply. His mind was too occupied with thought. He was wondering if he had reached the radio and called in the airstrike? For the life of him, he could not remember. He looked over to where the radio had been. He was still several yards away. If he'd had made the call, how did he end on the opposite side of Captain Branson? He looked back to the radio, now in the hands of the Taliban. Then the dreaded thought hit him--he never reached the radio; the call for air support was never made.

The blue turban shouted some orders in Pashto to a group of Taliban up by Toby and Sweeney. They promptly gathered the bodies. Having already secured their weapons and gone through their pockets for souvenirs and identifying papers, they dragged their bodies—the real prize, down toward the position of their leader and the other dead Marines. Others did likewise to Captain Branson, dragging him out by his legs, his head racking against the rocks, and Private Donnelly as well, picking his pockets clean, gathering up his rifle and equipment, and dragging him across the granite. They were all heaped into one pile.

Destined for some gruesome cyber display, Garner thought, or some kind of televised mockery.

"What is your company?" the Taliban leader asked again.

Grimacing into the sun, Garner looked up at him. He has the face of a goat, he thought.

When Garner did not answer, the Taliban leader reached down and snapped Garner's dog tags from his neck.

"Dax Garner?" he said, reading it. "A Sergeant?"

Garner did not reply.

"What's your company?"

One of the Taliban high up in the canyon began shouting something in Pashto. The Taliban leader acknowledged, shouting something back.

"So you are the only one," the Taliban leader said. He glanced over at the growing pile of dead Marines. "You will make a great prize nonetheless."

The blue turban poked at Garner's wound with the tip of his rifle barrel. Garner felt the pain radiate up from his leg and into his abdomen.

"Don't worry, you will live," the Taliban said. "I'll make sure of that."

And as he said it, a crackling noise came from the radio held in the one Taliban's hand. Garner gazed up at it, dazzlingly. The bastards have me, he thought. The bastards have us. The goddamned radio I never reached, into which I never keyed air-support coordinates.

The grisly image of comrades, disfigured and mocked on international television, flashed through his head. Such a pity; such a travesty; how could I have let them have me? How could I have let them win?

His mind began to wonder; the foggy unconsciousness returned. Then he began to see blackness again.

Vaguely he heard the blue turban speaking; "I asked you a question. Don't fall asleep on me now." And, vaguely, he heard the radio cackle again.

Then the radio spoke: "Inbound five sixty."

And a different voice acknowledged: "That's a Roger."

The blue turban glanced skyward.

In a fantastic white flash and gray roar of smoke, the entire earth lifted. In the same ten-thousandth of a second Garner heard it and saw it, it took his light away. Boulders and trees shot skyward, broken and splintered apart. What was once stone and wood was now vaporized dust. Shock waves rocked the forest on the northern mountainside as two tapered-winged birds came streaking out from the smoke clouds. Followed belated in their wake was the roar of jet engines—their afterburners thundering off the canyon walls. As the debris began their arching descent, the two jets dropped low on the distant horizon and became lost in the afternoon haze.

The Escort

Ray Keifetz

Wakened
by the click of ravens
pecking stolen watches,
blinking for the moon
which doesn't rise
where even starlight is stolen;
under hemlocks this night
I heard them singing.
Their singing drew me
and I crept in to them
because their firelight
seemed, even for them,
too bright.

A breeze blowing leaves,
a dry wind swirling dust,
I shake them to their roots
and away they rush
to veer and fall and wake
whole yet raked
by this back they clapped
like a back that could be clapped,
this water they poured
as if these lips could drink,
this hand they reached for in the dark
like a hand a child might take.

Picking needles from their hair
they will search the sky,
they will holler at the trees,
they will watch the sparrows
fly untouched through the rain,
hear the geese cackle
before the axe,
they will start for home
leading me
by the need …

Eyes of Realization

Alan S. Brown

The global tension surrounding North Korea is undeniable, especially in the wake of recent nuclear tests, missile launches and executions. News reports provide a safe, detached version, free from danger, but the standoff at the DMZ is palpable and ongoing. And U.S. soldiers are right in the middle of it.

In 2003, so was I.

Before I visited the Joint Security Area, about as far north as one can get without crossing into North Korea, my notion of the DMZ had been stereotypical: a thick cement wall, overlapping strands of razor wire and domino-spaced guard towers. Training calendars, soldier issues, and administrative backlog absorbed my days as a young Army captain in 2003 stationed at nearby Camp Casey. While I lived and worked within the totalitarian regime's close artillery range, I seldom gave it a thought.

Three colleagues and I wore camouflage battle-dress uniforms as we drove north on the only road to the JSA, the Joint Security Area. Our uniforms presented a stark contrast to the less threatening green Class As required of other Army visitors. We were excited for our personal tour by a fellow captain who lived and worked at Camp Bonifas, the tiny garrison with the mission of securing the JSA.

Also referred to as Panmunjom, the JSA hosted the negotiation of the July 1953 armistice between the United Nations and North Korea. To this day, the United Nations Command and North Korea oversee the terms of the ceasefire agreement in a portion of the JSA called the "truce village." The entire JSA encompasses an area just 800 meters in diameter, bisected by the Military Demarcation Line, the literal border between the North and South. Soldiers from the Republic of Korea and the United States secure the south side of this small powder keg and stand toe to toe with their North Korean counterparts.

After two separate ID checkpoints along the lone highway running north, we arrived at Camp Bonifas. Right away, the post seemed unremarkable. Barracks, a helipad among the sports field, tin-sided Quonset huts, and a tiny post exchange with toothpaste, shampoo and Kiwi boot polish. Nothing to indicate we were less than a mile from North Korea and its army of 1.5 million.

Our guide, Captain Worthington, ushered us into a small briefing room flanked by grainy black and white photos from the early 1950s. A rusted yellow metal sign with the words "Military Demarcation Line" hung on the wall. A 20-year-old infantryman delivered a crisp briefing as if he were a 20-year veteran. He outlined a history of the Korean War, the purpose of the JSA and several anecdotes of armed skirmishes within the JSA as recently as the early 1970s. One such anecdote recounted the murder of Captain Arthur Bonifas and First Lieutenant Mark Barret in 1976. Their deaths resulted from a North Korean uprising over the trimming of a large poplar tree near the MDL, Military Demarcation Line. The overgrown tree blocked the South's view, and the North's guards took exception to the South's initiative to trim it. One of the photos on the wall now made sense. The fuzzy, enlarged image showed five Americans overtaken by more than 30 North Koreans. A closer look revealed a North Korean striking Captain Bonifas with an ax.

Twenty minutes into my visit, I hadn't seen any of what I expected to see, but I quickly felt the weight of this place, this tiny area of land where war, fear and hate had sustained itself since 1953.

On a small shuttle bus heading north, we stopped at an official looking gate with a large sign announcing our entry into the JSA. Captain Worthington and his driver jumped out of the bus and took two steps to a guard shack where they locked and loaded their Berettas. My eyes followed with familiarity as their slides each racked a 9 mm round. I became acutely aware I was unarmed.

We drove a short distance along a single lane, freshly paved road through intermittent rice patties and dense vegetation. We passed an ordinary barracks where the combined U.S. and South Korean quick reaction force waited in full battle rattle to respond anywhere in the JSA within minutes. We stopped at a hilltop vantage point with a 180-degree view across the border. Immediately, we saw several large Korean signs, a mile or more in the distance. The officer-in-charge, Lieutenant Jones, quickly translated with a smirk—"Yankee Go Home." With the lieutenant's binoculars, I scanned the tree line, noticing rusty, yellow metal signs every 50 meters, identical to one in the briefing room – Military Demarcation Line. These signs marked the entire border: English and Hangul facing the south, Hangul and Chinese facing the north. With the exception of these uniformly spaced signs, no indication of the precise border existed. No wall. No fence. Only rusty, yellow signs.

I scanned to a North Korean guard tower about half mile northwest. It stood like a box on four stilts with a slanted roof. Quickly, before someone told me it wasn't allowed, I put the binoculars down and zoomed in with my camera. Later, the enlarged photo revealed the fuzzy but discernable figure of a North Korean soldier on an outside catwalk, staring back with binoculars.

North Korea made world headlines every week, but I never considered these two countries to be still at war. The terms armistice, ceasefire, and peace accords all carried more friendly connotations. However, I would not use the word "friendly" to describe the atmosphere at the JSA. The soldiers there worked every day with just four days off a month. When they passed a checkpoint or access gate, they double-checked to make sure their weapons were locked and loaded. I handled my weapon maybe once a month for a qualification range, routine maintenance or a training exercise. My family thought I was living dangerously on Camp Casey, about 20 miles from the DMZ. These guys saw North Koreans armed with live rounds and hate every day.

The bus continued to the Bridge of No Return, used to exchange POWs after the armistice. Once a prisoner crossed over the bridge, he would never be allowed to go back. The 30-meter, wooden bridge appeared weathered and worn, yet sturdy. It was sobering to stand on a bridge that had supported so many men, so many prisoners, so much hope, so much pain.

We walked to the rusty yellow MDL sign at the foot of the bridge's three-meter wide planks. A matchbox guard shack stood at the other side with a two-foot by two-foot cut out revealing a torso silhouette—watching us. I imagined he was relaying descriptions of our uniform, rank and activities to his higher headquarters. I knew he was armed, and I knew he had been conditioned at a young age to hate me. I stared right back, raised my camera and took several pictures of his position in defiance. The term "enemy" didn't seem right. But it was clear we were not friends.

As we turned to get back on the bus, a sudden boom stopped us cold. Close enough to be startling, but far enough not to raise panic, the detonation was not the pitch of a rifle or pistol and did not leave a visible plume of smoke or debris. Captain Worthington immediately spoke into his radio, while the rest of us got on the bus and held a wide-eyed conference. Perhaps a malfunctioning mine? The guard across the bridge made me uneasy. The ax murder had occurred 30 meters from where we had stood. And now an unexplained detonation? We exchanged nervous looks as we drove south again.

Our final stop of the tour was the truce village of Panmunjom. The simple placement of buildings within the village clearly suggested a standoff. Set back 40 meters from either side of the border, a mere line in the gravel, two formidable five-story buildings faced off. Between them, six narrow buildings, no more than 4-meters wide, 10-meters long and 5-meters apart, precisely bisect the MDL for the purpose of hosting multi-lateral talks: three buildings for the United Nations and three for North Korea.

Our bus pulled up to the south entrance of an expansive building, appropriately named the New Freedom House, having been rebuilt in 1998 with contributions from the Hyundai Corporation. Contemporary construction on the outside and eloquently detailed on the inside, it symbolized economic and political rebirth and stability. Our enlisted guide, Specialist Smith, joked it was a multi-million dollar doormat: uninhabited, no heat, no air conditioning. We walked through a palatial foyer to the other side, to see the North Korean structure 80 meters away. With a wide stance, perfect symmetry and granite facade, the structure stared back emotionless, revealing none of the oppression or economic depravity beyond its foundation.

Two flights up, a lone North Korean soldier in an olive tunic, matching pants, and saucer cap stood at the entrance. Reacting to our presence, he turned to a small window behind him and spoke to the blank glass. Less than a minute later, two soldiers in the same uniform appeared through the front entrance and descended the steps towards us. With the help of my zoom lens, I could make out black leather holsters on their right hip. They didn't stop until their toes nearly touched the line marking the MDL. They stared at us through binoculars, hard and purposeful. Unlike the soldier's silhouette across the Bridge of No Return, these soldiers had faces, uniforms, and a focused, military bearing I was only used to seeing in the faces of friendly soldiers. Again wishing I had a weapon, I raised my camera in plain view of their binoculars, staring back through the safety of the lens.

A South Korean soldier wearing a combat helmet, mirrored aviator sunglasses and pistol quickly marched up to mirror their posture, toe to toe. He spoke into his radio while blocking their view. The North Koreans simply stepped to the side to continue their reconnaissance, never once looking or acknowledging the soldier from the South.

I held my camera steady and captured the seriousness within their eyes. No emotion. Nothing visible to reveal a common thread of humanity between us. Perhaps they were memorizing our name and rank to add us to the list of soldiers who worked within the JSA. Were they trying to intimidate us? What advantage were they trying to gain? I thought my country's long-standing commitment to the people of South Korea.

Conflicting ideologies aside, was their sense of duty any different than my own? Could I find fault with that? After all, we soldiers must do what we are told.

My respect for the South Korean people grew. Over a million and a half North Korean soldiers stared in their direction and yet the people of the South never flinched. They lived with a fervent optimism towards the future, choosing not to dwell on their ever-present stalemate. I gained greater context for the frequent international headlines and rhetorical jousting, the importance of my own mission renewed. I was glad to see the North Korean soldiers turn around after five minutes and walk back inside. But their stares remain etched into my memory.

Issue 6 Contributors

Jeffrey Alfier's latest chapbooks are *Southbound Express to Bay Head* (Grayson Books, 2016) and *The Red Stag at Carrbridge — Scotland Poems* (Aldrich, 2016). Recent credits include *Cold Mountain Review, Southern Poetry Review*, and *Hotel Amerika*. He is founder and co-editor of *Blue Horse Press* and *San Pedro River Review*.

Tobi Alfier is a multiple Pushcart nominee and a Best of the Net nominee. Current chapbooks are *The Coincidence of Castles* from Glass Lyre Press, and *Romance and Rust* from Blue Horse Press. *Down Anstruther Way* is forthcoming from FutureCycle Press. She is co-editor of *San Pedro River Review* (www.bluehorsepress.com).

Emily Arnick was born and raised in Kodiak, Alaska and grew up working on her father's commercial fishing boats. She is employed as a Personal Trainer and is currently a student at the University of Alaska Fairbanks. She enjoys reading, spending time outdoors, and (usually) enjoys writing. She resides in Alaska with her four children, one of which happens to be a Labrador retriever.

Cécile Barlier was born in France, but has lived in the United States for over a decade, raising a family and working as an entrepreneur. She has been a regular student at the Writer's Studio in San Francisco for many years. Two of her short stories, *A Gypsy's Book of Revelations* and *Forgetting* have been nominated for a Pushcart Prize.

Tara Ballard is from Anchorage, Alaska. Her poems have been published in *The Southampton Review, Salamander, The McNeese Review, Bridge Eight*, and other literary magazines.

Lana Bella, a Pushcart nominee, is an author of two chapbooks, *Under My Dark* (Crisis Chronicles Press, 2016) and *Adagio* (Finishing Line Press, forthcoming), has had poetry and fiction featured with over 290 journals, *2River, California Quarterly, Chiron Review, Columbia Journal, Poetry Salzburg Review, San Pedro River Review, The Hamilton Stone Review, The Ilanot Review, The Writing Disorder, Third Wednesday, Tipton Poetry Journal, Yes Poetry*, and elsewhere, among others. She resides in the US and the coastal town of Nha Trang, Vietnam, where she is a mom of two far-too-clever-frolicsome imps.

Jon Boisvert grew up in southeastern Wisconsin & now lives in Oregon. He's a graduate of the Independent Publishing Resources Center's certificate program & of other programs, too. His first book, *Born*, is forthcoming on Airlie Press. You can sometimes see his new poems & drawings & stuff at www.jonboisvert.com. Ryan Boyd (@ryanaboyd) lives in Los Angeles, where he teaches in the Writing Program at the University of Southern California. His poetry and criticism have appeared in the *Los Angeles Review*, *Dialogist*, the *Texas Review*, *FIELD*, and other fine places.

Alan S. Brown, who was born in Alaska and raised in Oregon, attended the University of Portland before beginning his career as an active duty Army officer. Over the last 20 years, he's served all over the world to include Germany, Korea, Iraq, North Dakota, Colorado, Kansas, Texas and Alaska. Still on active duty, he is currently an Asst. Professor of English at the U.S. Military Academy at West Point, NY. He holds an M.A. in English from Colorado State University.

Ha Kiet Chau is a writer from Northern California. Her poems have been published in *New Madrid*, *Ploughshares*, *Mission at Tenth*, *Sierra Nevada Review*, and *Kalyani Magazine*, among others. She is a recipient of the 2014-2015 UCLA Extension Writers' Program Scholarship. Her chapbook, *Woman Come Undone*, is available from Mouthfeel Press.

Martha Clarkson manages design for Microsoft workplace. Her poetry, photography, fiction and non can be found in *monkeybicycle*, *Clackamas Literary Review*, *Seattle Review*, *Alimentum*, *Hawaii Pacific Reivew*. She has a Pushcart Nomination, and is listed under "Notable Stories," Best American Non-Required Reading for 2007 and 2009. She is a recipient of best short story, 2012, Anderbo/ Open City prize, for "Her Voices, Her Room." Find her: www.marthaclarkson.com

Michael Coolen is a composer, actor, performance artist, storyteller, and writer living in Corvallis, Oregon His poems, essays, stories, and memoirs have been published in a wide variety of print and electronic media. He is also a published composer whose works have been performed around the world, including at Carnegie Hall, the New England Conservatory of Music, MoMA, and the Christie Gallery in New York.

Daniel Corfield teaches writing at Golden West College in Huntington Beach California. His fiction appears in over a dozen literary journals including *Word Riot* and *Carve Magazine*. His poetry can be found in *Beside the City of Angels: An Anthology of Long Beach Poetry*. He enjoys surfing and playing beach volleyball in his spare time.

Dylan D. Debelis is a founding editor of *Pelorus Press*, publisher, poet, and Unitarian Universalist Minister based out of New York City. Dylan has been published in a diversity of influential Literary Magazines and Reviews including *Prairie Schooner*, *[TAB] Literary Review*, and *[apt] Poetry Review*. His first full-length book of poetry entitled *The Garage? Just Torch It* is forthcoming through Vine Leaves Press.

Alexandra D'Italia's fiction and nonfiction have appeared in *Meat for Tea*, *Arcadia*, *Red Rock Review*, *Arcadia*, *South Loop Review*, among others. Love Creek Productions staged her short play, *The Fix Up*, in New York in 2012. She had not one, but two plays, at the Last Frontier Theatre Conference. One of her stories won the Edward W. Moses Graduate Writing Award for fiction. She has her masters in creative writing from University of Southern California.

Jeff Ewing's poems, stories, and essays have appeared recently in *Sugar House Review*, *ZYZZYVA*, *Willow Springs*, *Arroyo*, *Southwest Review*, *Utne Reader*, *Crazyhorse*, *Catamaran Literary Reader*, and *Cimarron Review*, among others. He lives in Northern California with his wife and daughter. You can find him online at jeffewing.com.

Maureen Foley (maureenfoley.com) is a poet, writer and artist living in on an avocado ranch by the sea in Carpinteria, California. Her work has appeared in numerous publications, including, *Spittoon*, *The Nassau Review*, *Inlandia*, and *Ontologica*. Her novella, *Women Float*, was published by the Chicago Center for Literature and Photography and she won the Dead Metaphor Press Chapbook Award for Epilepsy. She completed an MFA in Prose from Naropa University and is currently working on a novel about the experience of new motherhood and loss.

Leah Freiwald lives in San Francisco with her husband and a Lakeland terrier. She is completing a novel based on her adventures as an organic farmer in the Virginia piedmont. Several of her stories have been published; one was the finalist for the John Gardner Fiction Prize.

Brandon French an assistant professor of English at Yale, a topless Pink Pussycat cocktail waitress, a playwright and screenwriter, Director of Development at Columbia Pictures Television, an award-winning advertising copywriter and creative director, a psychoanalyst in private practice and a mother. Forty of her stories have been accepted for publication by literary journals and she was an award winner in the 2015 Chicago Tribune Nelson Algren Fiction Contest.

J.K. Frerichs enjoys the good life of the Nebraska Panhandle with family and friends and is proud to be a Cornhusker.

Paul Gacioch holds an MFA from New York University. His short fiction has appeared in *The Columbia Review*, *Fourteen Hills*, *Watchword*, and *Sidebrow's* print anthology and chapbook. He has read at San Francisco's Litquake, been nominated for a couple Pushcarts, and was the featured writer at Watchword's first Whole Story art installation. He currently writes and teaches in Silicon Valley.

Will George has shot cannons, traded buffalo robes, and led hikes for numerous National Park units throughout the West. In the literary world, Will has penned stories and poems for *North Coast Squid*, *Hip Fish*, *Rain*, *The Eastern Iowa Review*, *FLARE: The Flagler Review*, *Prick of the Spindle*, *Shout Out*, and *Blood Lotus*. Will holds a M.F.A. in creative nonfiction writing from Goddard College, for which he is forever grateful and will be forever indebted.

Melinda Giordano is from Los Angeles, California. Her writing has appeared in *Lake Effect Magazine*, *Scheherazade's Bequest*, and *Vine Leaves Literary Journal* among others. She was also a regular poetry contributor to CalamitiesPress.com with her own column, "I Wandered and Listened" and was nominated for the 2017 Pushcart Prize. She writes flash fiction and poetry that speculates on the possibility of remarkable things—the secret lives of the natural world.

Kathleen Glassburn resides in Edmonds, Washington with her husband, three dogs, two cats, and a 50-year-old turtle. Besides writing, she likes to play the piano and spend time with her horse. She earned an MFA in Creative Writing from Antioch University, Los Angeles. For samples of published stories and more information, see her website: www.kathleenglassburn.com. She is the Managing Editor of *The Writer's Workshop Review*. www.thewritersworkshopreview.net

Sharon Goldberg lives in Seattle and was once an advertising copywriter. Her work has appeared/is forthcoming in *The Gettysburg Review*, *The Louisville Review*, *Cold Mountain Review*, *Under The Sun*, *Chicago Quarterly Review*, *The Antigonish Review*, three fiction anthologies, and elsewhere. Sharon was the second place winner of the 2012 On The Premises Humor Contest and Fiction Attic Press's 2013 Flash in the Attic Contest. She is an avid but cautious skier and enthusiastic world traveler.

Kathleen Gunton is a poet/photographer who believes one art feeds another. Her poems and images often appear in the same journal. After the convent, she graduated from CSULB and began publishing poetry. Recent work in *Rhino*, *Studio One*, *West Trestle Review*, *Perceptions*, and *The William Stafford Anthology: A Ritual To Read Together*—to name a few. While she completes her second collection, she posts to her blog: Discursion.

Sean Hennessey is an avid collector of empty notebooks, an obsession he claims to justify by composing short fiction and poetry in them. He holds an MFA in Creative Writing and is currently teaching at Portland State University. He moonlights as a stoner metal musician and lives with his dog and two cats in Portland, Oregon.

Sarah Isto is a writer of a certain age who lives in Alaska, dividing her time between coastal Juneau and a remote cabin near Denali. She is author of two non-fiction books published by the University of Alaska Press. Her poetry has appeared in *Cirque*, *Timberline Review*, *Windfall*, and *Perfume River Poetry Review*.

Ray Keifetz has published poems and stories in numerous literary journals including *The Bitter Oleander*, *Kestrel*, *The Ashland Creek Press*, *The Briar Cliff Review*, and *Skidrow Penthouse*. His work has twice been nominated for the Pushcart Prize. He lives in Northern California where he earns his living peddling wine.

Mercedes Lawry has published poetry in such journals as *Poetry*, *Nimrod*, *Prairie Schooner*, *Harpur Palate*, *Natural Bridge*, and others. Thrice-nominated for a Pushcart Prize, she's published two chapbooks, most recently "Happy Darkness". She's also published short fiction, essays and stories and poems for children and lives in Seattle.

Cameron Quan Louie lives in Seattle, where he interns at Wave Books and is working on his MFA at the University of Washington. In 2011, he received the Hattie-Lockett Award from the University of Arizona Poetry Center, and he was one of the 2016 Bill and Ruth True Family Fellowship recipients. His poems have appeared in *Persona*, *Rainy Day*, *Zócalo Public Square*, *Santa Ana River Review*, and are forthcoming in *Foothill*.

Briana Loveall is a mother of two, wife of one, and a current MFA student at Eastern Washington University's Creative Writing program. Her previous works have been published with *Northwest Boulevard* and *Mamalode*. When she isn't writing nonfiction or reading Orwell, Tartt, or Didion, she spends her time gardening, building tent forts, camping, skiing, and making sandwiches.

Cindy Maresic lives in San Diego, California, where she works as an elementary school teacher, and serves in her district's writing task force. She has an MFA from San Diego State University, and her writing has appeared in *Glass: A Journal of Poetry*, *Aperion Review*, and *Mapping Me: A Landscape of Women's Stories*. When Cindy isn't writing poetry, she is working on her first, young adult novel.

Michael Mark is a hospice volunteer. His poetry has recently appeared or is forthcoming in *Bellevue Literary Review*, *Cimarron Review*, *Cutthroat Journal*, *Paterson Literary Review*, *Poet Lore*, *Potomac Review*, *Rattle*, *Spillway*, *Sugar House Review*, and *Tahoma Literary Review*. His poetry has been nominated for three Pushcart Prizes and The Best of the Net. michaeljmark.com

Simone Martel's debut novel, *A Cat Came Back*, will be published in December by Harvard Square Editions. Simone is also the author of a memoir, *The Expectant Gardener*, and a story collection, *Exile's Garden*. After studying English at U.C. Berkeley, Simone operated an organic tomato farm near Stockton, California. She's working on a new novel based on that experience.

Linnea Nelson is an MFA candidate at Oregon State University, where she teaches writing. Her poetry has appeared in *The Adirondack Review*, *San Pedro River Review*, *Tule Review*, and *Tribeca Poetry Review*, among other publications, and is forthcoming in the anthology *Leaving My Shadow: A Tribute to Anna Akhmatova*. Prior to coming to Oregon, Linnea worked as a language assistant in France, where she learned you can cook a lot with only a microwave.
Toti O'Brien's work has appeared in *Subprimal*, *Atlas And Alice*, *Minola*, and *Indiana Voice*, among other journals and anthologies. Some of her poetry was translated in Serbian. She has contributed stories and articles to various Italian magazines. More about her can be found at totihan.net/writer.html

Lauren Paredes is a storyteller across the mediums with a soft spot for the unusual. She received her MFA in Fiction from Lesley University in 2015. Her work has appeared in *Commonthought Magazine*, *DigBoston*, *Spark and Fizz*, and the upcoming *Grapple Annual No. 2*. Lauren currently lives in Portland, Oregon with her partner and her cat, Louie Buñuel.

Frank Scozzari lives on the California central coast. He is an avid traveler and once climbed Mt. Kilimanjaro, the highest point in Africa. A multiple Pushcart Prize nominee, his award-winning short stories have been widely anthologized and featured in literary theater. His fiction has also been featured in *USA Today*.

Heidi Seaborn, an accomplished poet in her youth, took a very long break. After three decades, three kids, four marriages, 27 moves and a business career, she started writing again with the advantage of all that experience. Living in Seattle, she currently benefits from David Wagoner's mentorship. Her poetry has or will appear in *Into the Void Review*, *Flying South 2016 Anthology*, *3Elements Review*, *Windfall*, *Fredericksburg Literary and Art Review*, *Ekphrastic Review*, the *Voices Project*, the *Ice Dream Anthology*, and elsewhere.

David K. Slay completed two years of short story writing workshops, primarily in the UCLA Writers' Program, after retiring from a career as a clinical and community psychologist. He is interested in writing short literary fiction that has the potential to produce self-awareness in readers, or that helps to reveal an aspect of human nature. This is his first fiction publication.

Nancy Shobe began her career as an advertising copywriter in Chicago. Since then, she has written *The Insiders' Guide to Santa Barbara* (2008), the documentary film *Above Santa Barbara* (2010), travel guides for conference and visitor bureaus, and numerous articles for news portals. She has written essays about end-of-life that appear in literary journals throughout the United States. Nancy is also a certified yoga therapist and photographer. She may be reached at gobrainflowcom or nancyshobe.com.

David Shrauger is a freelance writer and veteran of combat tours in Iraq and Afghanistan. A graduate of Seattle University with dual degrees in History and English Literature, he recently completed an MFA in Creative Writing & Poetics at University of Washington. He lives with his family in Bellevue, WA.

Tracy Snyder lives in Salem, Oregon, the wife of one man, mother of two sons, and servant of two cats. She usually writes science fiction or fantasy, but occasionally pens a piece from the real world. By day, she is a lymphedema therapist. In the evening, she paddles on a competitive dragon boat team named the Angry Unicorns. You can find her at www.tracylsnyder.com.

Max Talley was born in New York City, graduated from a liberal arts college, and moved to Southern California, where he writes fiction and teaches music. His writing has appeared, or is forthcoming, in *The Rogue Voice Journal*, *Iconoclast*, *Two Cities Review*, *Chantwood Magazine*, *The Del Sol Review*, and the *Hardboiled* anthology from *Dead Guns Press*. Talley's novel, *Yesterday We Forget Tomorrow*, was published in 2014. www.maxdevoetalley.com

Janice Westerling is a San Francisco Bay Area writer who grew up in the Central Valley of California and studied with the late poet Philip Levine at Fresno State College. Her work has appeared in the *Christian Science Monitor*, the *Santa Clara Review*, the *Coachella Review*, *Reed Magazine*, *Forge*, and elsewhere.

www.ingramcontent.com/pod-product-compliance
Lightning Source LLC
Chambersburg PA
CBHW031348170626
46807CB00002B/873

* 9 7 8 0 9 9 6 9 2 3 9 0 3 *